What I

 ... out of 5 stars

"Vivid Worldbuilding and Relentlessly Bleak Tone"

Scob Nation explores power, control, and the consequences of ideological extremism through vivid worldbuilding and a relentlessly bleak tone. The writing is sharp, provocative, and unapologetically graphic, often favoring atmosphere over subtlety. Unsettling yet compelling, though the intensity can feel overwhelming at times. Appeals most to fans of dystopian thrillers, political satire, and speculative cautionary tales.

"A Dystopia Too Real to Ignore"

Scob Nation doesn't ease you in - it grabs you by the collar and drags you straight into a nightmare version of America that feels just a little too close for comfort. This is a world where caring about the planet has twisted into something monstrous - surveillance dressed up as virtue, punishment branded as progress, ideology performing its cruelty in broad daylight. The world Grit builds is bold and brutal, the kind that gets under your skin and stays there. But underneath all the horror - the moral scorecards, the camps designed to reprogram you into compliance - there's something fragile and stubborn hanging on. Human connection. Reads like a warning shot and a dare all at once. Fast, disturbing, and worst of all? It doesn't feel that far away. Highly recommended.

"Anxiety Inducing"

A fascinating story about a father on a mission to save his son in a world overrun by technology and destroyed by climate change. As you read, you will feel nervous about what is about to happen - not just to the characters but to the world we are living in. Highly engaging and anxiety inducing.

"Sacrifice, Freedom and Justice"

Races through a chilling near future shaped by so-called climate justice. The setting is uniquely strange and filled with altered enforcers, tracked citizens and engineered creatures. A rigid system of environmental purity is enforced at any human cost imaginable. Moral perfection becomes weaponized as algorithms, prisons and neural rewiring replace freedom. Works as dark satire asking how much liberty society will sacrifice when fear and virtue collide violently.

"A Bold, Unsettling Dystopian Thriller"

Imagines a near-future America where climate extremism has hardened into totalitarian control. The world-building is vivid and disturbing: body-modified enforcers, bio-engineered creatures, moral surveillance tech, and 'reprogramming' centers where dissent is corrected rather than debated. At the center stands Blonden Viate, the chilling Climate Overman, whose fusion of moral absolutism and machine learning turns virtue into an algorithm and obedience into policy. Despite its dark satire and relentless tension, Scob Nation finds moments of humanity in unexpected alliances and fragile connections. Sharp, provocative, and uncomfortably plausible.

SCOB NATION

BY
TEMPL GRIT

r26-0126

CHAPTER 1

ATASCADERO, CA

The circuits sewn into Gina's eyeballs were coming loose.

She had steadied her nervous stomach when the doctor strapped her into the LASIK machine and peeled up her corneal flap. Aside from a confused moment of blurriness, she felt nothing when the mini-solar module was sutured onto her iris and the wiring was routed under her eyelid. The doctor assured her that the microcircuit clusters at her tear ducts could withstand the moisture, and the procedure itself seemed easy enough. On paper, anyway.

In practice, however, her eyeball implants were a problem.

"Would this have happened if we'd fused them instead?" Gina asked.

The doctor shrugged. "Not sure. Remember, fusing stiffens the cornea, we gave William retinal astigmatism when we did it. He still can't see out of his left eye."

Gina nodded. She'd blinded four pigs testing out the fusion process, and it took her another six months and countless prototypes before she had a design that could be implanted. Bending the solar wafer into the curvature of the cornea had proven simple enough (use a thimble), and the wiring problem had been frustrating but solvable (tweezers and a toothpick). She'd fixed the location of the battery implant (the upper sinus cavity), selected mini-light strips to replace her eyebrows (5 millimeters tall), and had even developed the nasal laparoscopic procedure to connect all the components together. The hardest part of the entire design, as it turned out, was lasering into her eyebrow roots to ensure they wouldn't grow back into the circuits.

Gina stood at the workbench and fumbled with the cellphone app. She typed on the screen, hit enter, then looked into the mirror. Her right eyebrow lit up with the word STOP, her left eyebrow lit up with OIL, and she turned to Doctor James to reveal their creation.

"Damn, Gina, that's perfect," he said. He turned off the room light, held up his phone, clicked a picture, then showed it to her.

Gina stared long and hard at the selfie, admiring the way her eyebrows lit up the dark room, how she'd transformed her forehead into a human flashlight. She rotated her head back and forth, lighting up the mirror, then the sink, then the workbench. "My God," she said, "it's just…beautiful." Gina began to cry, and as she did her right eyebrow glitched and went dark.

"Tears short it out, Gina – you can't cry!" James warned. He swabbed her tear duct with a Q-tip.

STOP OIL lit up across her eyebrows again, and she held her eyes wide open to prevent the glitch.

"OK, so I can glue the corners down, but we'll have to use drying drops to make sure it doesn't short anymore," James said, shining his ophthalmic flashlight into her eyes. "We'll just have to make that part of the pre-game. Now, let me look at your nose."

Six weeks earlier Doctor James had sewn Gina's nostrils shut. They had the fusion versus suture conversation many times back then - Dr. James wanted dissolving sutures - but ultimately Gina made an aesthetic choice: always a San Francisco Giants fan, she'd chosen baseball laces to permanently close her nostrils. She wanted the world to see the red, cross-stich pattern across her nose at her unveiling. *Dirty, polluted air will never travel this way again*, she proudly thought. *One step closer to our Pure Selves.*

The Grand Reveal would happen on November 17, 2045, during the opening ceremony of the global Conference of Parties session. It was the 50th anniversary of COP climate meetings, and this year it was to be held in Washington D.C., its first time at the U.S. Capitol. Gina thought the white antebellum architecture - juxtaposed with the pure and natural beauty of the cherry blossoms - was the perfect backdrop for their Purification. If ever there was a location that showcased mankind's climate hypocrisy, it was D.C.: *rich white people enslaving us huddled masses with big oil pork. God wants oil in the ground.*

In exactly twenty-seven days, at precisely 16:40 p.m., Gina and all five hundred members of The Flagellantes would form a circle around the Capitol's Reflecting Pool and face west, towards the setting sun.

At 16:48 they would, in unison, drop their ceremonial robes to the ground, and reveal their bruised fleshpalettes to the media cameras. They would show the square grids inked all over their naked bodies, each square signifying a ton of carbon dioxide they had emitted in their lifetime, each bruise a cleansing step in their repentance. Older brothers and sisters would shine head-to-toe in their bruised glory, while younger ones would self-abuse around their breasts, or along their neckline, or on their exposed genitals. It was the first time Gina had ever wished she was a 70-year-old man: she wanted to welt her entire body and bruise her own testicles.

At 16:50 the group would tilt their faces up, open their eyes, and stare directly into the setting sun. Within twelve seconds their retinas would sear into useless crisps, blinding them all. Their solar panel corneas would soak up the sun's last rays, power up their nose battery implants, then light up their eyebrow ridges. When the sun set behind the Lincoln Memorial, conference attendees would surround the group and gasp at their commitment; and when full darkness hit, five hundred forehead lights would shine brightly and illuminate the United Nations flags with the words "STOP OIL." It would be magnificent.

At 16:52, all five hundred members of The Flagellantes would emerge as their Pure Selves in front of the world, butterflies breaking free from their cocoons, united in their climate despair. They would stand bare in purity, bruised in penance, blind in commitment, eyebrows lit in Nazarene glory, their message clear: *the only way to free our world of CO2 poison is to burn it out of our eyeballs and beat it out of our bodies.*

CHAPTER 2

TWO YEARS EARLIER
SAN LUIS OBISPO, CA

Lauren Anaya pulled the Umbili-Net disc out of its velvet pouch and held it in her palm. It felt solid and sleek, like something you wanted to rub against your front teeth. Sometimes, she did just that.

Like most people, she had been hesitant to adopt the new communication system, and when it changed its attachment method from a headband to a temple-magnet implant she took a hard pass. But then she saw the intimacy of Umbili-calls, how those connected seemed to actually *be connected*, temple to temple, like they were literally plugged into each other across the world. They seemed, well, happy. She implanted the quarter-sized magnet into her right temple and never looked back. Now every time it buzzed she closed her eyes to let its warmth soak through her eyebrows, let it soothe her entire forehead. *No wonder they called them Umbili-Calls*, she thought. *It feels like home.*

It buzz-buzz-buzzed at her temple, and she tapped it twice to answer. A holo-screen appeared in front of her face – six inches too close! – and she poked the air to adjust the settings. When she reset the screen to the correct distance, she answered.

"What's up Gina?" she said.

"Dad's climate legislation is coming up for a vote next week. We should both get to Sacramento to support it," Gina said.

"I don't know, G, feels kinda weird, don't you think? I mean, he passed last year. Like we're there honoring a ghost. Maybe we should just let it go."

"Lauren, it's the Cecil B. Montoya Climate Morality Bill. It's his name on the damn thing. How can we just ignore it? It's his legacy for Christ's sake." Gina pleaded.

"I don't even know what's in it. Have you read it?"

"He always wanted to hold people accountable for their own climate actions, and that's what this does. It requires mandatory reporting of everyone's personal carbon emissions, which ultimately gets rolled up into a scoring system. It's just a framework for now, but you can see where this leads, right? It can be the foundation for transformational change!" Gina said, bouncing in her seat.

"It's a big step, G."

Just then, her husband Mateo Anaya walked in, noticed the U-disc session, and asked: "Who you talking to, Laur?"

"Gina," she said.

"Put her on public, let me say hi." Mateo said.

Lauren tapped her U-disc, scrolled through the air, tapped a virtual spot, then stared back at the holo-screen.

"Damn Gina – what happened to your hair?" Mateo asked.

Gina rubbed her hands over her shaved-bald head and smiled. "Who needs it anyway? We have to purify ourselves for when life gets simpler. Might as well start now," she said.

"When 'life gets simpler'. You mean when we go back to living in caves?" Mateo said. He turned to Lauren and asked: "Bud?"

Lauren pressed a holo-button and the refrigerator door opened. Mateo reached inside, grabbed a Budweiser can, popped the top, then toasted Gina with it. "I'd better drink up then. Cheers," he said.

"You always joke, Mattie. I know we don't see eye-to-eye on this, but this is happening regardless. You can see the transformation happening everywhere: we've rebuilt the highways, redesigned cars, crafted new legislation, even built new curriculum. There's no more hiding from it. Change is happening, whether you like it or not," Gina said.

Mateo took a long pull on his beer, squinted, then pursed his lips. Lauren had seen this look a thousand times before, and she raised her palms to try and stem their never-ending argument. "Hey, maybe we can talk about this another ti-"

Mateo interrupted. "You know, Gina, I was watching them build that Jim Crow-i-dor up north of Gilroy, and all I could see was tractors and trucks and tree-clearing combines. The only EV I saw was when the damn mayor drove up, and he was only there for five minutes. All I saw were machines blowing black smoke up into the air, tearing through trees and grinding dirt. You're telling me we're doing this for the climate? No way."

"You know I hate it when you call them Jim Crow-i-dors," Gina said.

"You know I hate it when you call me Mattie. So, we're even," Mateo said, then belched.

"Come on you two," Lauren said.

Gina jumped in. "Daddy worked on The Great Jim Crow Interstate Reparation Bill of 2030 for years, and it changed the American highway system as we know it. We rerouted interstates away from Regionally Integrated Territories of Enslavement communities –"

"Your RITE just sounds so *wrong*," Mateo chuckled. He belched again.

Lauren gave him a side-eye glance.

"- and through White Responsible Omniracist Neighborhoods of Genocide…" Gina said.

"I was right – it is WRONG!" Mateo laughed.

Lauren squinted at him and put her hands on her hips. *Give us a break, Teo,* she thought.

"We fixed things!" Gina insisted.

"Did you? It's just alphabet soup if you ask me. You still going through with this DUH bullshit?" Mateo asked.

"You mean the Discriminatory United Heuristics system?" Gina asked.

"All I hear is DUH," Mateo said.

"It gives highway access to historically discriminated people of color," Gina said. "It's historic legislation. It's foundational. It's transformative."

"It's a Brown Score, Gina, just a way to assign numbers to people's skin color. C'mon. I'm a 53, by the way. Hooray for me." Burp.

"It gets you preferred access to highways," Gina said.

"It gives me preferred access based on my skin color; it IS discrimination. It makes discrimination law. DUH." Mateo said.

"You don't want better highway access?" Gina asked.

"I don't fucking want it, Gina. I don't need your...help."

"Yes, well lots of people do, *Mattie*," Gina said. "White people have been enslaving colored people with highways and technology for hundreds of years. This helps fix it."

"No, they don't, *Jim Crow-i-dor*," Mateo said. "It's just rich white people trying to fix poor brown people. Misdirected as always. It's just RITE, WRONG, and DUH. How can you not see it?"

Gina sighed, then asked: "So I guess you won't be joining Lauren tomorrow?"

"Not unless I can drive Big Red."

"Right. A bloody red Camaro at a landmark climate legislation ceremony, a testament to our father's legacy, surrounded by press. I don't think so. How is that world-destroyer anyway?" Gina asked.

"Gassed up and ready to go," Mateo said. "Vroom vroom."

Hearing enough, Lauren jumped in: "Let's talk about this later, G." She left the U-call and turned towards Mateo.

"What the hell, Teo?"

Mateo shrugged. "What do you mean 'what'? She shaved her head for this shit!"

"Well, we'll have to meet her halfway at some point. I've been getting calls about this, about Daddy's work on his scoring system, and well, let's just say the voices are getting louder."

"The voices? What voices?" Mateo asked.

"There's a push to link climate scores with U-discs. That means people will get to share their data with each other, and find other folks whose values align with theirs."

"Find how?"

"They're adding colors to the U-discs. And different interests would be different colors. So those who align with say, purple, can instantly see those who align with purple."

"So, the purples get together to hate the greens," Mateo said.

"No, they find the purples, they find each other quicker because they have similar interests. Think how much more efficient it will be. We don't have to spend our time figuring out who's on board, who isn't, all that politicking. We can just get straight to things. Instantly," Lauren said. *Why couldn't he see it?*

"We won't have to worry at all about talking to each other, about meeting each other, about doing the hard work of connecting with people. We can just judge them instantly and move on," Mateo said.

"You're so cynical!" Lauren said. She'd grown tired of his resistance to climate progress, even if she didn't fully align with Gina's radical agenda. Her dad had worked on climate legislation for decades and was a true pioneer in enlisting Big Tech for help. A partnership with Umbili-Net was going to be huge: with the company's reach, the brand name, its ability to put policy instantly onto the foreheads of billions of people with the press of a button…it could change the world. She'd seen the prototypes, and they were revolutionary. Like it or not, Mateo was going to have to get on board with it.

"Yellow arm bands, Laur. Like they did with the Jews. If you don't believe like us – if your thought isn't approved – you'll be labeled instantly. Now you'll know who the enemy is, just like that. Orwell." He snapped his fingers.

"That's extreme, it's not going to happen that way. There are other ways to look at it. We can use it for good." she said.

"Said everyone who ever wanted total control. It's Nazis marking the Jews, Big Tech-style. Instead of yellow arm bands it's glowing temples. Yawohl, meinen Führer," he said, giving a Sieg Heil salute.

"That's crap and you know it, Mateo. It will allow us to focus energies on where we need it the most, just like Daddy laid out. Just like he designed it. It's going change the world. Guaranteed."

Mateo stood, crushed the empty Bud can in his palm, and said: "For once, Laur, you and I finally agree."

CHAPTER 3

PRESENT DAY
SAN LUIS OBISPO, CA

Mateo woke up to sunlight shining through the bedroom window shades. Normally he was up with his 6:00 a.m. alarm, so sunlight through the windows was a surprise. Swiping up on his phone, he read: "Mumbai, India, 10:47 p.m." *Wait, what? I'm in San Luis Obispo. It's morning here.*

Walking to his wife's nightstand, he picked up her phone and swiped up: "Morning, Fucker", it read. Just then, the electronic motors in their sensor-pedic bed whirred, closing his side of the bed like a clamshell, lifted her side up, then alternated, back and forth, like a mattressed roller coaster.

"Damn it, Teo, I'm getting up," Lauren said. "Knock it off."

"I'm not doing it, Laur, the bed's gone nuts," Mateo said.

Suddenly, the wall TV lit up. An anchorwoman appeared: "Stampede CEO Gore Mecklenberg is calling it a glitch and expects to have it solved by noon. He said it's a 'hiccup caused by an over-air software update' and doesn't expect it to interrupt next week's Democan National Convention…"

Before Mateo could grab the remote, the TV switched channels to Wolf News, where an agitated Senator said: "It's the Great Correction, just what us Republicrats have been saying for so long. We won't say we told you so but, hell yeah, we told you so…"

The TV switched over again, this time to a steady, glowing Stampede feed. There was only one word across the entire screen: "CLIMAPOCALYPSE".

"What's going on?" Lauren asked, clearing the sleep from her eyes.

"Not sure." He opened the window shades and looked out onto a cul-de-sac of chaos. Grabbing his car key fob, walked out the front door and into his driveway. The headlights of his cobalt blue clEVer minivan blinked right to left, then left to right, and when he clicked again the hood jumped open, then shut, then open again, then laughed like some twisted EV hyena. One more click and the rear tailgate lifted, farted loudly through the speakers, then slammed shut.

What the fuck?

To his left, neighbors were running in and out of their front door, the wife pulling on a blouse, the husband still in a bathrobe. Their teenage son chased their Bernadoodle down the street, while their daughter stuffed a Tabby cat into a carrier. Then, as frantically as they'd been moving, they all just stopped and put their hands up to their right temple.

All four of their temples pulsed soft pink, and they stopped dead in their tracks. Not only had Mateo never seen U-disc pulsing colors before, he'd never seen a group stop together and wait. It was like they were all responding to an emergency alarm of some sort, except there was no alarm. They just stood in the street, breathing in unison.

"What the hell is going on, Mateo?" a man to his right asked.

"No idea, Jimmy," Mateo said.

In his driveway, Jimmy's MEVatron rolled down its automatic windows, yelled "your wife is fat!", then flattened its own tires, *ssssssssssssss*. Then Jimmy's U-disc flashed green, then yellow, then vibrated loudly. Jimmy reached up and slapped it off his temple like a dragonfly.

"The fuck is going on?" he said to no one in particular, circling his car, running back into his house.

Across the street, Mateo watched a couple tug at their garage door, one on each side, lifting with their legs a garage door that would not be lifted. The wife's U-disc glowed a steady brown, the husband's pulsed through color after color after color, despite his repeated "disconnect" commands. Finally, he just removed it and pulled at his garage door in futility.

At right, an empty golf cart circled the cul-de-sac, around and around and around it went.

And then, just as quickly as the chaos began, it all stopped.

Mateo's car stood still.

The neighbor caught his Bernadoodle.

The garage neighbors stared at their door, still closed.

The golf cart whirred straight, ran up a curb, then rolled into a rose bush.

The cul-de-sac went completely silent.

He pulled the U-disc out of bathrobe pocket and snapped it into place. It hummed and whirred and buzzed, and the holo-screen jumped into an array of images: local news, weather reports, an international Al-Jazeera feed. Shaking his head, he couldn't process the cacophony of images and messages and colors. Then, suddenly, the U-disc vibrated warm: throbbing in, pulsing out, resonating through his eyebrows and down his nasal ridge. Warmth crawled down his cheeks, and he found his eyes closing halfway, like he'd been given a lorazepam drip. It pulsed in rhythm, purring with a low hum, calming him. Feeling himself swirling into a foggy vortex, he reached up and quickly snapped it off his temple.

He stood in the middle of the cul-de-sac catching his breath, wondering what the hell just happened.

Oh my God. Nothing works. And the U-discs are fucking taking over.

Nothing worked.

Lauren tried her old-school cell phone, but it couldn't even find a network.

She pressed the remote control on the flat- screen, but instead the microwave started and said, in full volume, "tu pizza ya está lista."

She snapped on a flashlight, but it became too hot to hold so she dropped it.

Then her laptop screen lit up and cycled through various text threads: "the temperature at Vail Ski Resort is a frigid four degrees Fahrenheit", "today's movie showtimes are…", and "we're sorry, your call cannot be completed as dialed."

She ran around her living room and kitchen, looking through the flashing lights, listening to the whirring electronics, flipping the clapping switches. In a house full of electronics and smart devices, things turned on and off randomly, like she was in an amusement park fun house. It was a mess of alarms and clicks and screens and chaos. Nothing worked the way it was supposed to.

Then, she remembered: *Oh my God I have to find Reyes!*

She snapped her U-disc into place and immediately felt that calm sense of belonging. Saying "temple Reyes" it tried, but it kept bouncing back with busy signals, something she hadn't heard in decades. With each attempt, however, her disc pulsed and hummed, like it was apologizing for not being able to connect. *Don't worry, it's going to be alright, we'll find him soon enough.* Standing still in her living room, she felt overwhelmingly calm.

Mateo's voice entered her head as a barely audible whisper, yet it wasn't until she noticed his U-disc slide across the countertop that she saw him. She saw him, but his edges blurred into a soft fog, like he was floating towards her as a Thanksgiving Day parade balloon. His mouth opened and closed, a mawing goldfish, and she could actually see the words escaping: they crawled out of his open mouth, formed into a floating sentence, then slowly soaked into her irises. She heard him through her eyes, his voice soft and reassuring, even as he paced around the kitchen. *Do people hear through their eyes? Because I could get on board with that.*

And then, louder: Lauren! Lauren! Lauren!

She blinked, then saw Mateo's agitated face before her, his hands shaking her shoulders.

"Hi hun," Lauren said. He looked kind, and handsome, like she'd always remembered him.

"It's fucking nuts out there, Laur. Everything's gone crazy. Nothing works. Even the cars are fucking spazzed!" Mateo said. He scuttled around the room, opening drawers, looking for something.

Colors started to appear more distinct, the edges of furniture more pronounced. She felt like she was waking up. "Reyes," she mumbled.

"Did you get ahold of him?" Mateo asked, frantically.

Lauren shook her head. "I don't think so, hun."

Mateo looked hard at her. "What do you mean you don't think so? Did you try?"

"Yes."

"Did you talk with him?"

"No."

"How many times did you temple him?"

"It's still trying," she said calmly, patting her disc.

Mateo frowned, looked at her glowing U-disc, then said "motherfuck!" He slapped it off her forehead.

Lauren felt a pause, and then a shudder. Her gaze focused onto the butcherblock countertops, and she scrolled through mental images of its entire construction history: they purchased the wood from Peru, because Montana pine was in short supply; it took them over six months to get the corners curved exactly the way she wanted; and Reyes loved eating Fruit Loops off their bare surface, just putting his lips onto them like he was a giant vacuum hose, shloop, shloop, shloop.

"Lauren, what the hell is going on with you?" Mateo asked, his voice nearly screaming.

Lauren looked up and finally saw him. She was dizzy, foggy, yet focused. "Hi, Teo. Did you find Reyes?"

"You were templing him, Laur," he said. He sat down next to her at the table and spoke softly. "Are you OK? Can you see me? Does it hurt anywhere?"

"I'm fine," Lauren said. "I feel fine. Great, in fact. Better than I've felt in a long time actually. I was nervous, then I wasn't." Her eyes drifted to the U-disc on the counter, laying there peacefully. Unconsciously, she reached out for it.

Mateo pushed it away. "No, let's leave these off for now. They're doing some weird shit."

Minutes passed, and she watched Mateo pace and rant throughout their lower floor. She heard "Reyes" and "glitch" and "D.C.", but they were all just blurry snippets. Slowly her hearing and thinking returned, but even as they did, she felt strangely calm. She knew that something big had gone wrong, but she didn't actually feel it. They were just words.

"Janet across the street said it's one of those electromagnet pulse things, where something zaps and fries all the electronics," Mateo said.

Lauren looked around her kitchen. "No, wouldn't an EMP just fry everything? This stuff works," she said. "Or, some of it works, some just glitches. It's just random." She clicked a flashlight off and on.

"I guess," Mateo said and stared hard at her. Reaching across the counter, he picked up his U-disc. To him it was just a plastic disc, the color of a biscuit. "Was yours doing weird shit?"

Lauren said, simply: "I liked it. It calmed me. But then again, it always calms me. I like feeling I can walk right into his forehead."

Mateo frowned. "It's just a way to connect, Laur. And we have to keep trying."

Lauren smiled. "It's always been more than that. To me anyway." She remembered when Reyes had first moved to Washington D.C., when she could just Umbili-Call him and feel like he was sitting there at the kitchen table, like she was connected to him through her own umbilical. Now, she couldn't live without it.

"Mine tried this weird buzzing and humming shit, like it was trying to hypnotize me. Same thing happened with Jimmy. Kinda felt drunk."

Lauren nodded, then passed hers from palm to palm.

"The feeds are all over the place, can't tell if it's just a local thing or something bigger. But it's messed up D.C., and we gotta get ahold of Reyes. I tried the airports, but nothing comes up at all. Trains are the same way. It's freaking me out."

"I'm sure it's just a passing thing, Teo," Lauren said. For some reason she tried to make her voice sound reassuring.

"Didn't they say it was just a glitch and they'd have it fixed in a few hours?"

"What if they're not? What if it's complete fucking chaos and all the airports and train stations are down? How will we find out what's going on with Reyes?" Mateo asked, his voice rising.

"I'm sure it's fine," Lauren said, patting the tabletop. "Sit down and we can wait for everything to get up and running again." She felt it was all going to be OK.

Mateo stared hard at Lauren, squinted, then walked over to the keychain ring by the stove. He grabbed the keys to his Camaro, and said: "I've gotta go find him, Lauren. I have to know if he's ok." He dangled the car keys.

"You're going to drive all the way out to Washington D.C.?" Lauren asked. She was concerned but also unconcerned. It would be a long drive. He would need to stop for sandwiches.

"Nothing works, Laur. And Umbili-Net's going to fuck everything up." Mateo said.

Lauren smiled calmly and closed her eyes. "Nothing works, Teo. And U-Net's going to save us," she said. She had never been so sure of anything in her entire life.

CHAPTER 4

TEMPLETON, CALIFORNIA
OCTOBER 23, 2045

Mateo had been driving up California Highway 101 all of his life. As a child, he'd pile in the back of his father's Chevy Silverado with sisters Yolanda and Darlene, riding on hay bales and stopping for soft serve in Gilroy. Or Soledad. Or, on days when Dad celebrated a good picking month: Monterey. He always wondered if coastal fog somehow made ice cream sweeter, and Darlene was absolutely sure it did.

In high school he'd find his way into the hilly fields in eastern King City, up top along the ridges, in the late spring when the rains stopped, before the avocado trees bloomed, while the dirt was soft and powdery and clean. He would lay on a blanket with Jasmine and make out, or later, with Debbie, they would strip bare and couple in the warm moonlight. It was natural and innocent and slightly corrupt, which is what they were.

Then he met Lauren, and he was pretty sure they conceived Reyes in a Greenfield Motel 8. Or the Gonzales Holiday Inn. And if not those, he was sure it was in the San Benito Drive-On-Inn, that lazy motel where highway 25 squiggled past the dirty curves of 146.

Ah, Reyes.

Mateo reached into the front pocket of his faded blue jeans and pulled out a small, red Camaro Hot Wheels car, a trinket he'd taken from his son's bedroom. It felt solid and cold in his palm, and he held it up to admire its detail. Reyes spent years vroom vrooming Lil Red across their kitchen floor, racing it so much the front two tires shattered. Mateo set the toy into a crevice alongside the stick shift, and smiled: *Big Red coming to deliver Lil Red.* He remembered buying it at the Chualar Five and Dime, then Lauren feeding him later at City Park. It felt whole and complete, like nothing he'd ever experienced before.

Mateo turned north and hit the gas. That it had a gas pedal at all was a welcome feeling, and he put his palm flat on the dashboard to feel the engine rumble as it revved up to highway speed. Sure, his clEVer could climb Cuesta Peak in four seconds, but it always felt so…sanitary. He missed the slow build-up of momentum as the Camaro drank in petrol, like it was chugging a big, hot mug of confidence as it rolled forward. He thought of weekly walks up Bishop's Peak, where his Rottweiler would chase squirrels into crags. Guinness actually smiled the entire, drooling time, and it reminded him of a simple feeling: *sometimes you just gotta let a big dog be a big dog.*

Not that there was any dog left in the clEVer, not after the bump. Democans called it the Glitch, Republicrats the Correction, and social media was filled with the alarming and inane: Climapocalypse, The End, Axes of Evil, TrumpistManifesto were all trending. Mateo didn't care what he heard or read or saw, he just needed to find Reyes.

The problem was: how?

As Gina had reminded him, the Great Jim Crow Interstate Reparation Bill of 2030 changed the American highway system as we knew it and granted him preferred highway access through California's vast highway network. Mateo's olive skin gave him a 53 on the brown scale, which allowed highway access to all but the left lanes; carpool lanes were still reserved for DUH scores over 65 and, well, carpools. While he'd voted against the DUH framework, he allowed some guilty pleasure: he loved clicking the clEVer turn signal, seeing the display offer "DUH Access Granted", then passing the white swells in their Viszlas. *Score one for the brown guys*, he thought.

Driving up the 101, Mateo didn't actually know how he was going to get to Washington D.C. Jim Crow-i-dors required vehicles to have electric under-body induction systems in order to engage the all-electric highway network; they also required permissions and sponsors to cross. Driving his red, gas-powered Camaro up through California's farm community, Mateo had neither. He knew he could get as far as Port Morgan Hill, but he had no idea how he would get east. But first things first: Mateo needed gas.

He exited at Road 244 for Camp Roberts, an old Army-training base turned techno-hub, and pulled into an Authorized Fuel Station. By law all fuel stations were supposed to have gasoline and diesel ports along with slow and fast-charging EV ports, but their availability was inconsistent and usually a crap shoot. Despite the standard government-issue look and feel for each station, what worked and what didn't was typically left to local politics: good luck finding a working EV charger in Oklahoma, as Mateo once learned. And here in California, gas ports that operated three weeks ago were likely to have been dismantled as part of some weekend vigilantism.

Stepping out of his Camaro, he looked left towards Camp CyberSpoke and saw people wandering parking lots: staring at their phones, shaking them, clicking U-calls on their temples, mouths agape at each other, some of them actually talking to each other. He pulled the gas nozzle out of its holster, and, to his surprise, the station clicked to life; its display showed: "Welcome, Mateo Anaya, you are authorized for 14.6 gallons of unleaded fuel" and the speaker played a soft little jingle. *Success!*

Leaning against the trunk, he watched the Camp's techno-elite wander about, ants scurrying from a crushed hill. The Bump had thrown Camp CyberSpoke into a glitch-fest, with techies manically plugging and unplugging devices throughout the campus. Mateo breathed in the gas fumes, as he found the scent oddly comforting. It reminded him of simpler times, when you could just get in your car, fill it up and drive. Get lost? Who cares, just turn around and drive somewhere else. No approvals or technology needed.

Just then, the speaker stopped, and the screen went dark. Slowly, a picture emerged of a middle finger with the words "PLANET KILLER" underneath; the song stopped and turned into a heckling rant: "hope you're happy you sonofabitch, you're killing children and turning the world into a place where only rich, white people survive...we'll stop you, we'll find you and burn you down..."

Mateo let the station finish its rant. He'd heard that climate vigilantes had hacked into fuel stations, but this was the first time he'd seen or heard it himself. As the gas pump clicked and finished, he looked onto the highway overpass and a big orange sign: "Your WRONG DUH Dollars at work." *No shit.*

PORT MORGAN HILL

Morgan Hill, California, originally known as the last of Silicon Valley's somewhat-affordable bedroom communities, was now a full-blown port. Forty-eight white vestibules crossed the highway, each one 3.14159 meters across (those Stampede techies sure have a sense of humor!), each separated by a fully automated e-lane. To the right was The Rotunda, a spinning piece of asphalt-alloy borrowed from San Francisco's cable-car heritage; its job was to gather each vehicle, rotate to its desired vectors, then eject it into an open billet along each Jim Crow-i-dor. It was the traffic master: anyone wanting to travel east on a national corridor had to visit The Rotunda.

After the bump, however, the Rotunda was on manual control, with guards and techies on laptops approving all movement. Across a big electronic directional sign leaned a large piece of plywood, with "Enter Building for Approvals" painted in big red letters. Tow trucks and forklifts worked the roadsides, moving electrics to and fro, belching out gas fumes as they worked. A bright yellow forklift with "-illar" on it tried to slide forks under a stalled Viszla; after three attempts it gave up and just drove its forks into the driver's side door, lifted the car up, drove it ten feet away, then dumped it. A man with an EVStinguisher rushed over, doused the Viszla with foam, then turned to the hundreds of other men dousing Viszlas with EVStinguishers. Port Morgan Hill was bustling with life, dispensing fire safety, moving carcasses around a graveyard.

Mateo parked in lane 31 and stepped out of the Camaro. An orderly tech walked over, pulled a scanner out of its holster, beeped it at the license plate, then stepped to Mateo. "Keys, please," he said.

"Keys? No, I'm just going in for a permit," Mateo said.

"No keys, no permit," the tech said, holding his palm up.

Mateo eyed the tech up and down – *what was he, 23? 24? He better not scratch Big Red* – then tossed the keys. The keys bounced off the tech's palm onto his boot; he bent down to retrieve them. He pointed at the white office door.

Mateo stepped into the office. He sat in a beige metal chair in front of a putty-gray, metal wall; on the wall hung a plasma TV with the words "Want the Truth, Indeed? Try Stampede" scrolling across it. The door shut automatically; Mateo turned his shoulders left and put one palm flat on the wall, the other on the closed door. *Damn, this isn't even an office.*

The plasma screen lit up, twittered for a second, then a face appeared. An older, olive-skinned man looked back at Mateo, smiling softly, staring directly at him. "Hello, my name is Anthony," the face said.

Mateo squinted at the image. "Anthony? That's my brother. You even look a little like him." *Exactly like him*, he thought.

"We know," the image said. "Anthony Anaya, born in Taos, New Mexico on September 22, 1987, died in Eagle Crest, Colorado on June 22, 2042."

Mateo sat upright. "Yes. How did you know?" he asked.

"It's public knowledge, no need to be alarmed," it said.

"Well, I'm looking into my dead brother's face and talking to him. Consider myself fucking alarmed," he said. He stared at the face and couldn't process it: he knew the AI bots had chewed through the deep web to calculate Anthony's face, but he hadn't expected it to look so damn real. He'd buried Anthony, he was there when Anthony told him goodbye the last time. For *real.* It made no sense that he was now talking to him.

"We have found it often makes family comfortable," the image said. "73.27% of the time anyway. But other times it doesn't. Consider yourself exceptional," it said, and attempted a weak smile. The image chittered and glitched, then morphed into a female's face: brown hair, dark skin, green eyes, a face Mateo didn't recognize. "Is this better?"

Mateo shrugged. "I guess?"

"Very well then. Hello, Mr. Anaya, I'm Antonia," the new image said, now in a softer, female voice.

Mateo shook his head, like he was trying to knock the image out of it. "Look, I'm just trying to get a pass to go east. My son-"

"Reyes," Antonia interrupted.

"Yes, Reyes…he's in Washington D.C., and I need to find him. We can't reach him; all the networks are down." Mateo said.

Antonia nodded and looked down onto a virtual clipboard. She smiled. "Yes, all of your U-Link attempts are logged and available. We've made a note of the microwave glitch; that is certainly a new one."

Mateo was growing agitated. He had no patience to talk with a TV-bot when all he needed was a permit to get on a highway. "Is there a person I can speak with? I'm in a bit of a hurry."

Antonia smiled. "Everyone is in a hurry today, after the glitch. Unfortunately, there are no human units available to meet with you, but I can certainly help you." Antonia looked at Mateo and held his gaze, and then her hair slowly turned blonde, then her eyes blue. "Or perhaps Mykayla can help you?"

"That's my college girlfriend," Mateo said.

"We know. University of New Mexico. Sociology Major," Mykayla said.

Mateo couldn't look at the screen. "Fine, fine," he said.

"Well, you have a wonderful DUH Score, I trust you have enjoyed the benefits of being a protected citizen." Mykayla said.

"I'm a 53, don't know how protected I am."

"But I have some wonderful news, Mr. Anaya. Your DUH Score has been upgraded to a 65, which will allow you passage in the fastest of highway lanes. That is certainly a nice benefit," Mykayla said.

"How did I get upgraded? It's not like I got browner on the drive up," Mateo asked.

"Not browner, sir, just more discriminated against. Last week Bonka452 called you 'coconut' on a Stampede feed, which is a subtle but very direct racist comment, is it not?"

"Brown on the outside, white on the inside," Mateo said. "Not a compliment. I've been called worse."

"Yes, you have, sir. Last Thursday, NateHate2000 called you a beaner on your Twittoob feed, and you were awarded an additional 9 points for that. That's an especially egregious euphemism for a man of Hispanic heritage like yourself, isn't it?"

Mateo nodded. "I'm just an American."

"With 37.3% Mexican, 27.9% Spanish, 19.23% Portuguese heritage, sir. With a small spattering of other things as well too. You're even 1.23% African American. The discrimination you have endured has allowed us to protect you more, hence your 65 DUH score. Congratulations."

Fucking hell. Congratulations on my discrimination, are they fucking serious? Mateo leaned forward and put his elbows on his knees. He had no idea how to process any of this information. *Just give me my fucking permit.*

"By my calculations, your upgraded DUH score will save you 63.4 minutes on your trip to Denver. Congratulations! That's quite a discrimination benefit you'll receive, sir," Mykayla said.

"Denver? I'm going all the way to Washington D.C." Mateo said.

Just then, Mykayla's image turned sour. Her smile vanished, and horn-rimmed glasses appeared; her hair was pulled back off her shoulders into a taut ponytail.

"Well sir, you are approved for autonomous driverless service to Denver, with an overnight stop in Salina, Utah. You can apply for passage to Chicago in Denver. And, I hesitate to say this, but there is some unfortunate news as well," serious Mykayla said.

Before Mateo could respond, Mykayla continued:

"Your Climate Morality Index Rating has dropped dramatically, sir. Your Stampede feeds have contained many unapproved words and phrases, as I'm sure you know. For example, you used the phrase 'climate truth?' 34 times in the past 90 days, which gives you a Climate Denial Rating of .37/day, which is very high. At that level, you can legally be called a Republicrat, which would of course hurt your Political Acceptance Leaning Score – which is already working against you. 'Climate truth' is allowed as a statement, but not as a question. That was your undoing. Sir."

"You can't do that, the Climate Lexicon Act never passed," Mateo said as he stood up. He poked his finger at the screen and stepped forward. "You can't penalize me for asking questions about the climate. That's exactly why we voted it down."

The TV screen chittered, then continued. "There is only One Climate Truth, Mr. Anaya, and you're not approved to question it. I'm afraid that, by arguing with me right now, your CMIR has gone down again, sir. And, you are just thirty seconds away from being assigned a one-time Republicrat penalty. I can assure you that you don't want that, sir. I suggest you accept the very fair benefits we've assigned you."

Mateo stood at the screen, seething. He clenched his fist.

Mykayla's stern image began to morph again, this time into the face of Stampede CEO Gore Mecklenberg. It looked directly into Mateo's eyes and said: "as to the question of laws, we are authorized to approve and disapprove travel, we are authorized to dispense Climate Truth. Since the Glitch, we're the only ones trusted with the proper security. We designed the roads, we designed the autos, we control the entire network, so only we, Stampede, can assure your safety and the integrity of your communications. Both the climate and your political motivations are too important to be left to the uninformed, so we've been authorized to intervene. We will continue to monitor your beliefs, of course, and adjust the benefits you receive accordingly."

Mateo turned and opened the door.

"Mr. Anaya, thank you for the Camaro. We have confiscated it and upgraded your climate morality accordingly. Congratulations. Enjoy your tip to Denver."

CHAPTER 5

MONTE SERENO, CALIFORNIA
THE ALCHEMY OF PROGRESS EMERGENCY SUMMIT
OCTOBER 23-24, 2045

Dr. Colleen Forsythe stood in front of the esteemed room and felt that anticipation burn through her gut. It wasn't excitement exactly, but more like a feeling of exalted dread: *if we can't find the moral compass in this room, with these people, at this time, then there isn't one to be found.* The room itself was precisely what she had expected: sterile, but indulgent. She thought of it as nature adjacent: cold white walls, with enormous glass panels reflecting but isolating them from the immaculate greenery outside. The design was created by Silicon Valley's greatest minds, giving it a hum of something invisible working behind the scenes, but without any warmth of true humanity. This wasn't the place where souls found comfort; there would be no homemade mac-and-cheese lunches or fireside chats with grandma. Rather, this was a place where the climate ethnocracy told the plebian rabble what to think - and then built them widgets so they didn't have to.

The chairs around the grand conference table were set just far enough apart to hint at formality, but not so far that true connection was impossible. It was all just for show, of course, because no one would dare move closer. Each person was here because they thought their role, their company, their technology, their own self, was the key to saving the world. If anyone was going to move, it was going to be *them*: the other guys, the second-rate technologies, the ones from companies whose valuations were far below their own.

The tablet purred softly in her hands, enough to keep the silence but loud enough to remind her that the flow of information was never-ending. She could almost hear the hum of data, the eternal undercurrent of algorithms and feeds that these technologists lived and died by. It was always the same with them: they couldn't see the forest for the trees. *Shit, they don't even know what trees are. All they see are their tools, their precious fucking tools, and nothing else.*

She took a deep breath, straightened her carefully tailored jacket, then said in a voice with deep gravitas: "Let's begin." With a brief and almost imperceptible nod, the large video screen on the wall flickered to life, displaying the meeting's purpose:

"Ethos & Evolution: Moving from Techno to Ethnocrats. Quickly."

"As of yesterday, ladies and gentlemen, the world is *fucked*."

She let the words hang in the air, let their asses shift uncomfortably in their seats, let them deal with the conflicting images of a moral thought leader dropping an F-bomb to open a meeting. Nothing brought the technelite to submission faster than the realization that there was someone in the room who could, and absolutely would, do the dirty work.

"And we are just the group unfuck it."

She clasped her hands in front of her, standing tall and still. "Yesterday at precisely 12:03 a.m. Greenwich Mean Time, the country's energy, communication, and transportation systems were hacked into oblivion. From whom, we don't yet know, though undoubtedly some of you will have insight into that. Everything official has gone offline or is working in such a way as to be completely impotent. As of October 21, 2045, America is officially deaf, dumb, blind. And morally bankrupt." She paused for effect.

The room mumbled in agreement.

"And yet, we aren't, because we have you. As the old saying goes: one man's shit is another man's treasure, and today, ladies and gentlemen, we've been given one of those things. Which do you suppose it is?"

A voice from the back blurted: "A shitty treasure?"

"Ha! Fair enough, my friend. And now: introductions. You all know me, I'm Dr. Colleen Forsythe, Lead Scholar at the Institute for Ethical Futures and Climate Moralist in Residence. I've dedicated my life to studying the intersection of ethics, climate policy, and human behavior. My role here is to ensure that we move forward not just with technological solutions, but with a moral framework that can guide those solutions." She pointed to the woman on her right.

"Thank you, Dr. Forsythe. Sasha Monroe, Chief Architect of Communication Systems and Chief Morale Strategist at Umbili-Net. At U-Net, we understand that communication is the foundation of civilization. We create systems that connect people, empower them, and shape their behavior. Our job is simple: to make sure people are connected, informed, and ultimately, compliant with the broader goals of society." Her eyes darted between the group and the prepared intro on her laptop.

"*Compliant.* How appropriate for today," Dr. Colleen said, turning to the next seat. "Mr. Vance?"

"Thank you, Doctor, I'm Ellis Vance, Chief Curator of Autonomous Ecosystem Expansion & Digital Dominion." He recited his title clearly, undoubtedly like he'd practiced a thousand times in his bathroom mirror, or said countless times at Sand Hill Road cocktail parties, and quoted from memory: "Stampede is not just about moving people from point A to point B. We're building the future of global mobility. We're making the world more connected, more flexible. We're giving people the power to move freely, to control their own destinies."

"Wonderful. The car people," Dr. Colleen said, making sure not to give his title more bloat than it deserved. She nodded to the next chair.

"Dr. Alaric Helmann, Head of Transformational Sociotechnical Research, The Reimagined World Initiative. Geneva. Sociologist. Historian. Climate crisis." His voice was thick, phlegmy, British, and much too baritone for a man of his slight build.

"How did you get here so quickly, Dr. Helmann? Planes are down and such," Dr. Colleen asked, a question to which she already knew the answer.

"Presenting in Monterey. Glitch. Now I'm here," he said.

Hope he's more than an Oxford comma, Dr. Colleen thought.

"Last but not least!" the remaining woman said, to Dr. Colleen's left. "Juliette Medina, Global Impact Strategist, The New Ecumenical Collective. I'm an activist, and I combine environmentalism with tech, mostly socials. I've got 3.7 million followers," she said.

"Ah yes, our WowNow Queen. Welcome," Dr. Colleen finished. "Welcome all." She nodded affirmation to the fifteen or so technologists, sociologists, architects, researchers, advisors, and other 'ists and 'ors who filled the conference room.

The participants settled into their chairs for the long-haul, with anointed table-dwellers assuming stances befitting their echelon. Sasha Monroe had turned to face Dr. Colleen, at the front, while Ellis Vance pointed his chair directly at Sasha, his competitor. Dr. Helmann sat straight ahead, his palms flat on the tabletop, moving them only when he tugged his long, gray beard. Juliette Medina bounced and swirled, checking multiple phones and social media. Every few seconds she would pose for a selfie, click, then tap it into the multi-verse.

"If I may, let me suggest that we eschew formal titles for our time together. You earned your spot into this room, we all have the chops to prove we belong here. It would just be, well, easier, if I may suggest it," Colleen said.

"I don't quite share your opening salvo, Colleen," Sasha from U-net said. "Yes, things are down, things are chaotic, but we aren't nearly as fucked as you said we are. In fact, I'd say we are already decidedly unfucked."

Colleen smiled. She knew Sasha Monroe was an M.I.T. graduate, a Boston girl, and would not be put off by a mere show of language. The were just fucking words, after all. And like herself, Sasha was a dirt girl.

Ellis from Stampede jumped in. He stared straight ahead at Sasha – whose eyes never left Colleen – and added: "Jim Crow highway system is fully operational. Since the glitch we've had over 11.167 million vehicles traverse the system, totaling nearly 75.67 million miles. We have a 98.967% availability rate, accidents and casualty rates are within normal operating ranges. On socials, all systems are fully operational: WowNow, Twittoob, full Stampede feeds are available." He sat back, seemingly satisfied. "Decidedly unfucked."

Colleen chuckled. She didn't remember the last time she heard a Stanford graduate cuss, ever. He looked like it was his first time doing so.

"Regarding usage statistics, I can report that all North American Umbili-Net nodes are fully operational, our connection droppage rates are at our lowest since we launched the temple implant program, and we are a full go," Sasha said.

"What about the misdirected feed rates? We've heard they're off the charts," Ellis said.

Sasha shrugged. "A momentary problem as the main public backbones went down. True, we did have momentary misdirection rates above 27%, but once we switched over to the primary U-net backbones we neared full availability." She looked at Ellis directly for the first time, smiled softly, and said: "Today, we're at 100%. One. Zero. Zero."

Ellis leaned back and looked like he was going to shit through his nostrils.

"Decidedly *unfucked*." Sasha continued. "Our temple implant program has the highest availability of any communication service ever, and our Virident program has successfully integrated data inputs from over 63.47 million data sources. It's passed all required troubleshooting protocols, and we've been expedited for trials."

"Wait, so you're ready to launch the Virident Colors program?" Colleen asked.

"Virident Green has been green-lighted," Sasha said.

"Explain please," Ellis said.

Sasha pulled two U-discs out of red velvet satchel and put one to her right temple; it snapped quickly into place. A second later it glowed bright green, pulsed brightly, then morphed into the brightest tinge of emerald green available.

"We call it electric emerald, it's bright and vibrant, with just the slightest of blue undertones," she explained. "We have cross-correlated our system with thousands of climate factors, from personal food consumption, to home energy usage, to transportation mileages, histories, in addition to the Climate Morality Index Rating system – CMIR – of course." She handed the second U-disc to Ellis.

Ellis snapped the U-disc into place, waited, then looked confused when his temple lit bright yellow.

"Sulfuric yellow, bright and garish, with a touch of acid in it. Hex #FFDD00," Sasha said. "It suits you, Ellis."

He slapped it off his forehead; it clacked onto the tabletop. "What the fuck does it mean anyway? It's just a trick! Oooo, look, mine turned yellow, hers turned pink, his turned blue. Oooo, mine turned black. It doesn't mean shit," Ellis said, his hands fluttering in the air for emphasis.

"Actually, it means you're a climate criminal." For the first time in the discussion, Dr. Alaric Helmann, chimed in: "You're talking about visual identification of climate sensibilities. Something we've never seen before. You're going to put people's climate morality on *display,* for everyone to see."

Sasha and Colleen turned towards Alaric. *Not just an Oxford comma indeed,* Colleen thought. Ellis never turned. He sat seething, his face red, his hair gel cracked.

"What yellow means is you have some climate work to do, my dear Sir. It registered yellow for a reason, and you've earned those reasons. Or-" he turned towards Sasha – "did I miss something?"

"That's exactly right," Sasha said. She broke into a wide, full-mouthed grin. "It reflects his climate score. And, it obviously shows that the colors we chose are intuitive, like we thought they would be." She clicked something on her tablet.

"So what? We've had CMIR ratings for years, ever since they passed the legislation. We have a CMIR ticker in every dashboard, updated with real-time data," Ellis said, poking the table with his index finger. "Every vehicle displays a climate score."

"Well, there's more," Sasha said, reluctantly.

Alaric seemed to get it. "It's not just display, is it? You're talking behavioral control. You think you can actually change them in some way. You can exert control."

Sasha paused, then nodded.

"Demonstrate?" Alaric asked.

Sasha slid the second U-disc across the table, and he snapped it onto his temple. It instantly whirred and hummed, then settled into a solid green tint. He smiled with green satisfaction.

"Ready?" Sasha asked.

He nodded, yes. All eyes in the room turned towards him.

Sasha pulled up her holo-screen, scrolled down, then tapped a virtual button. Instantly, the U-disc hummed in pulsing rhythm, and almost as instantly Alaric's eyes closed halfway in response. He swayed back and forth slowly, his eyes open at half-mast, humming and purring softly.

"Can you hear me, Alaric?" Dr. Colleen asked, a bit concerned. He was obviously in some sort of trance, but she didn't know whether or not it was a good thing.

He nodded, then held up his right thumb. His U-disc purred in a dull, pink glow to signify his trance.

Sasha pressed the button, and the pink U-disc clicked off. Slowly, Alaric returned to the room.

"Beyond the pale," Alaric said. "Just beyond. Like a morphine drip. Just *calm*. I still feel it. Might I have more?"

"We've got most of the bugs out," Sasha said.

Alaric shook his head as if to clear his fog. "Now let's try black."

Sasha's eyes widened. "Are you sure? Black has a bit of a trap door. Not so soothing."

"Turn me black," he said.

Sasha paused, then clicked a button. Alaric's forehead buzzed loudly then went completely silent; but when it did, he grabbed the disc and shut his eyes tight. He held his temple and groaned, shaking his head back and forth. After a few seconds, he snapped it off his temple and set it gently down onto the tabletop. He waited, then opened his eyes.

In a soft and measured tone, Alaric said: "That is a uniquely painful and unpleasant experience. I don't know that I've experienced anything like that before that left me so violated. It hurts, yes, but more than that: it *invades.* I literally felt like you could reach inside me and melt whichever part you wanted. Like evil had physically entered my person. Perhaps…this is what rape feels like?"

Oh. My. God. We've built a way to cause someone to feel rape? Dr. Colleen felt an icy shiver run down her spine. She looked over at Sasha, whose cheeks had reddened. Ellis' forehead was pulled tight against his skull. This was some serious shit.

"You've developed the ability to control humanity, to influence and direct our behavior. How we feel. All of us," Alaric said. "You can render both pleasure and pain, while sitting in your chair somewhere. It's like nothing I've ever conceived of before."

"No. Fucking. Way. There is no way that thing leaves this room!" Ellis said. He spun his head around the room. "Anyone? That's Fat Man and Little Boy combined!" He was bouncing in his seat.

"It's already been approved as a foundational app in new models. The glitch accelerated our approval process. It's available now. Like, *today.*" Sasha said.

"We can't. Raping someone's head? Are we even talking about this?" Ellis said. The room murmured and buzzed.

"Well, that's why we're all here, to decide exactly what to do with this groundbreaking technology. Like it or not, we've been given this, shall we say, opportunity. The stars have aligned, whether or not we believe that, and we can do in one week what has taken humanity centuries to accomplish. We can do it today." Dr. Colleen said. She snapped her fingers and felt the silence hang in the air like a dull, arid, dust cloud. It didn't feel clean like fog, it just felt dirty. But then again, she and Sasha were the dirt girls.

Ellis sat back in his chair and put his palms flat on the tabletop. For the first time since he'd been there, he looked calm and formidable. It was like the opportunity had transformed him. Perhaps it had. Finally, he said:

"Do you remember the autonomous vehicle fiasco we had back in '28? We pushed our vehicles through local and state approvals – spent billions to do so – then turned them loose on the streets of San Francisco. Six weeks in and we mow down a busload of seventh graders on a field trip to MOMA. Eighteen of them! Talk about laying a big moral turd right there in uptown! We…fucking killed people." he said. His voice was calm and steady.

"We can control it. We've built in safety measures," Sasha said.

"So did we," Ellis said. "We still killed children."

"Think of the lawsuits. We'll get sued into oblivion," Ellis offered.

"Since yesterday's glitch, we're under martial law. Since U-net and Stampede are the only things working, we have full autonomy to launch. We can do as we see fit. Who's going to stop us?" Dr. Colleen asked.

"Who, indeed." Alaric said. "It's just us deciding how to control the rest of us. Pain or pleasure, at our fingertips. Imagine it." He shook both hands like he was trying to eject the responsibility off them.

"We can control it," Sasha reiterated. This time her voice didn't sound so sure.

Can we? Dr. Collen thought.

"Yes, but who controls us?" Alaric asked. "It's almost a form of torture. On everyone's head. To be adjusted by the click of a holo-screen by us, accountable to no one but ourselves and our moral compass. How can we justify it? How, pray tell, could we orchestrate such an unmitigated shambles? It would seem we are edging toward the abyss with undue confidence, wouldn't you agree?"

Dr. Colleen saw her cue and ran with it. "What choice do we have, Alaric? The technology is available, it's already begun, it will find the light of day with or without us. But It's us who have the moral authority, so we are just the ones to do it. In fact, the world needs us right now. The only communication that works is U-net. The only socials are Stampede. The only vehicles and roads are Stampede. Without us, the world doesn't work at all. Without us-"

"The world stays fucked," Sasha interrupted. "They need us. More than ever. It's ours to control. But we have the responsibility to make it available to everyone. All the more so when we roll out Phase 2." Her once-strong voice sounded weak and trilly.

Colleen added another point that, until now, she'd kept secret. "Like it or not, this technology is going to come out. I have it on very good authority that other companies have developed similar technologies and are competing in this space." She stared Ellis down, who didn't meet her gaze. *Anything you'd like to tell us? Or should I tell them the conversations I've had with the Stampede brass? No? Didn't think so.* After a few seconds, he nodded yes.

"So, if we don't decide this now, we'll be here in six months having a deeper, much broader discussion about the exact same thing. And we'll be six months behind," Colleen said.

The room hung silent for what seemed an eternity.

"Going to rape people's heads," Alaric said.

"That analogy stays in this room, Dr. Helmann. Agreed?" Colleen said, using his official title to enlist his cooperation.

Heads around the room nodded. No words were spoken.

"And now, the bigger question," Dr. Colleen said.

"Probitas," Alaric said. "What to do about them."

"They're madmen, just a bunch of sycophant climate lunatics," Ellis said. "Everyone knows that. Fucking army of minions."

"No one argues that. They are, shall we say, committed to the climate cause. But we could use an army right now, couldn't we? We've been working for decades to pass climate legislation, and now the world has given us an ability to put it out there – to literally put it on people's foreheads – instantly, like that. Now. No board meetings, no legislative hearings, no polls. We can make 20 years of climate progress by tomorrow morning. Couldn't we use an army of minions to get the word out?" Dr. Colleen said. She could feel the momentum building as she said it. They could be an unstoppable force.

"Imagine: we control the networks, the cars, the roads, the messages. We get instant climate morality on everybody's foreheads, there's just no more hiding at all. We know them. We can find them. We can correct them. We can make more climate progress than we ever dreamed possible," she said.

"Probitas has correction centers. They have disciples all over the country," Alaric said.

"They have a *Bible*," Ellis added. "Like, a real one. A Bible they wrote. Like they're God."

"They'll see the potential immediately. We bring it to them and they'll find a way to cut us out. But if we don't include them and they find out…we'll have no input whatsoever. We'll be out. We'll have unleashed the beast, as it were," Alaric said.

What damage could a system like Virident Green cause if left in the hands of the cultish Probitas Organization? Dr. Colleen thought. On one hand their reach was substantial – they had significant enrollment in every state - and were pushing hard into Western Europe, and could be a true ally to spread directed climate morality throughout the country. That was the good news. But on the other hand, they would certainly understand the total control that Virident Green would give them and could cut out her group entirely. If she ignored them, they could bypass her completely, and whatever climorality she could bring to the table would be gone. Their control consisted of conformity, obedience and a relentless worship of their elders, The Overmen. *No, if I leave it up to them they'll destroy the place. There's no choice. If I don't control them, they'll control us.*

"Leave Probitas to me," she said. "We have to steer the ship from here, keep the tech backbone secret within the confines of our confidentiality. It's the only way. I'll make them see not only the immense power we're allowing them to use, but also the tremendous responsibility we're entrusting to them. They'll see it. They'll see how Divinity bestowed this unto them," Dr. Colleen said.

If not, we're fucked.

CHAPTER 6

78 MILES WEST OF BOULDER, COLORADO

The facial recognition on the Stampede HERD wasn't working.

Or rather, it recognized Mateo's face, just not his eyes. He'd made it three miles east on Jim Crow-i-dor 470 when the HERD slowed down, pulled over, then just idled. For the past twenty minutes he'd been staring into the dashboard's retinal scanner, looking left, then up and down, trying to jumpstart the vehicle that was supposed to take him all the way to Denver. Ryan Reynolds joked "your retina is not approved for this journey" so many times that he began to slur, sounding like "yall'ss retinas oww blurrrrry". Mateo opened his right eye wide, stared at the sensor's fluctuating, whirring pulse, and then Ryan Reynold's face appeared, winked, and said "You looking at me? Cuz I'm the only one here," in his best Taxi Driver DeNiro voice. *Who thinks of this shit?* Mateo thought.

The HERD pulled back into lane 1, and Mateo felt it pause, then click when the inductor coils connected. It reminded him of stepping into Mr. Toad's Wild Ride at Disneyland, where you sat down and waited for that underbody clunk to know you were getting pulled along. E-corridors were smoother, yes, but mind-numbingly antiseptic.

He studied the HERD's interior. There was a simple steering wheel, behind which was the dashboard display, about 8 inches tall, that ran the entire width of the front seat. The seat itself was a leatherette-covered bench, as was the second in the back. There was no stick or shifting apparatus of any kind; all controls were electronic and therefore required no intervention whatsoever. The floor was utile black rubber-composite, magnetized so a metal container could be positioned to hold a drink or sandwich.

A large white circle showed on the display's left, with the speed lit up in black letters inside (74 miles per hour, approved); to its right was a vertical series of gages and dials, displaying some of the vehicle's inner workings. In the middle was a colored screen scrolling through commercials and various news sites, to the right was a knob that could be turned to navigate the display. He spun the knob clockwise, past Democan Facts Network feeds 1, 2 and 3, and when he clicked on Wolf Media News it displayed "We're sorry, this channel is temporarily unavailable." *Of course it is,* he thought.

Two hundred and sixty-two feet in front, another silver HERD drove; the dashboard indicated that was the proper distance between them to ensure full safety. Two hundred and sixty-two feet behind, another silver HERD drove, undoubtedly displaying that this was also the proper distance to trail. On the opposite side of the corridor streamed another row of HERDs, all silver, all undoubtedly driving the proper distance apart to ensure safety.

It wasn't dirty, it wasn't clean, it wasn't, well, anything at all, Mateo thought. *This may be the most boring cross-country trip ever.* Then, without warning, the dashboard display lit up, the volume loud. Mykayla, his Port Morgan Hill handler, was on-screen.

"Good morning, Mr. Anaya. I trust your journey has been satisfactory so far?" she asked.

Mateo shook his head to clear the cobwebs. "Well, sure. Not much to say either way. It's been fine."

"I'm very glad to hear it, sir. We at Stampede strive to make your user experience as pleasant as possible."

Mateo squinted at the display. *Was this a customer service call?*

Mykayla continued. "I wanted to give you an update on your trip to Denver, sir. There has been a deeper analysis, and I'm pleased to tell you that we have authorized another stop for you along your route."

"What do you mean another stop? I don't need more stops before I get to Denver," Mateo said. He was both surprised and agitated, and couldn't help but feel helpless. "And what do you mean by a deeper analysis?"

"You remember your 1984 Cherry Red Camaro you left us?" Mykayla asked.

"The car you took from me," Mateo corrected.

"Yes, the automobile that is now in our possession, that's correct. Well, we have had the opportunity to evaluate the vehicle, and it has caused us to authorize a course correction to your journey, Mr. Anaya."

"Define 'evaluate the vehicle'," Mateo said.

"Upon disassembly, we evaluate each component of the vehicle on its own to make sure that we have given you a proper total carbon score. This is of course standard when we receive a fossil-fuel-legacy vehicle such as yours," Mykayla said.

"Upon disassembly? You took my car apart?" Mateo yelled at the dashboard. "You have no right to do any of that!"

"It's standard protocol, sir. We have been authorized to perform a thorough accounting of the CO2 emissions embedded in your vehicle. When we first received the vehicle, we gave it a certain CO2 score based on standard assumptions, but upon disassembly we have modified your score."

"What are you even fucking talking about?" Mateo asked. He sat on the HERD's front bench in disbelief; he wanted to punch Mykayla's face through the dashboard.

"As you know, Mr. Anaya, each vehicle is built up of components from other suppliers, and each of those components has a CO2 footprint, the Scope 3 emissions. I'm sure I don't need to explain that to a man of your intelligence, sir," Mykayla said, pausing.

Mateo seethed.

"Upon disassembly, we came to understand that you had replaced the vehicle's carburetor three separate times, is that true, Mr. Anaya?"

Mateo stared at the screen. Finally, he nodded.

"I'm sorry but I'll need a verbal confirmation, Mr. Anaya. Did you replace the carburetor three times on your 1984 Chevy Camaro?"

"Yes, you bitch," Mateo said.

The screen chittered, Mykayla looked at her virtual clipboard and clicked off an imaginary action item. "Let it be known we have verbal confirmation of the vehicle's multiple modifications." The screen chittered some more. "One modification is allowed in your approved CO2 score, but since you've modified the vehicle multiple times it significantly affected your CO2 score." Mykayla stopped, and stared back at Mateo.

After what seemed like minutes, Mateo finally responded. "Are you expecting me to say something? What exactly does all this mean?"

"Yes, well your multiple modifications, as well as the long-term care and feeding of a vehicle that is no longer approved-"

"I have permits that allow it," Mateo interrupted.

"...no longer approved for ongoing use, it demonstrates an unacceptable commitment towards killing our planet. In fact, Mr. Anaya, your dedication to planet destruction now rates you as a Level 4 Climate Denier. That of course authorizes the standard Republicrat penalty, which makes things much more serious," Mykayla said.

Mateo sat in silence as the HERD zipped through Glenwood Canyon. It bent left, then forward, then swung right on a long thoroughfare along the Colorado River. Normally Mateo would have loved this part of the scenic drive, the red peaks shadowing his journey, but here he sat stunned, unable to respond.

Mykayla delivered the coup de grace: "What all of this means, sir, is that you have been assigned for climate reprogramming at the Probitas Correction Center in Boulder, Colorado. Your trip has been modified as such, and you are authorized for four additional nights at their facility. Congratulations on this wonderful climate atonement opportunity, Mr. Anaya."

———

The ceremony for her father's Climate Morality bill had gone well. Lauren usually loved the pomp of her father's achievements, and would seamlessly step into the background while her father did the heavy, public work. But since her father's death, smiling at the masses had proven tiresome; she preferred the behind-the-scenes administrivia underpinning all legislation. Give her a bill to draft and bullet points to create and she could spend a weekend in legislative, bureaucratic bliss.

Today, however, she could not get her foothold.

Mateo was gone, Gina was in full guerilla mode, and Reyes was nowhere to be found.

Anxiety bubbled up in her belly, so she reached for her U-disc, felt its cold hardness in her palm, then put it to her temple. Snap. Ah, that soft click against her temple was better than a Percocet drip.

Clicking the holo-screen, she tapped "CALM" and felt the U-disc hum. She thought of honey, warmed for 20 seconds in a microwave, slowly being drizzled across her forehead, across her eyebrows, down her cheeks, across the nose-bridge. She closed her eyes. Warmth down to her chin, across her lips, up into the gums of her molars, warming, soothing, smothering. She heard a low "ummmmm" but wasn't sure if she actually made the sound.

Opening her eyes, the holo-screen showed a red dot on a map; she clicked it. The screen filled with a breathtaking panorama of Glenwood Canyon, the sienna red valley in Colorado's mountains, like she was a hummingbird flying between the cavernous walls, atop the Colorado River. She felt the river mist along her face. Zipping past a sign for Boulder, she felt her hair slap against her back.

Click. She scrolled through and found "Reyes", clicked again, then she stopped mid-flight, hovered, then slowly sank down into a ski chalet couch. She sipped hot chocolate, licked the whipped cream from her lips, and put her hand on Reyes' knee.

"This tastes really good, Mom," Reyes said.

"It sure does," Lauren said. The U-disc purred. Somewhere the real Colorado waited.

CHAPTER 7

THE OVERMAN
BOULDER, COLORADO

The small, wooden crate was on his mahogany desk when he entered the office.

Blonden Viate, founder and Exalted Master of The Probitas Organization, couldn't believe that it had finally arrived. He was nervous. The artifact he'd been pursuing for eight years, nine months and seventeen days, the relic he'd hired a private investigator to procure, was suddenly here. On his desk. Even though he knew exactly what to do, his hands trembled.

Turning to his left, he stepped towards the custom liquor alcove he'd installed last year. Made of Macassar Ebony, a highly prized exotic wood known for its black and brown stripes, it embodied timelessness and elegance. The tree subspecies was now extinct, and his cabinet was the only one of its kind. Swelling with pride, he smiled at the children in his collection: a Château d'Yquem 1811, the legendary Sauternes, one of the best bottles of wine ever made; a bottle of Pappy Van Winkle's Family Reserve, a 47-year-old whiskey that would be perfect in four years; and a Dalmore 62-year-old Single Highland Malt Scotch that would never be opened. *Blood of the earth,* he thought.

He slid open a small drawer and pulled a wrought-iron skeleton key from its red velvet nest. Inserting the key into a keyhole, he turned it and gently opened a larger drawer. Inside was his precious: a bottle of Louis XIII Cognac, nestled into its custom velvet cradle, lying next to a wooden monogrammed corkscrew, also nestled into its custom velvet cradle. Resting above both was a small silver knife with the words "Our Love" engraved on it. He paused, hooked his right index fingertip inside a small hole, then slid out a long, wooden tray from the cabinet's belly. He set the bottle on the tray.

As he took the knife, he wondered how it had sounded when it sliced through his mother and father's wedding cake sixty-three years ago. As he removed the corkscrew, he wondered how easily its tip pushed into the champagne bottle cork at their wedding, how smoothly the screw burrowed into the bouchon, how easily it secured its purchase. *How many people cheered when his father popped open the bottle? Did it spill out onto the hand-woven tablecloths that lay underneath? Did his parents hook pinkies together in Le Nœud de l'Amour – The Knot of Love – playfully tugging them to and fro, signifying the give and take of marriage, before sipping their champagne and beginning their new life together?* He didn't know for sure, but he let the thoughts wash over him.

Viate pressed the knife tip into the bouchon wax and breathed deeply: sure enough, the wax released its scent of grape musk, legendary from France's Burgundy region, a visceral sign of its connection to the earth from whence it came. He twisted the knife, pulled off the wax plug, felt its monogram, smelled it, tasted it, bit it, chewed it, swallowed it, then set down the remains. Holding the corkscrew in his left palm, he curled it, letting its weight and heft remind him of the gravity of the moment. Then, he put his right middle finger onto the corkscrew's pointed end, pressed hard until the tip punctured flesh, and drizzled three drops of blood onto the cork; it hungrily sopped up the blood. He pressed the screw to the bloody cork, twisted once, twice, three times, then felt it give way. Gripping the bottle in his left hand, he tugged the corkscrew and opened the bottle.

I'm willing to do the little things to succeed, Daddy. You never believed me but I am. I'll even get bloody to get what I want. He sucked his blood off his fingertip.

The cork made a wet, dull "thwump" sound instead of the high, pingy pop of a lowly millionaire's liqueur. *How fucking satisfying.*

He poured a dash of The Louis into a snifter and let it breathe. Admiring the bottle, he spun it to and fro. *Are these my fingerprints? Why is there dust on the neck? Did my staff take it out to admire it? They know they're not supposed to – it's mine!*

He set the bottle down then stepped towards his desk, putting both palms flat onto the wooden crate. Foreign markings covered the aged oak, touchstones on its global journey; he recognized lettering as Old High German and Latin. At the top was a hand-carved emblem of a wreathed eagle atop a mountain, a salute to Friedrich Nietzsche, who had descended from the mountains to share his wisdom. Below the emblem was an inscription: "Wahrheit ist das Schicksal".

Truth is Destiny.

Twisting a rubber-tipped crowbar, he opened the crate's top. The scent of aged wood and old parchment filled the air, a fragrance that transported him to a time long past. On top was a handwritten note: "Here it is, I hope it's worth it. Expenses forthcoming – R.T." Below that, a book lay nestled within a bed of soft, hand-woven woolen cloth, dyed deep crimson, and lined with fine straw. Wherever it came from, Viate knew it wasn't from here. He liked to think it originated from an old Bavarian village, its rich color chosen to signify the importance of what it holds.

He lifted the book out – *fuck, it's heavy!* – grabbed his Louis snifter, sat down in a Hidebound leather chair, then rested the book on his lap. Peeling the soft cloth open, he finally saw what he'd been waiting a decade to see.

Sitting in his lap was an original copy of *Thus Spoke Zarathustra*, originally written by Friedrich Nietzsche and published in 1885. The first official English translation was by Alexander Tille in 1896, with the more well-known and influential translation by Thomas Common in 1909. All fine and good, Viate noted, but any run-of-the-mill billionaire could have those. He wanted a special version, and he knew where to find it.

He set his investigator onto a private publishing in 1894, by an obscure London press known for its limited and meticulous runs, completed a full two years before the official English translation. Lore had it that the original translator had been a close associate of Nietzsche himself, tasked with preserving the text's original power and nuance. Only 50 copies of this translation were ever printed.

Even still, he didn't want to be one of 50. He wanted the one written for *him.* He wanted *his* Bible. And now, he had it.

The cover was made of the skin of the now-extinct Pinta Island tortoise, a tortoise that had become a symbol of conservation efforts and climate change futility. Scientists had discovered the last known tortoise in 1991, named him Lonesome George, and tried for decades to find him a mate to continue his bloodline; but ultimately, they were unsuccessful, and Lonesome George passed away on June 24, 2012. It marked the official extinction of the Pinta Island tortoise, and the martyrdom of Lonesome George.

And now, Blonden Viate had a copy of Nietschke's historical tome, covered in Lonesome George's skin. It was the only copy ever made.

He licked the tortoise skin cover. It tasted salty and clean, like the oceans of divinity. *You'll never be able to taste this, Daddy. There's only one copy, and it's mine.*

Putting his hands flat on the cover, he ran through his normal routine. First, he checked the upper left camera, then the right, then those that lined the floorboard perimeters; all lit green, all operational, all connecting to both his own private system as well as the home's standard security system. Later he would compare the feeds from his private link to the home's security system, using the AI bot code he'd developed himself, to make sure they were the same, that no outside force had intervened. Next, he slid his U-disc into a small, lead-lined box in his chair's arm, the secret compartment he'd made to ensure complete silence from anyone *there.* Just in case. Then, he would whisper "daddy daddy daddy" three times into the chair's arm, checking his self-made cellphone app to see if it registered any decibels whatsoever; when it didn't, he knew he could count to five – one, two, three, four, five - then place his feet flat on the floor, then, and only then, he could lean back into comfort.

Finally safe, he exhaled deeply, smiled at the book, and opened it.

He read aloud:

"Once blasphemy against God was the greatest blasphemy; but God died, and with him died those blasphemers. To blaspheme the earth is now the most dreadful offense, and to esteem the entrails of the unknowable higher than the meaning of the earth!

The Overman is the meaning of the earth. He is this lightning, he is this madness!

I teach you the Overman. Man is something that shall be overcome. What have you done to overcome him?"

Blonden Viate sipped his Louis XIII cognac and savored his discovery. He said, in a voice that bellowed through the expansive room:

"God is dead. I am The Overman."

I have Lonesome George, the Louis XIII, and now, Nietschke's greatest work. I have his Bible, Daddy, not you, I have the only one ever made, from the skin of an extinct animal. It's mine, not yours, Daddy. I am the Overman, not you.

CHAPTER 8

PROBITAS HEADQUARTERS
BOULDER, COLORADO

"The meeting of Probitas will come to order," Exalted Master Blonden Viate said. He banged his gavel once, twice, then stood facing the group. One hundred and twenty-seven advocates turned to face him. Reaching inside his left inner robe pocket, he pulled out a picture of his unsmiling father - a wrinkled, wallet-sized black and white photo - and set it on the lower lectern shelf. From his right pocket he pulled out a picture of himself smiling in broad colors, a 3 x 5 laminated card. He set the pictures side by side, then pressed them together so the size difference was obvious. Unsatisfied, he grabbed his father's picture, folded and bent it, scrunched it, then reopened it and laid it next to his. There it sat, crumpled and atilt, meager next to his own magnificent image. *That's better. I'm over twice as big as you are, Daddy*, he thought.

He held up his right first, then began:

"Morales sumus!" he said, then extended his index finger.

"We are the morals," the group chanted, then extended their index fingers.

"Verum sumus!" he said, extending his middle finger.

"We are the truth," the group chanted, extending their middle fingers.

"Sumus progscientiae!" he said, extending his ring finger.

"We are progscience," the group chanted, extending their ring fingers.

Master Viate relished this moment: when he stood before his tribunal, his three-finger salute upright, their three-finger salutes in agreement, waiting for concurrence from other gatherings. The Umbi-link buzzed at his temple – agreement from Geneva! - and he raised his left hand to recite their motto:

"Progscience: Forging Truth, Fueling Revolution!" he chanted.

"Long live Probitas!" the group chanted in return. His temple buzz-buzz-buzzed in approval.

"These are exciting times, ladies and gentlemen. We are twenty-two days away from COP 50 and we have a full slate of items to finish, so let's get started. Lexicon, you're up!" Master Viate motioned the group on his right, and a tall, slender, bald man stood up.

Lexicon 1 scrolled to the first item on his holo-screen. "First, I must say that it is truly my honor to be placed in this position, to stand before the honorary tribunal of the most distinguished faculty, scientists, moralists, and thought creators…"

"The words please!" Master Viate interrupted. He tapped his fingers on the desk with impatience.

Lexicon 1 smiled. "Micro. Fusion. We have full approval for a complete and total ban of the words microfusion, nuclear microfusion, and all corresponding combinations thereof."

The room buzzed with applause and huzzahs.

"But that's not the best part," L1 continued. He looked left, then right, then smiled broadly. "We have full approval to ban…'Clean Nuclear!'" He jumped backward with excitement.

"Hear, hear!" a member yelled.

"Vivate probitas!" another screamed. Members hugged and kissed.

Master Viate let the room ring with excitement, let their temples buzz with approval, let Lexicon 1 soak in the communal respect he'd earned. Just last month Viate had publicly excoriated L1; his admonishment of "we have seventeen words to ban and all you have is 'gas gage'?" had gone Umbi-viral. It had been a calculation, of course, as Viate needed constituents to know he still wielded the bludgeon of climate language control. But now, on the cusp of COP 50, Viate milked the moment.

"And that is full approval for banishment. You have full legal?"

"All the way through Climate Court 7. Full legal, Supreme Court would be next." Lexicon 1 beamed.

Legal 1, seated on Viate's right, nodded approval.

"Penalties? Describe them please," Viate said.

Lexicon 1 counted them off. "First, social media scoring, Stampede at the lead. A full 10-point hit per usage. Second, after 5 Stampede hits we can drop their climate morality score, their CMIR, point-for-point. That's huge! And third – this is what I'm most proud of – we have received full-penalty approval for Offsetting Unapproved Children."

Master Viate turned to Legal 1 and asked: "Full OUCH?"

Legal 1 nodded. He motioned his hand in a karate chop gesture.

Master Viate turned to Lexicon 1 and nodded his head in approval. *Well done, my son, I didn't think you had it in you.* "So, you can now shame a language violator's children in full legal standing, is that correct, Lexicon 1?" he asked.

Lexicon 1 nodded yes, turned red, clasped his hands in front, then looked at the floor. "Yes, Master, we can even put Child of Denier banners at their school."

"Full OUCH, with COD banners, how impressive. And what was the secret to getting my esteemed colleague's full legal approval for this groundbreaking admonishment?" Viate asked. He winked at Legal 1, co-opting his participation in this demonstration.

"Honestly, it was the help I got from Communication, Master Viate. Communication 1 was indispensable, his tagline was sheer genius," L1 answered. He bounced on his feet.

"The tagline?" Viate asked.

Lexicon 1 pointed across the aisle, towards Communication.

Communication 1 stood and said: "Nuclear: it's the new N-word."

"Robes off, people," Master Viate said as he shut the door behind the four of them. He tossed today's New York Roast onto the desk: "What the fuck – I thought we killed print seven years ago. How did this even get out there?" he fumed. *One of these bastards planted the story, and I'm going to roast their nuts when I find out.*

Media 1 grabbed the newspaper and feathered the pages through her fingers. "Damn I miss these things," she said. She pressed the ink into her fingertips.

"I'm not here to have you fucking admire newspapers, Media 1. You're here to tell me how it got there in the first fucking place. Who did the interviews? How did it get printed? And where did they come up with this shit?" *Was it you? You used to work just down the street from the Roast, you could've dropped it off over coffee.*

The NY Roast's headline was ominous: "Blo-Viate, Climate Pirate". What followed was a 3,000-word article that roasted the Probitas organization, its members, and the progressive science techniques they employed.

"They're calling it Franken-psyence," Viate said.

"It's actually pretty clever," Media 1 said.

"Talk again and you're back in Lexicon," Viate snapped.

"They obviously kept the presses. And stockpiled paper from before," ProgScience 1 said.

"Yathink?" Viate said as he scanned the faces in the room. "I don't need you to tell me what I already know, I need you to tell me how we're going to fix this. I want you out in front of this. It's time to play offense, for fuck sakes!" *Maybe it was you, ProgScience. Maybe you miss the glory of those fat media dinners, the way those Los Alamos fucks pumped you up full of your own bullshit.*

He glared at Media 1 until she could no longer meet his gaze; she stared at the tabletop and waited for instructions. Taking a deep breath, he looked intently at each of his Guiding Forces, letting the tension build. When it peaked, he said in a voice much softer:

"There's a reason you're my Number Ones. You've earned these positions. I didn't give them to you, you've done the work. We're not here to advocate, we're here to transform." His voice tapered off at the end, with "transform" nearly a whisper.

"No one else can do this. You," he pleaded, "are the Guiding Forces. You have been Chosen. Our job isn't to respond, our job is to shape."

Media 1 closed her eyes, took three deep breaths, then let her open eyes raise off the table. She blew out through O-shaped lips.

Viate addressed her in his softest voice: "Media 1, you've got a Master's degree from Columbia University. You wrote The Probitas Doctrine, for crying out loud. You built the stone tablets, as it were. Those came from you." He turned and continued.

"Legal 1, you've got a whole team from Harvard Law, you've built the entire structure upon which our future depends. You will take down Big Oil and every single one of their Republicrat backers. It's you that will do it. Do you think Lexicon would have had their day in the sun without you?" He paused. "Your job is not to form a second court, it's to get into the Supreme Court. Your job is to own it." He patted Legal 1 gently on his left shoulder.

He turned to Lexicon 1 and smiled. "Nuclear, the new n-word. Nice. Now that's what I'm talking about. A bit blunt force perhaps, but our job is not to be subtle. Our job is to –"

"Transform," ProgScience 1 interrupted.

"Yes." Viate said.

After a silent minute, PS1 responded: "It's time to release the Polar Papers then. We've got a few weeks left, we can make it work."

"You can be ready?" Viate asked.

PS1 nodded.

"Lay it out for me," Media 1 said.

"Well, it goes like this: manmade global warming has melted the ice caps so much that Earth's physical properties – like its distributed weight around its rotational axis – has changed. That means Earth's rotation changes enough to even affect time. It may lengthen or shorten days, depending how we position it. That could heat the earth more, with the resultant societal effects, yada yada." ProgScience1 said.

Viate let it sink in. "Yes, that's it," he encouraged.

PS1 puffed up, then nodded.

"Let's get into it then," Media 1 said.

PS1 explained. "It's like your dryer at home. When you dry a load of wet towels or other heavy items, they sometimes gather in one spot and cause the bin to spin off its axis. That's why the alarm goes off: the weight is off-balance and can cause the dryer to tip over.

In this case the melted ice caps are the towels, they re-form elsewhere and knock us off our axis. Alarms and such go off, yada yada."

Viate nodded and pondered the suggestion. "I like the dryer thing, it's something Joe Everyman can digest." He turned to another and asked: "How about the Matheists?" *The Matheists, of course! The article was chockablock full of numbers and assumptions, where else would they have gotten them from?*

Matheist 1 sat forward and clicked off numbers. "The NY Roast has a 64.86% disapproval rating among Democans, so the story will score high on the Revile Index. But of course the Republicrats will jump, I predict a 4.74% bump in approval for the next 45 days; that's without countermeasures, of course."

Media 1 nodded. "Do you believe it?"

"Yes," PS1 answered.

"Can you prove it?"

"We'll work with Matheism, tweak the probability algorithms. We can measure how wet towels reallocate in driers, create four or five scenarios, then formulate climate extractions based on that data. We can probably get to two significant figures through peer-review by COP." PS1 looked at Matheist 1, who nodded.

"I'll need three," Media 1 said.

"Fine. Three significant figures," PS1 said.

Matheist 1 said: "I'm sure we can even get into the high twenties with it."

"No! It has to be in the upper 30s at least, preferably lower 40s. If the probability index is in the twenties, they'll call it the Ice Capades. You get that, right?"

PS1 and Matheist 1 looked at each other, paused, then nodded.

Media 1 asked: "you going to fill in the 'yada yadas'"?

"Of course, PS1 said.

Blonden Viate felt the power of divinity wash over him. The world was consolidating into his vision, the tectonic plates shifting, the gifts he'd been given were the signs. Probitas was ready to take their next steps.

He pointed outside to the auditorium. "They are the sheep, we are the Shepherds."

The group nodded slowly.

He was ready. They were ready. "I have one more thing for you, my Guiding Forces."

He pulled a U-disc from his front pocket and snapped it onto his right temple. As it clicked into place it cycled through colors: black, yellow, green, black, yellow, green, running through its own decision-making process. Which is, as it turned out, exactly what it did: when it hit green it stayed lit, bright as an emerald, pulsing brightly. Viate felt the light warm his temple and forehead; he saw the green tint reflect off his group's eyes.

"Welcome to Virident Green," he said.

"What the hell is Virident Green?" ProgScience 1 asked.

"It's one of the gifts we've been given. First was the bump, it gave our world a much-needed kick in the ass. Time for us to slow down and take stock of where we are and where we need to be. And the second is this new jewel from U-Net, something they've been testing - with my influence, of course - for years. It's color-coded to a person's climate score based on thousands of data points: it's like a litmus test for an individual's climate stance. They haven't divulged its algorithm, of course, but suffice to say it scrubs the data universe for every trace of climate impact and gives a score: green for those of us in-sync, yellow for those in-transit, and black for those needing correction."

The group sat in a green, pulsing glow, staring at his temple in silence.

"But…how will this happen, sir?" Media 1 asked. Her eyes sat wide, staring at his glowing temple.

"It now comes standard with all new U-discs, all existing units will be over-air retrofitted within the next 48 hours. Anyone choosing to use U-discs will have this feature implemented automatically," Viate said.

"Their visual climate score, on display for the world to see," ProgScience 1 said, to no one in particular.

"It'll take the guesswork out of it, that's for sure," Matheist 1 said.

"Aren't there legal concerns? Won't people sue the shit out of them?" Media 1 asked.

Legal 1 shrugged. "People can choose whether or not they use U-discs, it's their choice, just like lots of other big tech. If they don't want to use it then that's fine, they don't have to. But if they do, this comes with it automatically. That's the deal. It's voluntary, so we're protected." *Guaranteed Legal 1 was involved, he knows all the ins and outs of what we're doing, how we're all exposed. Damn sure he's bullet-proof – while tossing the rest of us under the bus.*

"I calculate a 33.47% adoption rate, sir," Matheist 1 said. "Interesting, but hardly transformative."

Viate shook his head. "We just had a magical bump, people. Nothing works. Nothing but what U-Net and Stampede operate, that is. Don't you see our chance here? We have voluntary martial laws in-place, and both companies have opted-in for this special dispensation." *Are you really not seeing what we've been given?*

"Meaning they can do whatever they want," PS1 said.

"Meaning it's their products, their networks, and they can implement whichever features they choose to. And they've been authorized by Federal to operate their systems until the glitch can be repaired," Viate said. "Given the chaos -"

"- Adoption will increase to 91.7%." Matheist 1 said.

"Exactly," Viate said. "We'll be able to aggressively implement and enforce our climate doctrines instantly."

"No standards, no laws, no votes, no statutes. It's the wild, wild west. Martial law. We can make twenty years of progress in twenty days," Legal 1 said, rubbing his chin. Viate couldn't tell if he was happy or pissed.

"It's our time, don't you see? Our divine right. This is no accident, this was meant to be. We have been handed the tools, literally. It's Us who've been given these gifts," Viate said.

He milked the moment, then, when the emotional current ebbed, he drove the point home: "King Ferdinand had his Inquisition. I have Virident Green. We're going to use it." *But Ferdinand left holes, which was his undoing. I won't make that mistake. Virident Green will reveal the apostates, the deniers, the frauds. There will be nowhere left to hide.*

Master Viate stood and held his hands out to the side. When the group stood and gripped, he saw it: they were a glowing circle, the righteous creators of climate justice and truth, an emerald halo of Divinity. He led their chant: "We are The Divine, We are the Chosen, We are filled with the Spirit."

They paused, then Viate finished: "I am The Overman."

"I am The Overman," the group said. *They don't understand it. Only I truly understand its gravitas, its weight. They've never seen Lonesome George. Only I've tasted him.*

"Let's go guide the flock," Viate said.

As the group disbanded, Viate stewed in his own thoughts. *More than anything, I need Virident Green to protect myself from these heathens. They don't believe it, they don't want it, they'll fuck me just to get a tenth of my power. They've always wanted what was mine, what I've earned, what I've spent my whole life building and nurturing. They're gnawing at the edges, gutter rats on a bone, waiting for my guard to slip. Virident Green will expose them before they even dare. It's my shield, my sword, the only way to keep Probitas from falling into their greedy hands.*

CHAPTER 9

PROBITAS CORRECTION CENTER
BOULDER, CO

Mateo tugged on the neckline of the black ceremonial robe. He hadn't worn a robe like this since college graduation thirty-two years ago, and that discomfort had been voluntary: the red, University of New Mexico robe was a sign of pride. Today, however, his black robe was a sign of climate shame.

Supreme Guardian Jeanette Littledove stood at the podium, adjusted her green gown, and welcomed the group. She stood, hands on lectern, and surveyed the front row: Mateo sat with four other climate sinners, all in their mandated climate penalty robes, in front of fifty other Probitas members in their green robes. Black was an indicator of their sinner status, the color of coal, and served as a visual reminder of their climate transgressions. In a few minutes they would be separated into five separate correction groups and would enclose themselves into five separate rooms with a sinner and ten correctors in each.

"Welcome, Climate Scobs," SG Littledove said.

The Probitas members said, in unison: "Ssssssscobs."

"Probitas: U-discs, please," she said.

All members reached into their robes, pulled out their U-discs, then snapped them to their temples. When they did, the discs lit up in bright emerald-green, matching their robes. The group seemed surprised, and "ooh'd" and "ahh'd" in admiration.

"We are honored to be the first tribunal in history to wear U-Net's new Virident Scoring system. From now on your U-discs will let the world know of your climate morality in full, clear, Virident Green Glory," SG Littledove smiled, "and leave no doubt as to your commitment to our cause." She rotated her head back and forth, smiling at the room's green-templed glow.

"And of course, it will remind us what work we have to do," she said, focusing on the front row. "Your U-discs, please."

Mateo looked at the other four supplicants; three fumbled in their robes, into their pockets, a fourth sat in defiance. She looked up at SG Littledove and shook her head. *No.*

SG Littledove persisted. "Scob Leslie?" she asked.

Leslie sat on her hands in defiance.

With a quick wave of her left hand, SG Littledove motioned towards three large Probitas members. "Very well, purity only comes to those who desire it. Remove Scob Leslie, please, brothers."

The three men grabbed her – Leslie fought and pushed and clawed – and pulled her towards the doorway. She yelled as they dragged her away: "I just need to visit my daughter at UCLA!" She grabbed Mateo's arm as she passed him, but the men wrestled her fingers off him. "Please help me…" she mumbled as she was taken away.

With Leslie removed, SG Littledove turned to Mateo: "Scob Anaya?"

Mateo weighed his options. He had no car, no approvals, nothing but the clothes he was wearing, and was in Boulder, Colorado. He could wrestle his way out of the procession, but then what? Who knew how things had changed because of the bump? He had no way to get to D.C., which meant he had no way to find Reyes. He had no choice.

He pulled the U-disc out of his jeans pocket and snapped it into place. The U-disc buzzed electric, pulsed, then turned black.

"Congratulations, everyone, for committing to Umbili-Net's Virident Program. You will now be able to show your climate morality instantly. Vivate Probitas," she said.

The group bellowed in green-temple-glory, fist-bumping and hugging each other. Mateo looked at the temples of the remaining three sinners: their U-discs shone inky black, pulsing with each heartbeat. They would now be marked as Scobs, until their correction.

"Probitas: all stand," SG Littledove said.

All members stood; they poked the four Scobs to stand up with them.

A Probitas member handed each Scob a thin, leather-bound notebook, with the phrase "OUR BELIEF" in gold letters on the front. Mateo opened it, and inside there was one page of text.

"As part of their cleansing, Scobs must recite each of the Probitas Core Truths. You must repent. Out loud, Scob. Say it," SG Littledove said.

You have to fucking be kidding me. Someone behind him poked him in the ribs, so he muttered, out loud:

"Core Truth 1: Manmade climate change is an existential threat." *Good God, they've completely lost it.*

The tribunal chanted, in unison, in voices unwavering: "Pillar."

Mateo looked around. *Really? We're Tibetan monks now?* SG Littledove stood, palms up, studying him intently.

"Core Truth 2: Fossil fuels cause it."

"Pillar," they said.

"Core Truth 3: The enemies: Fossil fuel companies and Republicrats." *Why do there have to be enemies? We're all using the same shit.*

"Pillar."

"Core Truth 4: Those who question are the enemy." *So just shut up and drink the Kool-Aid, huh? No room for thinking here?*

"Pillar."

"Core Truth 5: You are either with us, or against us." *Oh, I'm clearly against you, you cyborg-thinking fucktards.*

"Pillar."

Mateo looked at the next one and paused. He turned to SG Littledove and shook his head. "How exactly am I going to do this?" he asked.

"You must repent, out loud, Scob. Say it," she said.

Youbatshitcrazymotherfuckinglunaticsican'twaituntilIgetoutofherebastards.

"Core Truth 6: Thou shalt take a public, moral stand against fossil fuels and their companies."

"Pillar."

"Core Truth 7: We can prove this with Science and ProgScience. Both are approved." *And donkeys eat their own shit.*

"Pillar."

"Core Truth 8: ProgScientists must be followed completely. Their word is not to be questioned. They are in complete agreement. There is consensus." *Yes, mein Führer.*

"Pillar."

"Core Truth 9: We have all the solutions. They exist today. They are approved." *Maybe. Some. Kinda.*

"Pillar."

"And last but not least: Core Truth 10: All we need to solve climate change is the will." *And a fuckwad lot of money.*

"The Will. Pillar."

The tribunal then formed a tight circle around Mateo, shrouding him in a robed cocoon. They patted him on the back, gently slapped his shoulders and arms, then took turns congratulating him. Then, they simply started muttering his new moniker, the next phase of his metamorphosis, like he'd graduated from Cub Scout to Webelo: "unscob, unscob, unscob, unscob, unscob." *What: they think they're cleansing me?*

When it got to SG Littledove, she put both hands on his shoulders, looked him straight in the eye, and said, curtly: "Sign it." She handed him a plume, dipped in black ink.

A damn feather. Signing my confession like Friar Baldric the Repentant Dribbler.

The Probitas Doctrine

Core Truth 1
Manmade climate change is an existential threat.

Core Truth 2
Fossil fuels cause it.

Core Truth 3
The enemies: fossil fuel companies and Republicrats.

Core Truth 4
Those who question are also The Enemy.

Core Truth 5
You are either with Us, or against Us.

Core Truth 6
Thou shalt take a public, moral stand against fossil fuels and their companies.

Core Truth 7
We can prove this with Science and ProgScience. These are both Approved.

Core Truth 8
ProgScientists must be followed completely. their Word is not to be questioned. They are in complete agreement. There is Consensus.

Core Truth 9
We have all the Solutions, They exist today. They are Approved.

Core Truth 10
All we need to solve climate change is The Will.

So Let It Be Done
Vivate Probitas

Signature: *Mateo Anaya*

UNSCOB

"The problem is, ya cain't go east-west, ya gotta go south. Git yerself to Baton Rouge," the man called Houston said.

"Not sure I understand the problem, friend," Mateo said. They'd finished their first day of retraining and were allowed a 45-minute dinner. While within earshot, Probitas members stayed away from the four Scobs as if they were lepers. They looked over at and whispered about the sinner group, but none dared come near. Their retraining wasn't yet complete.

Houston leaned in. "Ya gotta git to Baton Rouge. Then you cain git down to the delta, then up onto the river."

"Let's pretend I know what you're talking about, friend," Mateo said, eating a plate of Probitas-issued food. He pawed at the vegetables on his plate: they were round like peas, but blue? Carrots were also blue, and the oval patty was…meat of some sort? Mateo poked at it with his fork.

"Ain't likin' that stoink?" Houston asked.

"Stoink?" Mateo asked.

Houston nodded. "Some hybrid kinda meat, they make it in labs. Company named BiOvine makes it, s'posed to have no methane at all. They say it's all 'planet friendly' 'n shit. Zero 'missions."

Mateo speared it with his fork and held it up: it was a perfect oval, with a uniform thickness of about ¾", colored a mottled gray. He held up a spoon full of blue peas and carrots. "Vegetables?" he asked.

"Yep. Them's veggies. You should see the taters," he laughed.

"I can't eat this shit," Mateo said.

"Turns out that's 'zactly the problem with stoink: gives most people the shits. So we's savin' cow farts and replacin' em with people farts," he laughed, slicing into his stoink steak. "You gonna eat yers?"

Mateo shook his head and pushed his plate towards Houston. "All yours, friend."

Houston chopped up the stoink into small, square bits, mixed in the blue peas and carrots and stuffed big spoonfuls into his mouth. "So like I's sayin', ya gotta git down to Baton

Rouge. I cain git ya there." Little bits of stoink and veggies spit out of his mouth when he spoke.

Mateo looked at the Probitas members surrounding them; other than snide, scornful glances, they paid him no mind.

"What makes you think I'm looking to get to the delta?" Mateo asked.

Houston shrugged. "Just a feelin' I git." Chomp, chomp, chomp.

"Let's say for a minute you're right. What are you thinking?"

Houston held his spoon in his fist and leaned forward. He lowered his voice: "You gotta git south, all them east-west Crow-doors is 'lectrified. Cain't git no vehicle 'tall on 'em if it ain't 'lectric. But north-south don't have it 'n such, they never finished. Y'all can jus' drive like normal."

"All the way to Baton Rouge?" Mateo asked.

Houston shook his head and pointed with his spoon. "Down inta Texas. Still hard to find gas, but I got 'nuff to git us down into Oklahoma, then down to Texas."

"I thought you said Baton Rouge."

Houston shrugged and chewed. "Yeah, well, we go straight down, but to git to Loosiana y'all need to get more creative."

"Y'all? You're not coming with me?" Mateo asked.

"Just to Texas. They's lookin' for me in Loosiana, so I cain't go there. But I got ways to git ya there."

Mateo pondered the plan. He liked the idea of getting out of this crazy climate fucking looney bin but didn't know how that would affect anything else. No gas cars in Colorado? If he made it to Baton Rouge, could he find a way to get east? He had no idea. Plus, was he really going to walk around with his temple-disc pulsing black? How else did the bump fuck things up?

Mateo grew suspicious. He shrugged: "Not sure, friend. Maybe you're just working for them and are trying to bust me?"

Houston stopped chewing and laughed. "I look like some'un who'd work for them?" He finished his stoink plate and rubbed his scraggly beard.

“OK, but tell me…why me? Why can’t you just do this yourself?” Mateo asked.

“Well, it’s jus’ part of my sentence is all. I cain drive in Colorado, just not ‘lone, I cain only drive my fam’ly ‘round. If it’s not kin, they’ll arrest me all over again. So if they stop us, yer my brother,” he smiled.

CHAPTER 10

DR. COLLEEN FORSYTHE AND BLONDEN VIATE
UMBILI-CALL: TEMPLE TO TEMPLE
LOCATIONS UNKNOWN

Dr. Forsythe made sure to temple him at 10:45 local time, precisely fifteen minutes before his strict bedtime of 11:00 p.m. She could be gracious, transparent, and forthcoming, all while fully honoring his busy and extremely strict schedule. His hard stop would limit the questions, soften the emotional ramblings, and give her the control she needed to steer this ship.

She could have called via cell phone, if only to maintain the distance, to lessen the emotional gravitas of temple-to-temple linking. But he would have taken that as a slight and, given her news, another slight would not go so well. She was about to wrinkle his thrice-pressed-suit, shall we say, and he wouldn't tolerate a coffee stain on his tie as well.

Or so, that was the plan.

She decided to temple him in her barren home office, with nothing but a slate gray wall behind her. No pictures on the wall, no framed family photos, no electronics of any sort; no, well, anything at all that he could see. She'd heard of the U-net pirate apps that could electronically sense a background wall's history and recreate it: it could tell where a painting frame nail had been, then extrapolate the type and originality of the painting itself; or a picture frame that had recently been removed but left the trace of an electronic shadow, to be reconstructed by advanced AI bots that could sense color and pattern trails in the ether. A colleague had reminded her of a lost business deal because a contract had been left out on a desk after a U-call, only to have the U-disc's holo-screen capture the contract image and send it to the recipient. U-discs sometimes had ghosts, and those ghosts sometimes had cameras. Best to just remove everything from the office and take no chances.

Even still, as was her custom, she allowed herself one small indulgence. She unzipped her briefcase and pulled out a small, white-sand-filled vial. It said "Aloha" in red letters across it, with a small cork sealing its top. It still bore the $6.95 price tag. She gripped the soft memento of her daughter, estranged for nearly three years now, as a stark reminder of the costs of her purpose. Motherhood, as she often said, has many responsibilities. Some hurt more than others.

Snapping her U-disc into place, checking her own image in the holo-screen, she scrolled down to "Viate" and pressed.

His face appeared on her screen, though he said nothing.

"Blonden?" she asked.

He nodded, then said "Viate."

She felt his voice ring across her head, like a small train circling her forehead. U-calls always affected her this way, and it was especially more pronounced with a deeper, male voice. Undoubtedly Viate knew this, and made sure his words echoed with baritone.

"Good evening, Blonden, thank you for templing at this late hour. I know we've got just a few minutes, so let's get into it, shall we?" Tick tock, his strict bedtime allowed her to forego the pleasantries.

Viate nodded.

"Right, well, first off: how is the Virident trial going? I understand it launched at your tribunal yesterday and that it's kick-off, shall we say, went off with a bang? A fair assessment?" she asked.

"It was met with moderate enthusiasm," Viate said. "I would not say it went off with a bang. But certainly a loud whisper, if I may articulate that."

Of course it did. Can't get too excited about what you don't control, can you, Blonden? "Well fabulous, I'm glad to hear it. Launches are always difficult, especially with something so far-reaching and complex. I assume your tech-folk have logged whatever bugs they found and will coordinate with my team to fix it."

Viate nodded.

"I'm curious as to what you thought of Virident Black?" she asked.

"In what way?" he said.

"Did you find the instant visualization of climate criminals to be, shall we say, enlightening?"

"They seemed adequate. It does save us on some paperwork, which is always a positive." He took a sip of cognac, then asked: "Colleen, is this a customer service call? If so, perhaps we could just have our tech teams perform this necessary function."

OK, you pompous ass. I'll drop the bomb. "No, you're right, let's get right to the heat of it. You've seen how Virident Black works, how all the different colors work, so your group is up on that. Fantastic. But there's more. There are other capabilities that we're launching that I want you to be aware of. Do you have a minute for a quick demonstration? Post-haste of course."

Viate frowned. "As you wish," he said.

"Right. First, I'm going to show you the hypno-net feature that's now standard on all models. Ready?"

He nodded.

She pressed the button and saw it light up, then heard Viate's temple buzzing from the other end. His eyes closed halfway, his head rocked back and forth, and he let out the slightest of hums, like a drawn-out "burrrrrrrrr." Letting it buzz for ten, eleven, twelve seconds, she hit the button a second time and switched it off. His eyes slowly opened fully, he blinked, then he shook his head lightly. *I can control your entire brain if I want, Blo-Viate.*

"Pleasant. Somewhat soothing. Felt like a shiatsu massage on my brain. Moderately enjoyable," he said.

She saw him look up at the holo-screen clock: 8 minutes left.

"Wonderful. Now let's go to black. It's a bit, shall we say, less pleasant than the previous. Slightly painful – I'll make sure to turn it down – but certainly a wake-up call. It's something we'll be able to control from HQ," she said.

"Ready," he said.

I'm quite sure you're not. She pressed the black button, it purred, then his forehead crinkled deeply. He closed his eyes, clenched his jaws, and shook his head back and forth. Groaning, he just shook his head, no no no. *He looks like a dog trying to shake the meat off a bone.*

She clicked it off.

"Decidedly unpleasant. What a supreme punishment for hardened criminals. They won't even know what hit them, which is, I suspect, precisely the point. Virident Black will set a new standard," he said. He looked almost proud to have endured the pain, something that made her very uncomfortable. *Masochistic bastard.*

He looked up at the timer: 4 minutes left.

"Blonden, there's one more thing I want to show you before we finish. U-Net's calling this Phase 2, but it's already available. And it's already embedded into every controller."

"Fine, show me please," he said.

"It's not something I can show you, actually."

He tilted his head in confusion. "What is it exactly?"

"It's a new feature that will ensure complete compliance. It will turn what we're doing from a voluntary system into something compulsory."

His eyebrows raised with interest. "Compulsory?"

She just said it: "With Phase 2, we have the ability to attach the U-disc onto the magnet permanently. To make its removal, shall we say, inconvenient."

"What does that mean?" he asked.

"It means that we have a control where the implanted magnet and the disc fuse together, and become permanently attached to one's temple. The implant will have an external component. It will remain on the head until the entire apparatus is surgically removed," she said.

She saw the holo-timer: 1 minute, 30 seconds left. Perfect. And now for the coup de grace.

"We can control this at HQ, of course, the technology to render this is quite proprietary and under U-Net's strictest of confidentiality policies. As such, we'll only render this with your full approval, of course, after we deliberate and agree."

"You won't put that capability out in the field?" he asked.

No fucking way are you getting your hands on this. "U-net has very strict confidentiality requirements. They prefer to keep it under tight control. I'm honored to be on their approval team, so thankfully we have a say in this manner. I'll consult with you as we need to implement it, of course. But it will be a headquarters-based capability. I'm sure you understand."

30 seconds left. Perfect.

Viate thought, then blinked, then nodded three times. "I understand. It's an interesting development. It will certainly give you – give us – a way to hold climate criminals accountable. I assume we'll have more discussions as we need it implemented. I thank you for showing it to me."

"Of course. We'll be partners in its roll-out, so I view you as a critical link in this chain," Dr. Colleen said.

Viate smiled and nodded. "By the way, tell your daughter Janet hello from me. Will you see her for the holidays?"

Fuck, that bastard. Even my ghosts have ghosts. Dr. Colleen nodded gently. "Thanksgiving, hopefully. She'll be honored to hear your greeting."

11:00 p.m. Click.

Blonden Viate had spent the last fifteen minutes arranging his chair in the middle of his study, in front of his awards and diploma wall. It was his standard backdrop: let the world see how esteemed he was, how educated he is, let them bask in the glory of his righteousness.

He practiced how to sit. Should he be casual, with his right leg crossed over his left, as if he was simply taking time out of his relaxation to indulge her call? Or should he sit formally, knees at ninety degrees, palms atop, like he was awaiting his next international award. Summertime coquettish, where he let his chin drift up towards the sunlight? Or wintertime formal, where his face stood strong and confident, like his neck was framed by his tuxedo collar and tie?

He decided on award formal and placed his feet three inches exactly in front of the chair's. Twenty minutes earlier he had removed his family wooden monogrammed corkscrew from its velvet pouch, and he held it in his right hand. He loved its heft, its burled finish, its smooth veneer. It felt heavy and clean and pure, exactly what he needed for this moment.

At 11:00 p.m. exactly, he clicked his holo-screen to accept her Umbili-Call. She knew his schedule and that he bedded the same time every night, so she chose 10:45 on purpose. It was strategic.

He reached down and tore a pancake-sized hole on his right pajama pant leg. Riiiip. *I know what you're going to do, Forsythe. I'm ready for you.*

When he put the U-disc to his temple and she turned it pink in soothing massage, he put the corkscrew tip, the very part that punctures a champagne bottle bouchon, to the skin on his thigh. An hour earlier, he'd shaved the top of his thigh completely to make sure nothing stood in the way of his commitment. When the U-disc buzzed and hummed and soothed and turned pink, he pushed the screw tip into his thigh. Just the tip.

You have no idea the strength I have.

When she mentioned black, he turned the screw clockwise a quarter turn. He already knew of Virident Black, *did she really think someone of my stature wouldn't have already heard of it?* He gave it another quarter turn to make sure he could feel the blood crawl down his shaved thigh.

When she pressed the pain button, his head echoed with trauma, like a parasite had burrowed into his skull, made its home, then had babies. It felt like his skull was going to burst from the inside, out onto his silk robe, down onto his imported rug. When his head throbbed the most, he turned the corkscrew a full turn, making sure to keep his face still and unbothered.

I am ten feet tall, I am the king of the world. The pain you give me is nothing, it doesn't even begin to test my strength. Is this all you've got? Daddy gave me ten times more. And I can take a hundred.

He felt the blood flow down his thigh; he was sure it soaked into the chair fabric.

When she said those words "under headquarters control", when she smiled on the inside but not on the outside, when she made it known that she controlled him and not the other way around, he gave the screw one more full turn and released it. It stood straight up, buried into his right thigh, oozing blood out the sides.

His heart pounded, yet he calmed his breathing. His thigh screamed in pain, yet he said nothing. She chopped his brain into nibbly bits, yet he took it all. She tried to exert her control, yet he displayed his.

Look at the man I am, Daddy. Look what I can do that you could never do. Even when betrayers and interlopers and vampires bare their fangs, I stand tall. I am stronger than they can ever imagine. There is nothing she can do that I can't minimize. Her biggest is my smallest. She is nothing. Like you, Daddy.

When he clicked off the screen and disconnected her treachery, he sat for exactly two more minutes. At 11:02 p.m. - two minutes late! – he gripped the corkscrew's handle, turned it counterclockwise one, twice, thrice, then pulled it out. As the blood gushed out of the wound, he turned the pain into freedom. He felt her fake control bounce off him like raindrops: small and wet and impotent. He turned the pain into purity, into cleansing, into salvation.

I eject you from me, Daddy. It's the blood of purge, of purification, of transformation. They think they can do this without me, just like you always did. I'll show them.

I am free. I am clean.

I am The Overman. You never will be.

CHAPTER 11

ESCAPE FROM PROBITAS
BOULDER, COLORADO

At 6:13 p.m. on October 29, 2045, Mateo and his new friend Houston walked out of Probitas Correction Center.

When he retells his story of escape in twenty years, he will say that he proudly strode out the glass doors in triumphant glory: he will have fought his way through green-templed henchmen bent on his imprisonment, tossing bodies and misplaced climate morality aside. He would escape as a bloodied, righteous vigilante, rescuing his friend, venturing forth to spread climate justice and truth. He would be a true climate hero, freeing others on his quest to save his son.

Today, however, he snuck out the side door and ran like a motherfucker. Houston reminded him at dinner that "we ain't 'rrested or nuthin', we just agreed to this shit 'cuz they own the roads." True words, perhaps, but it did nothing to quell the adrenaline rush when the side door clicked behind them. They looked at each other, eyes wide, and ran like hell. He suddenly felt fifteen years old, like he'd stolen a Hustler magazine from a 7-11 and wasn't going to stop running until he got to the crick.

Ten gasping minutes later, Houston stopped and veered into a wooded glen; Mateo followed. Houston went down a small hill, turned left into a thicket, then pushed through shrubbery into a clearing. There before them was a white, rusty, Ford F-150 pickup truck.

"Please tell me you don't call it Mater," Mateo said.

"K. Won't tell ya," Houston said, softly patting the hood like a reunited lover. "But she's always been good to me." He leaned down, kissed the hood, then said: "Missed you too, darlin'."

"Now *that* answers a few questions I had," Mateo said, chuckling.

Houston flipped him off, then ran to the driver's side door.

The pair climbed in and began their trek towards Tyler, Texas. They couldn't drive on main highways or roads – the Jim Crow-i-dors were fully off-limits – so they turned south towards Boise City, Oklahoma. It would be a seven-hour drive through hills and wintery farmlands, and Mateo settled in for what was to be perhaps the most interesting part of his journey. *I'm actually looking forward to just driving.*

They drove for hours, neither saying a word. Mateo rolled down his window and made his right hand into a wing, letting the air flow over and under it, lifting and dropping, like his dad showed him forty-five years ago, like he'd showed Reyes twenty years ago, like every dad showed his son for time on end. Yes, it was cold, but that's what made it great. It felt simple and cleansing. It was just pavement and dirt and trees and cold and gray and tires and hills and, well, freedom. They were men on a mission, no schedule, no overlords, no technology pumping real-time data into their feeds or brains. Three miles before the Oklahoma border, he remembered how happy he could be without all that technology.

And then, technology reminded him how quickly it could take it away.

In unison, their U-discs buzzed loudly and turned black. The buzzing was so strong it made him dizzy, and its intensity increased to the point where everything blurred. The disc burned into his skin like molten metal, behind his eye sockets, blurring his awareness into a dizzying swirl. Mateo tried to rip his off, but it felt welded to his skull, the pressure increasing so much he thought an alien would burst out of it. Houston had gripped his and was frantically trying to tear it off, but he couldn't; he just drove and slapped at his temple like a wasp had burrowed into it.

Then, as suddenly as it had begun, it just stopped. Crossing into Oklahoma, their U-discs went dead. He sat breathless, shaking his head, his mind trying to catch up with what his head just felt.

Mateo's first clear thought was that he'd been shot. His window had been open, maybe some rednecks were out shooting beer bottles and happened to sling one his way. Maybe he'd taken a bullet to the temple and was just lucky to be alive. But, he found no blood, and no wound. Nothing had hit him, and nothing had hit Houston. It was just their U-discs.

"What the fuck just happened?" Mateo finally said.

"No fucking idea," Houston returned. He kept trying to slap the disc off his head. He twisted and tugged, but it stayed attached.

"Yours come off?" Mateo asked.

"Nope. It's like somebody burnt it on or somethin'," Houston said. His eyes were wide, and he put both hands on the steering wheel to steady them.

"Yours still burning?" Mateo asked.

"Nope. Just stopped like yours did," Houston said.

"Like it turned off at the border or something," Mateo said. He was confused, but no longer in pain. He kept tugging on his U-disc, but at least he could think clearly. "That Virident shit must have had a trap door or something," Mateo offered.

"What's a trap door?" Houston asked. He pressed his thumb into the disc.

Mateo shrugged. "Don't know, really. All this Virident Green bullshit, maybe there's like some way for them to zap you if you go too far. Maybe they're not going to stop with just colors, maybe it goes way deeper than that. So they can control you," he said.

"That's some messed up shit, then," Houston said.

"Yeah. Messed up. But maybe it's worse. If they decided they could zap us like that, if they decided they were going to use these to punish us, what's to stop them from doing more?" Mateo asked.

"What do you mean more?" Houston said.

"Maybe there's a kill switch. Like if we don't come back then just press a button and it blasts us dead." Mateo said. He had no idea what they were capable of. They obviously knew they'd escaped, otherwise why would this have happened? *Are they tracking us now? Are they just going to hunt us down and zap us with these things?*

"That's some Mission Impossible shit," Houston said.

"But then they stopped working once we got into Oklahoma," Mateo said, trying to figure it out. "Maybe there's a limit to this stuff. Like we just reached its limit or something."

"That makes sense actually. Everything stops working once you git to Oklahoma. My first wife said I couldn't ever git it up once we hit the border," Houston said, grabbing his crotch.

"Could you ever?" Mateo said. He laughed.

They both drove in silence, holding their temples, pondering the crazy, painful world they'd entered.

They made their way down into Boise City, neither of them saying a word in the ten-mile drive. They pulled into a gas station, an old, four-nozzle Union 76 gas station; the rotating orange globe atop the sign pole still spun. Mateo stepped out, flipped open the gas tank door, unscrewed the gas tank lid and pumped gas, once again finding solace in the simple act of filling his tank. It reminded him of how far the world had come, but also how far he still needed to go to find Reyes.

Houston walked out of the store with a loaf of white Hillbilly Bread, a can of Peter Pan peanut butter, and a jar of Motley Gourmet jelly. He tossed the jelly to Mateo and said: "welcome to Oklahoma."

Mateo studied the label. "Sand Plum jelly? What the hell is that?" he asked.

"Oh, you're in for a treat, brother," Houston said, spreading the ingredients across the truck hood like he was preparing a gourmet meal. He opened the peanut butter, then the jelly, then looked around for a utensil to use; finding none, he just jammed his index finger into the peanut butter and scooped some out onto the bread. He did the same with the jelly. He smeared them both into a frothy mess, closed the bread together, then shoved it in his mouth. "Crunchy," he said, though it sounded more like *kruthy.*

"What, we're savages now?" Mateo asked. Reaching over to Houston's belt, he slid the Bowie knife out of its holster and held it up. *See? We're not apes.*

He dipped the pointy knife into the jelly first, spread it evenly on one slide, cleaned the blade on the second slice, then dipped it into the peanut butter. Spreading it just as evenly as the jelly, he cleaned the knife with the slice, put it back in the holster, then pushed the slices together. Admiring his work, he took a bite. Taking his time with things that matter, where he could take time to let his nurturing side, like he did when he made Reyes' PB&J sandwiches all those years, somehow centered him. He loved it, in fact. *Just take the time to do something right, even if it's not that important. Because damn, this sure does taste good.*

"Dangit, you'll starve yourself if you eat that way," Houston said, which came out as *dungyallstaffselfthatway*.

Mateo shook his head, and chewed, Houston nodded and chomped away. He had peanut butter on his lips, chip salt on his cheek, and Coke in his beard; he chewed hungrily.

"Hand-made PB&J. Who knew it'd taste so damn good?" Mateo said. He fist-bumped Houston. They stood, leaning against the rusted Ford F-150, eating peanut butter and jelly sandwiches at a Boise City, Oklahoma Union 76 station. They finished their sandwiches then shared the bag of Lay's. They chugged their Cokes, breathed deeply, then belched. Life seemed pretty fucking good at the moment.

"You a Blood or a Crip?" Houston asked.

"Huh?"

Houston held up a red and a blue bandana and said: "We cain't go 'round with these bloody bolts on our heads. Folks'll think we 'scaped from some nuthouse or somethin'," he said.

"Well...didn't we?" Mateo said. "What the fuck have we gotten into? Is everyone going to have these things? Will they become permanent now? Is that what the bump did?" He had a million questions.

Houston shrugged. "Don' know, but we're in country now. We drive trucks with gas, and punch folks in the jaw that piss us off. We're home."

"I thought Texas and Oklahoma were enemies," Mateo chuckled.

"True that. Or used to be, anyways. Now we just see eye-to-eye is all. We wanna eat BBQ, drink Lone Star and watch football on Saturdays. Pretty simple shit. Not like them Jim Crow-i-dor nutshits."

Mateo nodded. "I'm in a Crip mood, I think" he said, and grabbed the blue bandana.

"Gonna tear this thing outta my head at some point, even if I gotta cut it out myself. I ain't Frankenstein, no neck-bolts for me," he laughed. "But for now, guess I'm a Blood." He grabbed the red bandana, folded it, then tied it around his forehead.

"No shit, brother," Mateo said, then tied the blue bandana over his U-disc.

CHAPTER 12

CADILLAC RANCH
AMARILLO, TX

"James Dean in that Mercury '49,
Junior Johnson runnin' through the woods of Caroline,
Even Burt Reynolds in that black Trans-Am,
All gonna meet down at the Cadillac Ranch."

– Bruce Springsteen, "Cadillac Ranch

Mateo clicked off the radio as they pulled into a barren wheat field in west Amarillo. He stepped out of the car and viewed the exhibit: ten 1960s-era Cadillacs sat, noses buried in Texas cow pasture dirt, their tailfins pointed up towards the sky. Built in 1974, Cadillac Ranch had grown to signify America's car culture, a celebration of wind-in-your-hair independence. Over the years millions had visited from across the world, spray-painting the cars, snapping selfies, turning the junky art exhibit into a colorful array of pop culture history. It symbolized freedom, driving, and, well, Texas. Giddyup.

He'd always loved that song and couldn't remember how many times he'd listened to it cranked up, top down, driving up the California coast. Cadillac Ranch always meant freedom, except now, it had morphed into something much darker. As he stepped up to the cars, Mateo felt that those you, free days were long gone.

All ten Cadillacs were painted flat-black, including the windows and undercarriages. Across each car was a red letter, the entire panorama spelling out the word: "L-I-K-W-I-D-E-A-T-H". Bloody teardrops dripped from some of the letters, giving it an apocalyptic scowl. It was ominous and poignant on its own, but like most things, Cadillac Ranch had grown into a much bigger climate testament.

Mateo looked left at Mount Lithium, an enormous pile of dead batteries. What had started as a collection of dead EV battery packs had since morphed into a collection of dead batteries of all sorts. Mount Lithium now stood as a teeming dump of auto, flashlight, computer, phone, and countless other battery types, like it was mocking the anti-gas outrage of climate activists. Mateo could almost hear Mount Lithium saying: "Fuck me? Well fuck y'all too!" He picked up a rusty AA battery, juggled it like a hot potato, then tossed it at Houston. It hit Houston's shoulder and dropped into the dirt. They laughed.

Houston pointed to a small hand-written sign on the right, in front of an enormous black-sludge lake. The sign said: "Lake Shat-too."

"Wadda ya s'pose that means?" Houston asked, holding his nose. "Fuckin' thing stinks."

Mateo chuckled and shook his head. "I read about this. We moved all our manufacturing to China, back in the 20's, and these factories would just pour out sludge into the dirt. Started in this area called Baotou, so they called it Lake Battoo. Just big toxic lakes of manufacturing sludge."

"Lake Shat-too?" Houston asked.

Mateo shrugged. "Well, Texas, right? Like: 'them Chinese just shat, we can shat, too'."

Houston laughed. "Texans. They can shat, too. Shore does smell like they shat all over. Fuckin' A."

"Damn, no kidding. That thing stinks." Mateo said. This is what climate progress looks like? All that yelling and screaming, all we did was swap digging one hole for another. Lithium's better than oil? No difference at all, we're still digging graves. He shook his head, pretended to strum an air guitar, then sang:

"Cadillac, Cadillac
Standin' by, a lake called Shat,
Pulled up to, my house today,
Came and threw them bat-ter-ies a-way!"

He played a couple more bars of the song on his air guitar, then stopped in frustration. *That song's worthless now, all this climate shit even cost me Springsteen.*

"Ya lost yer rhyme there," Houston said.

"Nothing rhymes anymore," Mateo said. "You think that's what Springsteen meant?"

"Prolly not." Houston kicked at the dirt, then walked back to the truck. He opened the passenger door, then the glovebox, and pulled out a long, leather sheath. He tossed it on the seat.

Mateo looked at it, then Houston, then back at the sheath. "More PB&Js?" he asked. "Good man, keep your damn fingers out of my peanut butter."

"Y'all trust me?" Houston asked.

"Trust you…how?" Mateo asked. He squinted at Houston and stepped back.

"Been meanin' to talk with ya about this. Now that we're in Texas, well, where we're goin' they see things a bit different." He lifted his chin towards Mateo's forehead.

Mateo touched the blue bandana around his forehead.

"Now listen, don' mean no disrespect here, you gotta know what I'm all 'bout by now. Ya reckon?" Houston said.

Mateo nodded.

"But here, y'all wearin' a blue bandana and all, I mean…"

Mateo squinted. "Because I'm Mexican," he said.

"Well, yep. Cuz o' that. In Dallas, they'll think you run with Los Locos. You don' want none o' that, trust me," Houston said. "No disrespect…"

"None taken, fair point. You're the guide. I just need to get out to D.C." Mateo said.

Houston grabbed the leather sheath and pulled out the Bowie knife. He motioned at Mateo's temple and said: "we gotta get rid o' that. Mine too."

Mateo held up his palms, then shook his head. "No fucking way."

"What choice we got?" Houston said.

———

Skriiiiiiitch is the sound an implanted metal disc makes when it's ripped off your temple.

Well, it wasn't exactly ripped off, it was more like a knifeblade slicing around an electrical wire and pulling off the insulation. But still, it tore flesh.

Houston had pulled a paper bag out from under the driver's seat and yanked out a glass bottle.

"Jack Daniels?" Mateo asked.

"West Texas Crude, make it myself," he chuckled. He took a long pull on the bottle, chugged it, then handed it to Mateo.

Mateo pulled the same amount, then a little more, then chugged.

"Nasty," he said, holding his hand over his mouth. He took another swig, then another, then slowly felt the heat rise up to into his head. When he felt numb, he took hold of the Bowie knife. Houston pressed his left cheek against the door jamb and sat down; he held a torn oil towel to soak up the blood.

Mateo pressed the knife blade flat against Houston's right eyebrow then slid the edge under the U-disc; he pried up a bit to see if it would give, but it didn't. He rotated the blade around like he was peeling an apple, then around again, and gave it another tug. This time the skin bled just a little, and the disc gave way. "Gonna work," Houston said, and chugged the moonshine.

Again, Mateo pressed the blade flat but pushed further into the middle and spun; he held the handle and asked: "Ready?"

"Fuckin' A," Houston said.

Skriiiiiiitch. Mateo popped the U-disc off, like he was flipping a quarter off a hot railroad track with a spatula. He mashed the rag to Houston's temple and did his best to ignore the blood, only succeeding when he focused on an image of Reyes' face. *I'll see you soon, son.*

"Fuckity fuck fuck!" Houston yelled, mashing the oil rag onto his temple. He kicked at the dirt but held the rag firm. In a minute, he pulled it off.

Mateo nodded. "That's gonna work." He pushed the rag back up until the bleeding stopped, then put a big square Band-Aid on it.

They switched positions.

Mateo chugged the whiskey, held his breath then nodded. Houston quickly jabbed and spun, then jabbed and spun again, then quickly skriiiiitched the U-disc off Mateo's temple.

Pain shot through Mateo's forehead, his eyes went blurry, he thought he was going to pass out. He sat for what seemed like hours, holding the blood rag up to his temple at the quarter-sized injury. *Damn it, boy, this is what I have to do to find you.* Slowly, the blood flow stemmed, and the pain subsided.

"No more Crips," Houston laughed.

"No more Bloods," Mateo laughed back.

"Fuckin' A," Houston said.

Lauren clicked open The Big Texan Steak Ranch on her U-disc holo-screen and leaned back on her living room couch. Famous for its 72-ounce steak challenge, the restaurant was the epitome of cowboy kitsch. Reyes joked that he could eat the entire steak and get his family's meal for free, so there he was, seated under the stuffed elk head and buzzing neon "Saddle Up, Hombre" sign.

Or so he thought.

As the waiter slapped the gigungous T-bone onto the checkerboard tablecloth in front of him, Reyes just opened his eyes and mouth as wide as he could, in mock surprise. *There is just no fucking way*, his expression seemed to say.

Gina leaned in, opened up her non-sewn-together nostrils, and breathed in the steak's aroma. "I don't think a cow's ass ever smelled better!" she joked, licking her lips. She pulled her hair back and tossed it over her right shoulder, clearing a path to the food.

Lauren loved her like this: spunky, alive, natural, before she'd destroyed her face and head and body in acts of climate self-mutilation. This was her sister as she knew her, as she loved her, as she wanted her. *Full of life, full of hair, full of beef.*

Mateo reached over, jammed his thumb into the steak until it oozed juice, then sucked his thumb clean. "Yum!" he declared.

"Dad, that's gross!" Reyes said, tucking the white napkin into the neck of his T-shirt.

"That's a cow's ass the size of San Antone. And *I'm* gross" Mateo chuckled, tucking his own napkin into his own T-shirt. "It's feedin' time. Yee-fucking-haw!"

"Language, Teo," Lauren said, smiling.

Mateo stuck his tongue, then jammed his fork into the steak.

This was it. This was her whole, her world, her life, her soul, her all. This was...*her.* All she ever wanted, seated around the table in front of her. She drank it in. She smelled the raw steak. She listened to it sizzle on Reyes' plate. She drank in their laughs, their giggles, the soft squishy sounds of their chewing, and swirled in pure, unfiltered, U-disc bliss.

CHAPTER 13

UNIVERSITY OF NORTH TEXAS, DALLAS LAW CENTER FORMER DALLAS CITY HALL AND POLICE HEADQUARTERS DALLAS, TEXAS

Three hundred miles east of Cadillac Ranch, in the fifth-floor hallway of the University of North Texas Law Center in Dallas, Texas, Governor James Fritz looked into an empty room. The jail cell, spotlessly preserved for the past 82 years, still had the original mattress on which Lee Harvey Oswald spent his last night. He stepped in and poked at the mattress, absentmindedly looking for any signs of blood, any last remnants of John F. Kennedy. Governor John Connally had been hit along with JFK on that fateful day in 1963, and while Connally would recover from his injuries, America would never recover from Kennedy's.

On the second floor was his grandfather's office, also immaculately preserved. John "Will" Fritz had been the captain of Homicide and Robbery at Dallas PD the day Kennedy was shot, and most people assumed he was the "man in the white cowboy hat" that held Oswald's arm when he was shot in the basement. But Will Fritz typically stayed out of the spotlight and instead did the hard, detailed work their family was known for: he'd interrogated Lee Harvey Oswald himself in the cold, white, windowless basement room of 106 South Harwood Street. It was John Fritz who earned Oswald's confession after murdering President Kennedy, the most famous confession in Texas history. The Fritz family name would be enshrined in Texas and America's hearts forever.

Governor Fritz touched the nameplate of his grandfather's office and shook his head. He was about to oversee a meeting between the Texas Attorney General and the Dallas Police Department to discuss the state's response to Federal Climate Immigration Morality legislation and he burned with irony: his granddaddy jailed a real killer in this very office, and *now they want us to search for pretend killers. Twelve pounds o' bullshit in a ten-pound hat,* he thought.

In many ways, Fritz welcomed the glitch. Life before technology, life before we're-going-to-die-by-the-weekend-because-of-climate-change was just, well, simpler. Hell, he was staring into the actual scene where his grandfather solved a presidential murder, events that etched their family into the gristle of Texas history. No computers, no cell phones, no U-discs, no discs of any kind whatsoever. It was just men looking into the eyes of other men and making up their minds: guilty or not. If not, the prairie's your rodeo. If so, we'll lock ya up just like we did Good Ole' Lee Harvey. *Piss me off and I'll knock yer teeth out, then hand 'em back to you at the Bar-B-Q.*

Stepping into the first-floor conference room, he called the meeting to order. The glitch had blitzed all the lights and electronics, so he'd just shut the power off and went old-school: an open-window conference room, boots and shirtsleeves, just like law and order should be decided. "Hook 'em 'Horns," Governor Fritz said, tugging at his burnt orange University of Texas tie.

"Sooner Nation," Attorney General Susan Loving III said. The granddaughter of former Oklahoma AG Susan Loving, she always wore Oklahoma University dark crimson on her fingertips; today she tap-tap-tapped them on the desk.

"Let me just say: this is a steamin' pile o' Odessa bull-shit," Governor Fritz said. "We already got us a immigration problem, now we got a glitch, or bump, or whatever the hell else they wanna call it. And now they want us to climatize these illegals?"

"That's not what they're calling it, Jim. They want to make sure everyone gets the proper respect, the proper benefits best suited for their status," Loving said.

"'Their status.' That's DC-speak for them fixin' to spend our money," he said.

"Well, they'll send a lot of money too, Jim," Loving said.

"Tell me how this works, Susan."

"Since the glitch, the only networks that work reliably are, really, just Umbili-Net and Stampede. Just them. The highways, the autos, all linked by U-Net. So far, it's been the only reliable system," she said.

"Now it's *their* system? Cost us billions, too."

Loving nodded, then continued. "Their proposal is to use the U-Net as the core backbone, until we can get everything back online. We'll use U-discs as the primary communication pathways: visual, audio, information."

"Ain't we doin' that already? Mostly, anyway," he said.

"They want to expand it. They've added a new climate capability to the network, where they color-code a person's climate status automatically. They call it Virident," Loving said.

"What in Sam Houston are you talkin' about, Susan?"

"They tried it out in Boulder already, and it works. The discs are color-coded to a person's climate stance: green for approved climate thought, yellow for those working towards approval, and black for those that need…well, correction," Loving said.

Governor Fritz sat in silence, tapping his fingertips on his belt buckle.

"From what we've seen, they just light up with the color of their approval. If you're climate approved, you'll be green during waking hours, off at bedtime; yellow will blink every 10 minutes, off at bedtime; and black will just stay on always."

"Yella arm bands. Hey, at least we know who to shoot," Police Chief William Winton said. He'd been silent until now.

"No one's shooting anyone, Bill," Loving said.

"Dallas PD out huntin' Jews." Winton said. He pointed his finger at each empty chair in the room and shot. *Pew, pew, pew.*

"That's exactly what it's gonna feel like, Susan. We're gonna label people," Governor Fritz said.

"There's a potential problem with the black ones," Loving said.

Police Chief Winton said: "Ain't there always a problem with us darkies?"

"Not like that, Bill. Explain it please Susan," Fritz said.

"It works like this: we give each immigrant a U-disc, it gets synced with their ID and then their climate history. Those 'Who Believe' go green, they get uploaded automatically with bank accounts, temporary shelter, clothing, food credits, all that. Yellow gets somewhere in the middle, they go to a temporary shelter where they can 'Get Right', then qualify for more benefits," she read.

"But not the black," Fritz said.

"If it turns black, they'll be classified as Scobs. And Scobs get 'approved for climate reassignment' facilities for further training," she said.

"Concentration camps?" Chief Winton asked. "You kiddin' me?"

"Reassignment facilities. But that's not the worst part," Loving said. "If someone goes black, the U-disc attaches itself to the temple. Permanently. And the only way they can join society again is to have it removed surgically. So they can be 'Proven Green.'"

Police Chief Winton leaned back in the chair and put his hand on his holster. He chewed on a toothpick and shook his head. "So, lemme get this straight: illegals will put on this disc, if it goes green they're hunky-dory, they shine bright as baby Jesus' ass. We feed 'em, we clothe 'em, we house 'em, we pay 'em. If they're yella, we do that for a bit o' time till we can get 'em straight," he paused and looked at Fritz and Loving.

"But, if they go black, this disc burns into their forehead forever, and we bus 'em off to some camp. For retraining," he said. He snapped his holster open, pulled out his department-issued Glock 26, held the barrel and pushed the handle towards James Fritz.

"Shoot me now, Fritzie, ain't no way I'm doing this," Winton said. He clanked his pistol down onto the desk and slid it across.

"Calm down, Bill, that's not what's gonna happen. I don't even know what to say. We're just gonna let them U-boys run everything now? No votes, no nothin'?" Fritz asked, to no one in particular.

"Just until they fix the glitch," Loving said.

"I tol' you this was gonna happen, Governor," Winton said, his demeanor suddenly formal. "Didn't I tell you? Been saying it for years. Ever since they passed them Jim Crow highway laws – ever since we let California tell us how to run our own damn roads – we knew this was gonna happen."

"A lot of jobs in those highways, Bill," Fritz said.

"A lot of California dipsticks got a lot richer," Winton said.

"A lot of your men got overtime, too. How do you like your new patio, Bill?" Fritz asked.

Winton shook his head back and forth. "Fair 'nuff. But now tell me: how'm I s'posed to do my job? California's settin' the rules, tellin' us what we can and cain't do, how we can drive, who're criminals and what-not. And they're doin' it here in Texas. In *Dallas*. In *your* Dallas. You look me in the eyes and tell me how I'm gonna do my job, how we're gonna keep the people of the great state of Texas safe?"

"What do you suggest, Bill?" Fritz asked.

"Let's arm 'em all. Every U-disc gets a gun too. Let God sort 'em out," Winton said.

"God damn it, Bill, enough with that crap. You and I've been fightin' on this for years, we ain't gonna solve it now. Just…enough." Fritz held up his palms flat. *Truce.*

Winton held up his U-disc and said: "maybe this thing is gonna tell me which criminals to shoot? Got a aim-finder on it?"

Fritz pressed his palms flat in the air. *Enough.*

"When do we have to respond, Susan?" he asked.

"We have to formally accept by next Friday or else they limit access to the Jim-Crow-idors 20, 30, and all '35s. If we don't do anything that will be seen as non-compliance."

"That'll shut down the whole state," Fritz said. "God save 'em."

Governor James Fritz stood at the Centro de los Trabajadores Agricolas Fronterizos bus station in El Paso, Texas and studied the line of immigrants. He was used to this, of course, as he'd been redirecting immigrants away from Texas for the past 13 years, towards St. Louis, or New York, or Chicago, more steps in his never-ending battle with DC and sanctuary cities. Three years ago, he'd reached a DC détente: he would ship away the exact number of immigrants that had been agreed to by DC's think-tank spreadsheets. Washington would tell the press how Republicrats hated mothers and children, Governor Fritz would tell the world that Democans loved opening other people's borders then taking credit for the "wonderful contributions to America by people of color." Both stories earned their respective huzzahs and critiques, and the money kept flowing. It was win-win by lose-lose.

Green-glowing temples lined up for the all-electric Umbili-Network buses, heading straight for St. Louis; Fritz could hear the air conditioning whirring and see the plasma displays scrolling through advertisements and Stampede feeds. Yellow-glowing temples lined up for the all-white buses, penitentiary castoffs that had been electrified. Each had a TV that displayed Stampede climate messaging: "it's not too late to be great - for the climate" and "you've been blessed to do your climate best". Air conditioning on the white buses was a crapshoot, and it would surely flicker during their 12-hour drive to Chicago. Immigrants with black temples, however, loaded up into smoke-spewing school buses; no one bothered to paint those buses anything at all, to make sure it was obvious they needed retraining. It was the climate equivalent of a perp walk: yellow buses were headed straight to Mississippi, in full view of gawking traffic. Air conditioning was an open window.

Governor Fritz watched a family of five – two men, a woman, and two children – try to board a yellow-temple bus. The handlers blocked the bus door entrance, and the Dad grew increasingly agitated. Voices grew louder, fingers tapped and poked U-discs, the handlers yelled "negro, aqui" and pointed to other buses. After the two men were shoved out of line, the wife, now crying, gathered her kids and walked towards the school-bus-turned-deportation-train. The handler in their new line looked at their black temples – all five – nodded, then stepped aside so they could board.

Police Commissioner Winton looped his thumbs inside his belt and said, softly: "This is a sad day, Jimmy. Ain't no other way to say it. Can you imagine your Daddy – or your Grandaddy – doing this? I cain't either." He shook his head then spat into the dirt. "We're Texas. We do it our own damn way. Always done it, always will."

James Fritz seethed. Seeing the U-discs aglow as the immigrants boarded buses, he thought: *Good ol' Will took down real killers without no damn colored doohickeys. Now here I am, starin' at Mexicans with glowin' temples like we're sortin' cattle. Ain't what Granddaddy signed up for.* He pointed his chin to a group gathering behind the three buses. "That them?" he asked.

Winton nodded. "That's them. Got thirty right there, but there's plenty more who want in. Every'un wants to tear up them Crow-i-dors."

"Two thousand each, that gonna be enough?" Fritz asked. "Cuz there's more if needed."

"Hell, they'll do it for free if we ask 'em. Give 'em each a sledge and they'll chain gang that thing," Winton said. "Every-un hates them 'lectric highways."

"How long will it take?"

"'Bout two weeks. Most of 'em'll probably tent it, pull away from the road and sleep by day, then hammer them roads all night. They can get all three of them Crow-idors done in 'bout two weeks. Them roads'll be useless for anythin' after that," Winton said.

"Make sure of it, Bill. Damn Morgan Hill bastards," Governor James Fritz said. "They're gonna tell us where and when we can drive? We're Texas, for damn sakes, we don't do that Silicon Valley bullshit. I let it happen too much already." He turned to Winton and poked his finger in the air, for emphasis. "And remember: I want it messy. Tell 'em to shoot 'em, sledge 'em, pull 'em up by the roots for all I care," he seethed.

"The big climate conference is in twenty days, and I want them roads long gone by then, you understand? I want them U-cars gettin' lost in the desert, sendin' pics of sand all over the world. I want those Democans asking *me* for permission to drive my own damn roads. See how many of those fick-fucks can saddle up," Fritz finished.

Police Chief William Winton laughed. He pulled his Glock from his holster, pointed up, then fired a shot into the air. "Lone Star, mothafuckers."

Solved JFK, for damn sake. Now we're tellin' people where to drive, what color to wear. This is my Texas. We drive where we wanna drive.

CHAPTER 14

TYLER, TEXAS

Mateo stepped out of the Ford F-150 onto the front lawn of the McClendon House Museum. Built in 1878, the McClendon house sat on two acres in east Tyler and represented a Victorian and Italianate architecture style that harkened back to simpler times. Walking across the graveled path, he slowed his pace to hear the crunch: *nothing like the sound of boots crunching in soft gravel to ground a fella.* Stepping out onto the estate's lawns, he felt like a hundred years of technology never existed in the first place. He wanted to lay down on the big white porch, wrap the wooden planks around him, and take a nap.

Houston walked to the right side of the manor onto a gravel driveway, then continued towards the expansive back field. A hundred yards into the field sat a long prairie wagon, its white canvas gently fluttering in the breeze, led by four strong, spirited horses. Their coats were a mix of chestnut and gray, and the two lead horses bucked and snorted at each other; the other two chomped grass under their feet. Seated on a long wooden bench atop the coach was a large, white-hatted cowboy, his arms splayed wide on the bench, face up, eyes closed, drinking in the east Texas sun.

"Git yer ass up, cowboy," Houston said.

Brock Porter stood up, smiled, then clicked his tongue in his cheek: "Sic 'em, girls!" he said.

The two front horses snapped their heads toward Houston and snorted; Houston jumped back and put his hands up. "Bastard," he said.

He motioned for Mateo to come over, and he did. "This here's your ride," Houston said, then turned back to the wagon.

"Good one," Mateo said. He eyed the horses, the wagon, the grassy fields, and the large white cowboy standing on the bench. *Holy shit that's a big boy. He looks like a Marlboro ad.*

"Ain't fuckin' with ya," Houston said. "My boy Brock here's gonna get ya on down to Baton Rouge. He and his girls been makin' this trek for years."

Brock Porter's boots crunched on the gravel when he jumped down, and he strode over to Mateo.

"Mateo Anaya, meet Brock Porter. Brock Porter, meet Mateo Anaya," Houston said.

Mateo gave a confused look to Houston, extended his hand, then watched it get swallowed up in Brock's enormous grip. With a grunt and a shake, Mateo had met his chauffeur.

"Quit fuckin' with me, Houston," Mateo said. "How long did it take you to set this up?" He actually couldn't figure out how they made it happen.

Brock hooked his thumbs into his belt above his shiny "Porter Ranch: Tyler" belt buckle and squinted at Mateo. He studied him up and down – well, mostly down, because he stood almost a foot taller than Mateo - looked right, spit down into the grass, then looked over at Houston. "We good, H?" he asked.

Houston looked over at Mateo. "Y'all OK, Mateo?"

Shit, they're serious, Mateo thought. He looked at Houston, then Brock, then the covered coach, then back to Houston. All he could say was, "Um…"

Houston chimed in. "Look, tol' ya them roads is all messed up. Some are 'lectrified, some ain't, just have no way of knowin' what's gonna work and what's not. Me and Brock here been runnin' this route fer years, we know it back an' ferth. Guar-an-fuckin-tee we can git you down to Loosiana, 'cuz we been doing it for years. And no one can trace *shit.*"

Brock nodded and spat. He motioned for Mateo and Houston to follow him, which they did. Brock and Houston jumped up onto the wagon; Mateo followed. Brock stepped inside the wagon, shoved his thumb into a floorboard hole and pulled: underneath was a collection of metal parts and electronics, all nestled in together, a collection of motors and circuits and displays and gears. Mateo stepped back.

"You smuggling guns?" he asked.

"Rig parts," Houston said. He pointed at the various widgets in the floor. "Bits, drill collars, mud pumps, top drives, and the big daddies: blowout preventors. They made all new parts illegal, seein' as how they didn' want any more oil drillin', and they just figgered that the wells'd run dry once the parts ran out. So we make 'em down in Galveston and run 'em up through Lufkin, down into Loosiana. Keep them wells runnin' for the next twenty-ot years," he said.

"Now I run tours, and yer my fare," Brock said. He released the floorboard, it plopped back into place, and he pulled the beddings over it.

"So you smuggle oil rig parts in this, and I'm your cover," Mateo said, nodding his head.

"Done it five hunnert times now, prob'ly," Brock said. "Best wagon tours east o' the Pecos," he chuckled. Houston chuckled back.

"I've never even been in a coach before," Mateo said, nervously.

"Never tore a U-disc off yer head 'fore neither, till two days ago. Now look at us," Houston said, turning his head for Brock to admire.

Brock pulled up the bandage, squinted, then pushed it back down. "Shit damn," he said. "Y'all do that to y'selves? Nasty."

Houston grabbed the Bowie knife on his belt holster and smiled.

"Well shit damn. Maybe your California boy ain't as soft as I thought he'd be," Brock said.

"Oh, I'm a badass," Mateo said.

"That right, Houston? You bring me one o' them California *chingons*?" Brock asked, pronouncing it as *chin-gee-own-ays*.

"That mean he like his sushi cooked," Houston said.

Brock reached into his front pocket, pulled out a Bic lighter, then flicked it aflame. "Well alright then. I can work with this."

They all laughed. *Didn't think he was gonna buy it,* Mateo thought.

The three jumped down into the field, and Houston approached Mateo. He stood, face to face, and held out his fist. "Listen, brother, ain't nothin' the same now, we just gotta get ourselves back to basics is all. This is some good livin, trust me on that. Brock and me done this a thousand times, you'll wish y'all could do it always. Have you into Baton Rouge by noon Thursday."

Mateo knew he had no choice. *I'm not in Kansas anymore, and definitely not in California. This is the next step, like it or not. If I wanna see Reyes, I gotta go cowboy.*

He turned to Houston: "Don't know what to say, Houston. Woulda never made it this far without you." His voice cracked; he had to pause before continuing: "Thanks, brother. For everything."

"I aint one for no tears, Teo, you know that. You just keep on keepin' on, ya hear me?" Houston said, holding out his fist. "Be good to Porter here. Ain't his fault he's a Good Ole' Boy."

Mateo bumped his fist and nodded. *Thank you, brother. Really.*

"Ain't yer fault yer an Okie," Brock said, bumping fists with Houston. "I'll take care o' yer California boy here. Give him a taste o' good Texas livin'." Brock said. He jumped up onto the carriage.

"Lone star," he said.

"Lone star," Houston said.

"Yee haw," Mateo said.

CHAPTER 15

90 MILES WEST OF CHIRENO, TEXAS

"Y'all got two choices," Brock Porter said. In one hand he held up three vacuum-sealed gray bags, in the other he held a Winchester Ranger rifle.

"You going to shoot me if I choose wrong?" Mateo asked, holding up his hands in mock surrender.

"For dinner. We got these, or we can Texas it," he chuckled. He held the rifle out towards Mateo, showing a clear preference.

"What even *are* those?" Mateo asked, not really wanting to know the answer.

Brock turned the packages and read the labels. "Sez right here: 'BioBuffets are a complete meal, right out of the package. Contains 22% protein, 58% complex carbohydrates, and 20% fats. Just twist the package and it heats itself! Bone-in product available.'" He laughed, twisted the package, shook it, then tossed it at Mateo.

Mateo caught the package, now heating in his hands, and held it up. "This meat? And what is that, more blue veggies? Damn." He tossed it back and forth in his hands like a hot potato.

"It's a BioBuffet, veggies 'n meat right in the package. Sez so right thar," Brock said. He tossed the other bags aside, then stood. He wiped his brow on his shirtsleeve, then put his cowboy hat back on. "We jus' called 'em Stoink bags at first. Took us pert near a year to come up with BioBuffet," he said, pronouncing it as *boo-fay*.

"Wait, you invented these?" Mateo asked.

"Not the beast, jus' the name. That stoink is guv'ment issued, born 'n bred, we just licensed the formula 'n got the

Texokiana contract fer it. We breed 'n slotter 'em. But the feed? That's all us." Brock said.

"Not sure I understand," Mateo said.

"I'll tell y'all 'bout it. But for now ,we gotta git some dinner. You ever shoot one o' these 'fore?" he asked. He held up the rifle.

Mateo stood and shook his head. "You know I can't," he said.

Brock pulled the magazine out then pushed the rifle butt towards Mateo.

"Class 2 felony, just to hold it," Mateo said, holding his palms up. "Government Firearm and Weaponry law of 2030."

"Yeah, but have you ever shot it?" Brock asked.

"Course. I'm a badass, remember. Just testing to make sure you're not a spy."

Brock chuckled, then snapped .30-caliber bullets into the magazine as he spoke: "Sir, yer now in the great state o' Texas, we don' do none o' that GFAW bullshit down here. Look 'roun'. See any Californians? 'Sides you I mean." Snap, snap, snap.

Mateo shook his head.

"It don't matter anyways, we get ours off the grid, these 'r clean. Y'all could hold this up to the sensors and it wouldn't register shit, we know how to scrape the guts out of 'em." He snapped the magazine into place and pumped the first bullet into the chamber. "And since the glitch, hell, we're on our own down here. And it's just the way we like it."

As it turns out, the best way to attract wild turkey in east Texas, ninety miles west of Chireno, is to light a BioBuffet bag on fire.

Brock Porter did just that, tossed it onto the soft, Texas dirt, then walked away. He paced twenty, thirty, forty, then fifty steps, turned, and laid down on his stomach. Mateo did the same. Brock handed the rifle to Mateo, who wrapped the leather strap around his left elbow, pulled it tight, then adjusted the sight. "Well damn, look at you, actin' like you know how to shoot. Fifty yards ain't much, but at least feels like we're givin' 'em a chance, don' it?" Brock asked.

Mateo nodded, then squinted through the sight at the flaming bag.

Dark smoke billowed from the bag, and the night air carried it over to the pair. Mateo waved his hand across his nose: "Damn, that shit stinks," he said. Just then, as if they were air-dropped in, a flock of wild turkeys appeared and stormed the bag, pecking at it with their beaks. "Holy crap, where'd they come from?"

Brock laughed. "Them's crafty little fuckers, that's fer sure. They bury themselves sometimes, 'specially when they see wagons."

Mateo closed his left eye, focused his right through the scope, then pulled the trigger – BANG!

A puff of dirt went up five feet to the right of the flaming bag.

"I thought you said you shot before. Aim it," Brock said.

"I am aiming it!" Mateo said. He pulled the trigger again – BANG! – and a puff of dirt went up three feet to the right of the bag. *I hit every damn beer bottle I aim for. Usually.*

"Aim better," Brock said. "Just pretend you're shootin' out one of them Viszla tires."

Bang! This time Mateo got it. "Like fishin' in a barrel," he said.

"Or, like shootin' in a bag o' stoink." Brock said.

The biggest turkey lay headless and bloody, but the flock kept pecking at the bag and each other until it was gone. When empty, one of the smaller ones grabbed the bag in its beak and ran off into the shrubbery; the flock followed it, clucking along.

An hour later, Mateo and Brock sat on a tree stump by a campfire, grilling turkey and drinking whiskey. Brock had sliced corn cobs and carrots lengthwise and tossed them into the pan, so they poked the turkey and veggies together and ate, a Texas prairie kebab. *Some damn good eatin'*, Mateo thought.

"How do you even get into the stoink-farming business," Mateo asked. He cradled the Winchester rifle in his hands and felt its burnished wood hull; it felt solid and heavy and dramatic all at once. He took another swig of whiskey, passed it to Brock, then tossed a turkey bone onto the fire. It sizzled.

"We're in the regular ranchin' business first, but the regulations were gettin' hard. Had to start capturin' the gas, we were gettin' fined all the time, it was just gettin' tougher 'n tougher. We thought we'd breed stoink fer a spell jus' to keep 'em off our backs, but then they ran into a problem. Turns out their problem was somethin' we could fix," Brock said. He looked at Mateo with whiskey-blurred eyes and asked: "you a Washington-type? Y'all ain't got workin' hands. Maybe I shouldn't say nothin'."

Mateo looked at his hands and how unburdened with callouses they were. He shook his head, no.

"Took 'em ten years to develop them stoinks, designed 'em to not make any gas 'tall: no methane, no CO2, no nuthin'. They's all proud of it, thinkin' they'd solved the cow-fart climate problem. But it turns out when ya fuck up somethin' in one part of a hog, somethin' else fucks up back," he chugged, then spat. "Hell, I coulda tol' 'em that. Ain' no such thing as a free lunch."

"What do you mean?"

"So, Washington, right? They design these fuckin' cow-hogs, these stoinks, and they emit no methane or CO2. Magic, right? They redid their stomachs 'n shit, bred in all kinds of 'mitigating measures', they called it. Bred this whole new kind o' animal."

"Sounds perfect," Mateo said. Chug. "Isn't it?"

"Not to us. They redid the stomachs, the esophagus, bred in all kinds of new digestion 'n shit. But hey, guess what? When you git rid o' one gas, another comes to bite ya in the ass. Turns out they got rid o' methane and CO2, but then these cows made nitrous oxide instead. And not like a little, like tons," Brock said, shaking his head.

"Laughing gas?"

"Yep, N2-fuckin'-O. Laughin' gas. And these cows are shittin' this stuff out, and hey, turns out it's worse than CO2.

Turns out these fuckin' stoinks shit laughin' gas, which stays in the air for even longer and makes it all worse! No fuckin' shit," Brock said.

"I don't even know what to say about that," Mateo said. He just sat there nodding and chuckling.

"But ya come to Texas, ya git a Texas-sized solution," Brock said. "We been makin' feed for three generations down here, and turns out our special blend o' Texas weeds just sucks up that N2O. Turns out our feed solves their gas problem. Our feed is the only thing that unfucks them DC cows, the only thing that makes them stoinks 'missions free. And we're the only ones who kin make it," Brock said, smiling. He tossed another log onto the campfire

"Wait – RumenEase is yours?" Mateo asked. He'd seen the bags in all the hardware stores, and never really knew what they were for.

Brock nodded. "We invented that shit. First, DC tells us that we gotta breed their cows, so we breed their cows, got no choice in that, they got us by the short hairs. Then we find out their cows is all fucked up and our feed is what fixes 'em, so now we got *them* by the short hairs."

"I'm not sure having the government by the short hairs is such a great idea," Mateo said. "Look how they fucked everything up already. Hell, that I'm sitting here at all is because they just screwed it all up. They're gonna find a way to have you get outta their business."

Brock took a few moments to answer. "Well sir, the Porter fam'ly goes back more'n two hunderd years. We may not know much, but we know land, we know horses, we know ranchin', and we know Texas. Ain't never been a law we don' know where it begins, and where it ends," Brock said, poking his knife absentmindedly into the dirt. "We build that feed with 'gredients only us know, plus some that ain't 'zactly on the up and up. We built in a certain kinda deficiency, know what I'm sayin'?"

Mateo shrugged.

"After a few months them stoinks get addicted to our feed, they can only survive by eatin' it, and if they don't git our secret blend, they just haul off and die. Jus' happened to a big herd up in Iowa last month," Brock said.

"Insurance, Porter Ranch-style." He tipped his hat.

Mateo nodded.

"And now we're makin' most of it down in Messy-co. What we make up here is jus' fer show, for when the inspectors come in an' such. But the real stuff comes from down south, so anyone fucks with us Porters, them stoinks start gassin' up the planet all over again. And the only ones who know what happened, is *us*." He stabbed the knife into the ground.

"Well, and now *y'all*," he said.

Mateo put the whiskey bottle to his lips and took a pull. The heat of it made his eyes squint, and he focused his gaze onto a group of lights off in the distance. Try as he might, he couldn't make it out. Lifting the bottle, he pointed with his pinkie: "what's that?"

Brock Porter grabbed the bottle and swigged. "Nag-a-doches. Nuke plant. Guess they figgered we already makin' mutant meat, might as well make mutant babies too."

"There's a visual I didn't need," Mato said. "Nuke-shriveled nuts. Thanks for that."

"Yer welcome," Brock said.

CHAPTER 16

SUNSHINE FUSION NUCLEAR FACILITY
NAGOCDOCHES, TX
100 MILES EAST OF TYLER, TX

Choreographer Melody Rivers couldn't get her dancers to drop their nuclear-melted skin onto the ground properly.

Or rather, she couldn't get her lead dancer, climate activist Maja Andersson, to do it. The nineteen professionals had already learned that the best way to have the prosthetic masks drop off their faces was to wobble their heads gently, along the ear line; and when they did, their nuke-masks splatted properly into the dirt. But Maja Andersson couldn't get the hang of it. In take after take, Maja shook her head violently, like a dog trying to rip the meat off a sparerib. After a dozen tries, Melody Rivers realized it wasn't going to work.

"Maja darling, it has to look natural. Like your face just *wants* to fall off," Melody said.

"Nothing natural about nuclear fallout, faen også," Maja said. She kicked the rubber mask into the dirt.

"Now hun, you know I don't speak-ey Swede-ey," Melody said. "That's why we agreed-ey to speak-ey Eng-ley, didn't we?"

"Except I'm from Norway, so I don't speak Swedish, do I? Du ku," Maja said.

Melody turned to the mask maker and said: "Jimbo babe, we'll need those magnets. Toot suite, s'il vous plaît!"

Mask-man Jim pawed through the masks atop his worktable and grabbed one with ear hooks. The mask could be hooked over ears like glasses, with magnets that could be activated to drop the front skin away. Someone would have to press the magnetic switch, but it could certainly work. He handed the new mask to Melody.

"Let me see that face, my beautiful Meatish Sweetball," Melody said. She slid the mask onto Maja's ears, then pressed it to cover her nose. It looked pretty good, actually. She stepped back, clicked a handheld switch, and the front skin dropped off Maja's face. "Look at that drippy drama! Gorgeous, just oozing authenticity!" she said, clapping her hands gleefully.

Maja Andersson huffed away in disapproval. "If I don't get paid in the next twenty minutes there won't be any flash mob to have," she said, storming away. She scrolled up and down on her U-disc holo-screen. *No, goddammit, my Bam-mo account is still empty. So unless those fuckers fill it soon they can go ahead and open up this damn nuke facility. Let 'em all burn, see if I care.*

She walked over to the merchandise table and pawed through the goods for sale. She looked at the black t-shirts with dripping gray letters, unfolded for her final approval.

"I Used to Have a Full Head of Hair. Thanks, Sunshine Fusion". *Hmm, for the bald men crowd, not bad.* She tossed it on the approved pile.

"Ask Me About My Smile" and then, on the back: "Sunshine Fusion Burned Off My Lips." *Uff da. Cringy, but it'll work. Approved.*

"I Wasn't Going to Have Kids Anyway. Thanks, Sunshine Fusion." *No one'll get that one. Disapproved.*

She moved on to the pants.

"Sunshine Fusion: Because Who Needs Stable Genes Anyway." *We won't sell any, but kinda funny. Approved.*

She picked up another pair that said, across the crotch: "After Sunshine Fusion, These are Just for Decoration". *Ack!* She threw them down, then laughed.

She pulled up the holo-screen again and looked into her Bam-mo account. Then, she saw it: numbers spinning, dollars filling her account. It scrolled, scrolled, scrolled, then settled onto the agreed-upon protest fee: $125,000. Her eyes grew wide, and she bounced on her feet. She tilted her head back and bellowed: "let's protest, bitches!"

Mazel Maven, Editor and Chief Orchestrator of The Manhattan Machiavellian, pulled a bullhorn to her lips and beckoned: "camera angles, people!"

The dance troupe circled around Mazel, who was in front of a 72" plasma screen. The images were a patchwork of shots from 36 different angles: some on tripods, others from handheld cameras in the crowd, still others from the top of portable towers. The video network was built so it could provide live, full 360° views of the "accidental" flash mob protesting the nuclear facility's grand opening. Their protest had been planned for months, both Maya's and the dance troupe's fees paid for, in full, by The Manhattan Machiavellian. The MM would have full rights to the event and exclusivity, of course, which is exactly how the other MM wanted it.

"Let's see how the condiment parade looks from overhead," Mazel said.

Nine of the dance troupe members stood in line with condiment bottles in hand, three with Kapitalist Ketchup, three with Mercenary Mustard, and three with Ransack Relish. They stood in line, arms up and out and down, holding their condiments in protest. "Ketchup," Mazel said, "we have to see the labels. Gotta make sure we see them from all angles." The three ketchup holders turned their bottles to make sure the labels were visible.

"Let's run through it again, Mel. Let's get all three lines there, Maja up front, let's run it from all angles," Mazel said. "I want to make sure we get all angles, all of it, in HD."

Melody Rivers gathered all 20 dancers in front, held her right hand up, then cued the music. They swirled from the sides, from the front, from the back, in reverse, all moving on cue in their impromptu flash mob. They turned and gyrated and then, as the song finished, the back row held their condiments in proper position and, on cue, sprayed them towards the cameras.

"Yes, yes, yes!" Mazel said, staring at all images on the screen. "That's perfect. Damn, look at all the colors," she said.

“Perfect-ey Maj-ey!” Melody squealed, catching Maja’s melting expression.

Climate protestor Maja Andersson looked straight up at the overhead cameras, smiled broadly, then felt her face slide off into the dirt.

As the camera rolled, Mazel Maven watched, practically salivating at the image of a “face-free” Maja staring up, ketchup-and-mustard smeared across her cheeks, ready to dominate every media outlet worldwide.

In just three days, one week before COP 50, Mazel would stream live from the Sunshine Fusion Center, flashing Maja’s dancing protest on Umbili-Net, Stampede, WowNow, and Twittoob in a torrent of anti-nuke fervor. Never mind that the facility could power millions, nuclear energy was neither approved nor tolerated by ProgScience or The Machiavellian. Mazel Maven would make sure it died a drippy, splat-filled death.

CHAPTER 17

STOINK FARM
CHIRENO, TEXAS

"Covering 800 acres, the BiOvine Nutrition and Preparation Center in Chireno, Texas is home to 100,000 head of sus bovigenus, the world's only methane- and CO2-free livestock. Employing more than 400 people, BiOvine is eastern Texas' largest employer and, since 2035, its largest food exporter.

From Pasture to Plate:
BiOvine's livestock leaves no trace!"

– BiOvine 2045 Annual Report

Here's a little-known fact about Chireno, Texas: the "Welcome to Chireno, Texas" and the "BiOvine Nutrition and Preparation Center" signs are exactly the same size. Another fun fact: Chireno's 75937 zip code is exactly the combined weight of eighty BiOvine Sus Bovigenus livestock, in pounds. Exactly.

Brock Porter told Mateo those factoids as their wagon pulled into the front lot of Stoink Farm. Having driven by California's Harris Ranch multiple times, Mateo had prepared himself for the eye-melting reek of industrial cow farms. Years earlier, he'd visited the Monfort slaughterhouse in Greeley, Colorado and it soaked him in a death-stench for weeks afterwards. Jumping down off the covered wagon, he clamped his thumb and index finger over his nose and held his breath.

Brock Porter laughed. "Ain't what ya think, cowpoke," he said.

And indeed, it wasn't. Mateo breathed in the farm air deeply and had his first eureka moment: Stoink Farm gave off no odor whatsoever.

Mateo's second eureka moment: the only sounds stoink made were staccato "moots," which sounded like they were spitting the words down into the dirt. Mateo stood in front of the vast stoink fields amid a chorus of moot-moot-moots and wanted to spit himself. So, he did. Brock walked up next to him, rested his elbows on the metal fencing, and also spit.

"They're all the same size," Mateo said.

"Yep. And weight too. Each one grows to be 949.21 pounds, can't grow no more'n that. We just feed 'em 'till they stop eatin', then we take 'em to slotter," Brock said. He pointed to the warehouse on their right.

"Damn, those are some weird-lookin' fuckers," Mateo said. He wasn't sure what else to say. Each stoink stood about 4 ½ feet tall, with a round, wide body set atop short, tree-stump legs. It was grayish white all over, with bright pink circles scattered throughout. The cow tail hung low, with the end curly like a hog's: when it swatted flies it looked like it was slapping itself with a yo-yo. The forehead was wide and flat, the snout long and piggish, as if stuck on as an afterthought. The ears were tipped round and sat atop the head, giving it a Mickey Mouse look: if Mickey Mouse had pink, hairy, pig-ears, that is.

But, the eyes.

It had two, one on each side of its blocky head. While normal livestock eyes pointed forward, stoink eyes pointed sideways: one looking left, the other looking right, and they blinked out of sequence, like a chameleon. It was almost as if brain signals never even reached the eyes which, as it turned out, was exactly true.

"Their brains is the size of a walnut," Brock said. He made a circle with his thumb and middle finger. "They don't need to do nuthin' but eat 'n grow, so didn't really need to think none. They just bred the thinkin' right out of 'em. They just kinda wander 'bout, bumpin' into each other. They's as dumb as the Panhandle is flat."

Mateo just stood there and watched them. They wandered slowly, moot-mooting into each other, bumping into the fences. They were alive, but just barely. It was like they were just wandering, meat-covered robots.

"You'll like this," Brock said.

A loud, dull siren went off and the stoinks – thousands of them – lifted their heads, turned right, got in lines one after the other, and slowly trudged towards the feeding warehouse. Mateo thought they looked like the autonomous Viszlas on the highway, moving the same speed with the same distance apart; but instead, these robots were made of flesh and gristle and were, ultimately, food. It was feeding time, and off the stoinks went.

Brock and Mateo followed them up towards the feeding warehouse.

"Now, I'm no cow-guy, but where's all the cowshit?" Mateo asked. This was his third eureka moment: despite thousands of livestock, there was no shit. None to be found.

Brock smiled. "Well, that's part of the patents actually. When they mixed the cows and pigs' digestion, they had to combine 'em together. Put some pig stomach enzymes into the cow rumen bellies and, with some tweakin', they was able to figure out how make 'em shit inside. They turned one of the stomachs into a little shit-catcher, so it shits inside itself."

Mateo stopped and gagged; he caught himself from throwing up. "You're fucking with me," he said.

"Priciest part of the animal," Brock said. "Turns out that stomach o' shit is damn near pure protein, so we can sell it for ten times a stoink steak into the pro athlete market. Might even toss in a few steroids here and there for extra kick."

Mateo fought the gag and wiped his mouth. He looked up at the big "RumenEase" lettering on the side of the grain silo, then watched the stoinks wait in line for their turns at the trough.

"So this is what climate-friendly meat looks like," Mateo said.

"Long as they eat our feed," Brock smiled. "If they don't, they'll gas up the planet. Laughin' all the way."

Mateo stood and watched, shaking his head. He couldn't quite get his thoughts around it.

Brock pointed to the non-descript white warehouse in the field's corner. "Slotter-house right thar," he said.

Mateo shook his head. *No, no, no, no fucking way I'm going in there*, he thought.

———

By the time they reached the slaughterhouse, Mateo was in a full-blown sweat attack. Not only could he not get over what Stoinks looked like, he just couldn't process the entire thing. These were live beasts – but just barely! – things we engineered for our own consumption, like Dr. Frankenstein digging up graves just to make his sandwich. It wasn't just surreal, it was just plain messed up. And now he was stepping into the slaughterhouse, to see how we turned these robo-beasts into Stoink Steaks. He didn't think he could handle it. Wiping his forehead onto his shirtsleeves, he fought his stomach and his panic, and prepared to turn and run.

Long lines of stoink threaded throughout the warehouse, like a Disneyland ride queue. It circled left, then right, then up a long straightaway, then right again, and so on until they fed into a middle station area. The stoinks stood a standard distance apart, then moved forward as if on schedule. They were calm and unbothered.

And here is when Mateo had his fourth and biggest eureka moment: there was no killing, no cow-bolt pistol into the forehead. When each line ended at the finishing station, each stoink stood, then almost on cue, just died. There was no pain, no anxiety, no blood, nothing. Stoinks walked to the end of a line, waited, then tipped over dead.

They dropped dead, not coincidentally, onto a conveyer belt, which hauled the bodies away towards the sectioning room. Mateo knew this because the big open door they went through had a sign above it that said: "Sectioning Room."

Mateo looked at Brock, his mouth agape. "Suicidal cows?" he asked, lamely. "What the hell's going on?"

"Nah. 'Member I said the feed had some mods in it? Well sir, we built in some things that help. Each pellet has some brain tranq in it, then some cyanide. Eat one of 'em and nuthin' happens, but eat a million of 'em and they kick in. So when they've eaten enough to get to their full weight, they reach a certain threshold, then boom, it kicks in. Pretty precise, actually. The tranq dulls the brain so they feel nothin', then the other stops their heart. Just like that," Brock said, snapping his fingers.

Brock reached into the line and put his palm flat on a stoink's side. He slid his hand down under the belly, stopping at a round nub. He tapped it twice, then motioned to Mateo: "This here's the blood plug. Once they're dead we just flip this open and empty 'em, don't even need to string 'em up like we used to. Just pour 'em out through this hole. They got less than a gallon inside, and here's the best part: they bleed clear. So even when you bleed 'em, it jus' looks like they pissin' out syrup."

Mateo lost the battle with his stomach, and he puked into the dirt straw. He stood, hunched over, spitting into the straw, trying to catch his breath.

Brock patted Mateo on the shoulder and waited for the lurch to subside. "Yeah, buddy, it's some wild shit. Stoinks ain't barely even alive."

Mateo spit again.

Brock slapped Mateo on the back. "Blood plugs get 'em ever' time," he chuckled.

CHAPTER 18

BAYOU DRIPPERS
LEESVILLE, LOUISIANA

Mateo woke up as the wagon stopped. He'd been asleep in the back, under canvas, across the Louisiana border, and he shook his head to clear the confusion. After five days riding in a covered wagon across Texas, he had gotten used to constant bumpiness; that, combined with the horses' gait, actually lulled him to sleep. *Like a prairie metronome*, he thought.

It wasn't the lack of motion that woke him up though, it was the quiet. It was dead calm.

He pulled open the flap and pushed his head out. Brock Porter had put his hand up, and Mateo's nose smashed into it.

"Quiet," Brock whispered. "Move slow."

Eight people sat on horses before them, blocking their passage. Dressed in blacks and browns, hats and bandanas, they had formed a semicircle in front. Each of them held weapons befitting the bayou: bolo ropes, boar spears, knee clubs made of cypress root, cane spears. By the looks of it, this is where they lived.

"Who's ya friend, cher?" a female asked. She was in the middle and steered her horse forward.

"Evenin', Mudslide. Jus' passin' through," Brock said, calmly.

"Wha' happened to Houston?" she asked, pulling her horse closer to the wagon. She wore a long black prairie jacket and black cowboy hat bent at the front and back; her left ear lobe dangled with a long, peacock feather. The other seven members moved their horses closer to the wagon as well, closing their arc around the wagon's front.

"Has to sit hisself out o' Loosiana fer a spell. Don' worry, he'll be back in all his drawlin' self 'fore too long," Brock said.

Mateo sat on the bench next to Brock and watched the group close in around them. He looked left to right, then back. All of their eyes were focused on him. He thought about running, but where would he go? He was in the middle of nowhere.

"Hoo-wee, look at dat fella. He ain't from 'roun' here, is he now?" a man on Mateo's right said. He poked at the side of the wagon's canvas with his knotted, brown club.

"Non, sho' ain't," a man on Mateo's left said. He held the boar spear in his gloved hand, tip up, and wore a black T-shirt that said "Bawg" in white letters. He smiled broadly, displaying six brilliant teeth, then spit into the dirt.

Brock moved slowly and spoke softly. He held the reins in his left hand and put his right hand flat on his leg. "Jus' 'nother fare is all, Mudslide. Our usual. Got the usual payment too." He stood, towering over all of them. "Y'all gonna club me 'fore I get it?" he chuckled.

Mudslide pointed her chin at Brock, giving approval.

"Don't do nothin'," Brock whispered as he moved into the wagon. He foraged inside a large wooden chest and pulled out three bags of meat; he tossed one, two, three, up forward onto the bench. Mateo looked at them, then down at the group around them. He pushed one bag forward with his boot.

Brock sat down on the bench, picked up a bag, and tossed it to Mudslide. "One fer you, one fer Thibo, then Bawg." He tossed the second to the man on the right, the third to the left.

"Best not be any o' dat faux meat," Thibo said, squeezing the bag in his hand. "Y'know I hate that stoink."

Bawg bit the bag until it tore, then sucked out the juice. He laughed: "Ooh, dat good."

"Ain't our arrangemen," Brock said, shaking his head.

Mudslide turned and tossed the bag behind her, to a horseman in her group. She shook her head, looked at Mateo, then back at Brock, and said: "Three bags fer our usual fare, but things done changed, ain't dey? Da world done gone all messy an' such. Three ain't gonna be 'nough dis time, cher," she said.

"Trois, sûr, ça va pas suffire," Bawg said. He let the Ziploc bag dangle from his mouth, dripping meat juice onto his saddle. He laughed and stared at Mateo.

"What's goin' on, 'Slide? How come yer squeezin' me?" Brock asked, raising his voice just slightly.

"Whole lotta people comin' down here dese days. Not sure what happened, but we's seein' it. Mo' people, need mo' payment. Ain't we, mes frères et sœurs?" Mudslide said. She turned her head to the entire group as they nodded and whooped in agreement. Thibo held his knee club up and rested it on his saddle. He nodded.

Mateo didn't know what to do. He tried to copy Brock's calmness, but couldn't. Suddenly, he was Ned Beatty in the movie Deliverance being bent over a log by a snaggle-toothed Appalachian hillbilly who woofed: *"He shore got a real pretty mouth, ain't he? Bet he can squeal like a pig. Weeeee!"* He couldn't get the image out of his mind. He began to hyperventilate, his gaze dancing from horses to riders to Brock. He mumbled: "whuss happening?"

He reached inside the wagon and grabbed the Winchester rifle butt.

"Oo-wee, he a nervous one, ain' he?" Thibo said. He tapped the knob of his club on the wagon's sideboard, tap tap tap.

"Lui, il est nerveux, sûr, sûr," Bawg said, slurping at the bag in his mouth, letting it dangle and bounce.

"Where you from, beau garçon?" Mudslide asked.

Mateo tapped his chest with his fingers. "Me?" He gripped the rifle.

"Oui, toi, beau," Mudslide said.

"California," Mateo said, not sure if he should have said it. *Maybe I should've said Colorado*? he thought, for no apparent reason.

"Oh, ils sont jolis en Californie," Bawg said, slurping the bag.

"Oui, sûr, sûr," Thibo said, nodding his head repeatedly.

Mateo panicked. He grabbed the rifle and stood up quickly, aiming it skyward. He pumped a round into the chamber and put his finger on the trigger. He realized at that exact moment that he had never done that before, and suddenly wished he could take it back. But there he stood, dripping sweat, panting, waiting in silence.

A hard stick hit his right hand, which caused him to drop the gun. Then, a bolo rope wrapped across the barrel and pulled it sideways. Next, his right ankle was hooked, and he was pulled over the side, into the hard dirt, amidst a flurry of swings and thuds. By the time it stopped, he lay on his back on the ground, with two sharp poles at his throat.

"Ooh, tell us we kin stick dis pig," Bawg said. He'd dropped the baggie from his mouth and pushed his spear tip at Mateo's Adam's apple.

Squeal like a pig – weeee! Mateo heard.

Mudslide stepped over and stared down into Mateo. "Y'think you're de first one who t'ink he tell us what to do?" she said. She turned to Brock: "Mebbe you should tell California who we are, cher, so he don' think he can do us like dat. We done protec' the bayou, we live off the land, usin' just what we got right here, ain't no need for nothin' else. No guns, no oil, none o' that merde. Best tell him this don' end the way he think it do."

"Best be a good boy," Thibo said, pushing his spear tip at Mateo's throat.

Quickly, Brock jumped down and put his body between Thibo, Bawg and Mateo. He stood, palms up, put his boot to the spears and gently moved them away from Mateo's throat. "Damn 'Slide, sorry 'bout that, I had no idea he was gonna do that." He glared down at Mateo.

He shore do got a pretty mouth! Mateo heard.

"He's mine, you know I'll take care o' this boy. But what's it gonna take for us to git goin'?" Brock asked.

Mudslide looked at Brock, then Mateo, then the wagon. She pointed to the horses, then held up her index finger.

"Fuck. You serious?" Brock asked. "How 'bout we just cut off a finger or somethin'? Hell, let Bawg do it!" he said.

"Hoo-weeeeeeee!" Bawg yelled.

"One horse," Mudslide said. "You pick which one. And we get somethin' from him too."

———

Mateo ran his fingers over his shaved head. It felt warm, sticky, but also bumpy. Mudslide directed Thibo to shave off Mateo's hair, but the machete's length prevented it from doing much of a job. That, or maybe Thibo just wanted to leave some lumps here and there to remind him of what the Bayou Drippers could do if they wanted. But as it was, Mateo's head was now a patchwork of skin, hair tufts and bloody slits. It looked like someone had tried to shave a gourd and lost.

He leaned into the campfire and looked at his reflection in the steel coffee pot. Not only was his head now a bloody, hair-lumped patchwork, the bandage over his U-disc wound had fallen off and exposed the large scab. Between the scab and his hair patchery he looked like, well, a Bayou Dripper.

"You're one lucky sonofabitch, you know that? Coulda gone much worse fer ya. They coulda taken an ear for prize, and there'd be nothin' we could do about it." Brock said. He tossed a handful of sticks onto the fire and poked at it. "I told ya to hang back."

"Yeah well, this isn't my jam," Mateo said.

"Yer what?"

"Sorry. I ain't from 'round these parts," Mateo said, in his best faux drawl.

Brock studied Mateo through the campfire haze and said: "Damn, brother, you look a sight. Lost yer hair, drippin' blood, damn near shat yerself. A mustang off the prairie. Why are you even doin' this?"

"My son."

It took that question to remind Mateo why he was making this journey at all. He hadn't thought of Reyes in days, and the thought left him feeling alone and cold. He had always felt his paternity deeply, and it shocked him to realize he'd lost that contact. No phones, no U-links, no nothing. He couldn't talk to Lauren, and he couldn't find Reyes. He was just stuck in the Louisiana bayou with a stoink-farming Texan, he'd lost his hair, his dignity, and damn near his ear within minutes of each other, and his sad reflection stared back at him from a prairie coffee pot. He felt lost, not just because he literally was, but because he had no contact with his son. The thought made him want to swim up the Mississippi River alone.

He reached into his right front jeans pocket and pulled out Lil Red. It had lost a third wheel and was now just one plastic tire and three pokey axle stumps. No matter, it belonged to Reyes. He gripped it firmly in his palm, then answered. "Yeah, gotta get to DC. The bump made everything stop working, or at least we couldn't find a way to contact him. Just set out to find my son. Reyes," he said. He let the words hang in the air. It hurt to say it out loud, way more than he thought it would.

"What you got thar?" Brock asked.

Mateo held up Lil Red, then tossed it to Brock.

Brock caught it, then held it up to the campfire. "Now that's what I'm talkin' about," he said. "That his?"

Mateo nodded.

Brock tossed the car back to him. "What's it like out in California?" Brock asked. "How they handlin' all this?"

"What's it ever like in California?" Mateo answered. "It's fucked. Tech companies control everything, government lets them, and when something goes wrong, tech just takes over. Until it can't, that is," he shook his head. It made no goddamn sense.

"Are you all climate crazy like California?" Mateo asked, thinking that he'd never asked that question before.

Brock chewed on a stick and shook his head softly. "Don' even know how to answer that. We're all climate crazy, jus' in different ways. Texas crazy means getting' what we need how we need it. Need a windmill, we just put one up. We need oil, we dig fer it. Need solar? Sure, we'll string 'em out back. Just practical is all."

He poked his knife at Mateo and continued. "Now y'all Californians, that's another breed entirely. You drive them Viszlas just to show off yer green badge, then the rest of y'all use enough energy to light up Vegas. Just showboatin', that's all it is. Ain't got no room for that out here."

Mateo tossed some dirt into the fire. "True, that."

"Then ya got the Drippers. They always lived off the land, just more so nowadays. Paid 'em for years, no issues. Hell, sometimes I stay with 'em. They in tents, off rivers, no 'lectricity, no runnin' water - don't need it. They figure they're keepin' the bayou the way God made it, an' the less folks mess with it, the better. They'd sooner pull a hog out the mud than take a handout, an' they don't want a damn thing from nobody."

"Sounds like not a bad way to be," Mateo said.

Brock spit into the fire and nodded. "Maybe so, they're they own kinda crazy, not like us. They get pissed, they go kill a hog and roll 'round in its blood. We get pissed, we find someone to blame then 'spect Uncle Sam to fix it."

He jabbed the fire with a stick. "I mean, take these parts we's bringin' with us. Fer oil rigs, right? People want their EVs, but we keep burnin' oil to make 'em. Tennessee's churning out cars while burnin' gas to do it. Shut down coal, burn oil. We go in circles, call it progress. Make no damn hog-sense to it, if you ask me."

Mateo shrugged. "They force us to buy EVs in California, but I got a Camaro too. Or…had one, anyway. They took it."

Brock shook his head.

"So how do you do it? I mean, I'm going through Oklahoma and now Texas, it seems like things were kinda…normal? There's all these rules, all this craziness, but you all seem to find a way to get through it all. Not sure how you do that," Mateo said.

"We're Texas, we're used to fendin' fer ourselves. We always say: 'if yer hungry, grab a rifle.' Guv'ment always thinks they can come in and fix stuff , but hell, they never stepped one boot in our dirt. So, we just go along and say 'yessir' and 'yes'um' and go 'bout our business. When they go back to DC we just round 'em up and keep on keepin' on," Brock said. He spit into the fire.

"Listen, I hear there's some shit up ahead, jus' wanted you to know. Ever' now and then we can get a call out, or in, but I been hearin' some chatter. Like goin' up the river ain't gonna be no picnic, all I'm sayin'. You git to Chicago, you can git yerself a train, but it'll be a haul. Just be ready to saddle up, alright?"

Mateo nodded. He felt his stomach tighten up again at the thought.

Brock slapped him on the back. "You'll be fine. No one's gonna fuck with ya anyway. Y'all got that look."

"What look is that?" Mateo asked.

"Like ya got a few cactus needles in yer hatband," Brock said.

"And I'm not even wearing a hat," Mateo said.

"'Zactly," Brock said.

CHAPTER 19

BATON ROUGE, LOUISIANA

"Hoo-eee, is dis dat California boy you brought me right heah?" Lucien Dupont asked.

"Yep. Mateo Anaya, meet yer ride: Lucien Dupont," Brock said. He pointed back and forth at them both.

"Nice to meet you, Lucien," Mateo said. He extended his hand, Lucien studied him, then extended his, and they shook.

Lucien Dupont walked around Mateo in a slow circle, inspecting him up and down. As he did, he made a whispery tuk-tuk-tuk sound, like tsk-tsk with a Bayou drawl. He clasped his hands behind him like a general, circling, inspecting. "What you wan' me do with dis boy, cher? Sho' do look a sight," Lucien said.

He stopped in front of Mateo, a full head taller, then looked down into his eyes. He squinted and said: "This what Cali-forn-i-a do?" he asked.

Mateo didn't know what to do or say. He scratched his patchy bald spots; he hoped they didn't look as vacant and lost as he suddenly felt.

Lucien laughed out loud. "Ooh, got a twitchy one, eh?" He slapped Mateo on both shoulders. "Jus' messin' with you."

He stepped aside and raised his right hand, like a gameshow model offering up the prize. "Bienvenue à La Petite Gator," he said, pointing to the shantyboat.

Mateo looked at the small cabin atop two pontoons and squinted. The roof was rusted corrugated steel; it had two glass windows on each side. There were front and back doors, each leading to small, canopied porches. Tealights hung around the eaves, and the front right wall had a small insignia: "La Petite

Gator" next to a smiling alligator wearing a bent Cajun straw hat.

Brock jumped onto the boat and it dipped low under him, like it was ready to dump him into the river; he steadied himself with a post. "Fuckin' A," he said, nodding. He pulled his cowboy hat off, swabbed his brow on his shoulder, then put it back on.

"Dem dirt boys don' take much to water, do dey?" Lucien asked Mateo.

Mateo could barely understand him. It had taken him days to train his ears for Houston and Brock's Texas drawl, and those made Cajun sound like fifth grade English. With all the "who deys" and "dis deres" Mateo thought he'd fall into the Mississippi within an hour. He looked blankly at Lucien.

"Fine, fine, now I know what I'm workin' with here," Lucien said, his accent suddenly barely noticeable. "This boy's nevah been south, nevah been on the bayou, he lookin' at me like I'm Chinese," he said.

"I understood *that*," Mateo said.

"Good, good, we'll need that. This here's how it gonna go. When it just you and me, I'm talkin' like this. We have ourselves a good conversation 'n such. When t'ings get serious, I'm gonna talk bayou, y'hear?" he said.

"Got it. When I can't understand a fucking word you're saying I know to shut the hell up," Mateo said. He chuckled and tossed his bag inside the cabin.

Lucien applauded softly and smiled broadly at Brock. "Sho' nuff, look at dat big brain on Ma-te-o. Better than them Texas rednecks you send."

Brock rotated his fists over and over each other, like he was punching a speedbag, then stopped with his middle fingers extended.

Lucien bowed, and said: "Et pour toi."

Mateo stepped onto the boat and watched the two friends say goodbye. They spoke in whispers and smiles, touching each other's shoulders, exchanging soft handshakes. About the same height, Brock looked like he could eat four stoinks in one sitting, while Lucien was slim as an eel, one who could steal both your car and your girlfriend. Brock's hulk got them through east Texas, but Lucien's suavité would navigate the Mississippi. He prepared himself for the difference.

———

"Tell me what I'm lookin' at here," Lucien said. Mateo sat on a stool as Lucien circled him, knife and scissors in hand. They slowly drifted down the river while Lucien studied Mateo's lumpy, patchwork head.

"There's a story," Mateo said.

"Always a story, cher," he said. "Tuk, tuk, tuk, we goin' cue-ball, 'Teo. Ain' nothin' else we can do."

With care and caution, Lucien shaved off the hairy tufts left on Mateo's head. He flowed with the river, pausing when a current hit, holding Mateo's head firmly but softly, then continuing in long strokes as the river did the same. He dabbed at his bare skin often, removing all the hair carefully. He didn't know why, but Mateo liked Lucien immediately, and knew he could trust him. With a final scrape and a dab, Lucien tossed the towel over his shoulder and offered up the knife blade as a mirror: "Voilà".

Mateo grabbed a bar of soap, dunked it in the river and lathered up his beard scruff. He scritched and scratched the stubble off, then wet a bandana and washed his face, his arms, his chest and stomach. Five miles up the Mississippi, Mateo felt clean and refreshed, almost like he was brand new.

"Smooth as a jus' peeled crawfish," Lucien said. "Much better."

Mateo smiled and sat back. The river was black but alive, and he could make out the shore and skylines as they floated along. It felt like they were sneaking along undercover, going on a rescue mission right under the swells' noses, which, as it turned out, was probably exactly what they were doing. Lucien sat in a wooden chair next to Mateo on the front porch, sliced off a piece of dried pork and handed it to him. They ate jerky, sipped Nawlins Whiskey, and floated up the Mississippi.

"Tell me 'bout your boy," Lucien said.

The question caught Mateo so off-guard he choked a little, and found his eyes tearing up. The question centered him.

"Smart boy," he said, surprised that those were the first words he chose to share. "A year out of grad school at Claremont, went into the intelligence business right after school. He's in DC. Working for some agency that he can't talk about, doing things he can't say."

"'Telligence. Sounds like some James Bond shit," Lucien said.

"Could be, we figured as much. We don't talk about it too much, actually. It's just his thing." Mateo said. He pictured Reyes' dark, curly hair, his broad smile, his confident yet shy demeanor. He couldn't believe how much he missed him.

"He look like you or 'mama?" Lucien asked.

"My color, Lauren's eyes. Green."

"Hoo-boy, bet he's a charmer then," Lucien said, stringing out the description. Mateo liked how it sounded and repeated it in his head: *chahmah, chahmah, chahmah.* He looked over at Lucien, who bore a soft grin and a look into a memory that only he knew; he nodded his head slowly.

"So, tell me about your kids," Mateo said, unsure why he thought of Lucien as a dad.

Lucien took a swig of whiskey, then a deep breath, then shook his head. "Non, mon ami. Lucien don' talk 'bout none o' that."

CHAPTER 20

SCOB NATION
SOMEWHERE IN WEST MISSISSIPPI

Mateo stood up as the boat slowed down to a crawl. He squinted into the blackness but couldn't make out anything at all, not even the black ridge where sky met shore. They were drifting forward into nothingness, with just the slap-slapping of water at the pontoons.

Lucien broke the silence, his voice barely above a whisper. "Hmm, this stretch usually got life. Ain't never seen it this black," he said. He'd gathered his long hair into a ponytail and pulled it away from his face. He tuk-tuk'd softly as the boat drifted forward.

Then, bright headlights lit up the front of their boat, spanning the riverfront. Before them were a dozen or so boats: shanties, silver trawlers, small Jon boats, skiffs and canoes. Mateo couldn't tell how many people in total there were, but there were enough to block their path. And all were armed with clubs or guns or both.

"Hey now, who's goin' up da river heah?" a booming voice asked. Mateo could see the man's outline in front, standing in the long trawler. Two more people sat in the boat, one held the light.

"Hey there, cher, no need to fret none. Jus' me, Lucien Dupont, got me a fare headin' up tawards Memphis," Lucien said. He winked at Mateo and whispered: "Dis might be heah."

Translation: *shut the fuck up*, Mateo thought.

Different boats broke apart from the flotilla and slowly circled around them until The Gator was surrounded. Lights shone down onto both front and back porches, and long sticks poked at the pontoons and cabin walls and wooden chests.

"Call't Mossback. D'où viens-tu, étranger?" the river leader asked Lucien.

"From Baton Rouge, cher. Three generations o' DuPonts up dere. Et toi?" Lucien asked.

Mossback touched his boat to the front of The Gator. "Right here, cher." One of his boatmen held the hulls together as Mossback stepped onto The Gator, slow and steady. He shone a long flashlight at Lucien, studied him, then stepped to Mateo. "You ain' from 'round heah, fo' sho'. And where you from?" he asked.

"Colorado," Mateo said. His voice sounded as weak as he felt. "Heard there was some good gambling up in Memphis, wanted to see for myself, decided to hire Lucien here to take me." He gave Lucien a thumbs up.

"A flatlanda'? An' ya hired a shanty upriver?" Mossback asked. He looked around at boys on different boats. "That soun' right to you fellas?" he asked, loudly.

"Hell no, sha" and "non cher, no way" came from different boats. "Mighty 'spicious!" a voice from the back called.

"Oui, sha,'spicious to me too," Mossback said. He shined his flashlight onto Lucien's face, who smiled broadly, then asked: "Where yo' disc?"

Lucien gently clapped his hands in submission, held a finger up, and said: "Sorry 'bout that, got dat disc right heah." He reached into his front jeans pocket, pulled out his U-disc, then snapped it into place. It hummed and purred, then lit up yellow, throbbing at his right temple.

Dammit, I forgot about the disc! How could I have forgotten the disc? Mateo thought.

Mossback flashed the light onto Mateo's face and asked: "Where you?"

These river boys haven't smiled since the flood. As he did when nervous, Mateo just started talking. "Funny you ask, had it when I left Denver, but reckon I lost it down Texas way. Ain't had much trouble yet, but yeah, need me a new one, don't I?" He stopped and wished he could just shut the hell up. He noticed the black U-disc at Mossback's temple shine dull; the rest had black discs as well.

Mossback stood face to face with Mateo, looking right into his eyes. He squinted, shone the flashlight up to Mateo's temple, squinted more, then looked back at Mateo. "Non, sha. Ya tore it off," he said.

Mateo could only muster a lame: "No…it…fell, I lost it."

A second boater joined Mossback up on deck and pulled a sawed-off shotgun from under his river coat. He cocked it.

Lucien jumped in: "Hey now, cher, we all friends heah. Ain't no need fo' dat." He stood in front of the boaters with his palms up, gently smiling.

Mossback pulled an enormous knife out of his waistband and held it up to Mateo's temple. He pointed the blade at Mateo's scab and said: "Now Crawdad, what you t'ink dis looks like heah? Looks to Mossback dat dis boy done yank't off his disc. Like he's tryin' to get 'way with somethin'."

Crawdad held the gun at Mateo's face and nodded. "Oui, sha, same here," he said.

"T'ink maybe we got ourselves a Scob runner, what you think, Crawdad?" Mossback asked.

Crawdad smiled. "Oui, sha. We got ourselves a runner."

Mateo and Lucien were marched down the dirt main street of Scob Nation as climate criminals, led by Mossback and Crawdad. Since Lucien's U-disc was yellow, he was allowed to walk without handcuffs, but Mateo did the full perp-walk right through the middle of town, his hands tied in front with cypress vine rope handcuffs. Mossback and Crawdad beat on small skin drums as they walked, while the remaining boaters clanked moonshine bottles hanging from poles. Mateo asked Lucien: "Exactly what is our crime?"

Lucien shook his head. "T'ink we's about to find out, 'Teo."

They walked by a large, fenced-in area full of dirty people with a sign that said, "Holding Area", while to the right was an outside dorm: beddings and grass mattresses were tossed about between makeshift firepits and stone walls. People lay about the beds, some sleeping, some playing cards, others just staring into the dirt. Mateo didn't know who they were, but all of them had black U-discs lit, pulsing with their crimes. As they reached the end of the fields, a female said from the holding pen: "I know that man."

The procession stopped. Mossback walked over to a lady and asked: "Who you know, lil miss?"

Scob Leslie, the woman who had been forcefully removed from the Probitas Correction Center in Boulder, Colorado, pointed at Mateo. "Him," she said.

Mossback motioned to Crawdad, who opened the pen and pulled Leslie out. "You comin' with us, ma cher." He grabbed her by the wrist and walked with her hand-in-hand. Mateo looked over at her, but she didn't meet his gaze.

"Where we headed, les copains?" Lucien asked. He didn't look nervous, but he didn't look calm either. His eyes sparkled alert in his U-disc's yellow glow.

The procession stopped at a long shack with torches hanging on the side walls. A corrugated steel door was opened from the inside, then Mossback and Crawdad walked in, Scob Leslie alongside. Mateo and Lucian followed them, followed by the rest of the boater group.

Stepping into the large room, a tribunal court was in session.

A scraggly-haired blonde man sat in a wicker chair, facing a table of seven tribunal elders, their discs glowing yellow. Torches lit up the room, as did strings of mismatched tea lights along the perimeter. Another man with a glowing yellow U-disc paced around the defendant – *his lawyer?* Mateo wondered – and listened to the elders.

"…We have been authorized to hear climate confessions," Elder 1 said.

"Authorized by who?" Lawyer asked.

"Stampede. Umbili-Net. They's authorized." Elder 1 said.

"Don' even know what that means," Lawyer said. "They make laws now?"

Elder 1 shrugged. "Since da blip, we got us a new set o' rules, cher. Guv'ment gotta protect itself, don' it? Only t'ing workin' now is Stampede an' U-net cars, roads. So we's workin' together as a team, to make sure we still got laws 'n order. That means we gotta make do. We now under martial law, you know what dat mean?"

"So, locals control the laws now, is that it?" Lawyer asked.

Elder 1 nodded. "Dass true, 'cause this an emergency now. Martial law means we got new laws heah. And I'm the Marshall." He stared hard at the defendant.

"No crime has been committed, as far as we know," Lawyer said.

"So sez you. Company sez otherwise. But that's why we heah now, ain' it?" the Marshall said. "You client has been accused of bein' a climate denier level 3, now thass a serious vi-o-la-tion, ain' it?"

"Explain that," Lawyer said.

"Got his own blog, The Sober Climate 'n such, where he talk about science and ProgScience as if they ain' facts. Even questions how his own dirty oil habits have no impact what-so-evah. We got pages 'n pages o' Stampede threads, even U-Net statistics. Wan' us to go through all 'em?" the Marshall asked.

Lawyer and defendant shook their heads, no.

"How do you plead?" the Marshall asked.

Lawyer turned to the defendant and huddled together, whispering. After a few moments, Lawyer stood and said: "He pleads guilty."

The Marshall smiled broadly and said: "Now dat's what we like! Saves us all da time, y'know. Guilty. Class 2 misdemeanor, forty-five days co-rection. One Utili-Net link a day, no more. Full surgical removal of U-disc at release, upon completion of final inspections." He tapped a squirrel-skull gavel twice on the desktop, clunk clunk.

Large enforcer Scobs herded the defendant through a side door to his sentencing. Lawyer sat down in a side chair, shaking his head.

"Next!" the Marshall barked.

Mossback stepped forward. "Got ourselves a bounty Scob runnah, cher. Fresh off the boat. Even a witness," he said.

"He a bounty runnah?" the Marshall asked.

"Oui. Full bounty." Mossback said.

"Bring 'im on up. Let's see what kinda trouble dis boy brought us."

CHAPTER 21

THE TRIAL OF MATEO ANAYA
SCOB NATION COURT

Mateo Anaya stood in front of the climate court defiantly. To his left stood Mossback, engaging with the court, to his right stood Lucien. Crawdad walked up behind, pushed Mateo forward, then shoved him down into the chair. He pulled Lucien next to Mateo, then stepped back. Mateo's nostrils flared with the odor: Mossback's stanky hair, bayou musk, and flaming torch oil. The mix made his stomach churn.

"You lawyer?" the Marshall asked Lucien.

Lucien shrugged. "Am I?" he asked.

The Marshall banged the squirrel-gavel down. "Court to order," he said. "Who dis, and what are the charges?"

Mossback grabbed Mateo's chin and twisted his head left, exposing his scabbed temple. He showed it to the elders, then said: "He Mateo Anaya, see dis here? He don' tore off his disc. Seems dis boy was in Boulder for reprogrammin', then 'scaped along with another runnah. Seems he t'ink he can git away with them Scob penalties, done tore it right off his own head." He pointed Mateo's right temple at the elders for emphasis.

"Now I'll be damn'd, dat true boy? You rip dis t'ing off yo' own damn head?" the Marshall asked.

Mateo shrugged.

The Marshall scrolled through his U-disc holo-screen, then looked back at Mateo. "We got ourselves a whole list o' violations, some of 'em serious. Might be here 'while," he said.

Mateo said nothing.

"Who da witness?" the Marshall asked.

Mossback pulled Scob Leslie to the front, next to him.

"How you know he?"

"I was in Boulder with him. He was assigned for reprogramming with me," she said. She was quieter now, not defiant like she was in Boulder.

"Dat true?" the Marshall asked.

Again, Mateo said nothing.

The Marshall said: "Do you testify dat to be true, to th' best o' yo' recollection?" he asked Scob Leslie.

"Yes, your Honor. He was there with me. I can promise you that for sure." Her eyes pleaded with the Marshall.

"Let it be entered into da record heah that Scob Leslie done bore witness to the defendant. She was arrested with him in Boulder, Colorado, at the Probitas Correction Center, where she sat as a Scob with him," the Marshall said. "Dat co'rect?"

Scob Leslie nodded profusely. "Yes, that's correct, your Honor," she said. She wouldn't look at Mateo.

The Marshall banged his gavel. "One week ration to our witness heah," he said. A man behind him came around and pulled Scob Leslie away, through a side door. "I ask't you a question," the Marshall said directly to Mateo.

"What exactly are the charges?" Mateo asked, through gritted teeth.

Lucien leaned in and whispered: "Mais, you might wanna tone it down a lil bit." He gave Mateo a wide-eyed warning glance.

The Marshall: "Fair question. Let's unpack dis whole t'ing right now. Charge 1: y'all been 'cused o' bein' a Class 3 climate denier. Charge 2: we add on a Republicrat penalty, which busts that up to Class 4 climate denier. Charge 3: we have you bustin' out o' Probitas Correction, and charge 4: we have you tearin' off your own U-disc, in clear violation. And charge 5: you runnin' out on da bounty."

He looked hard at Mateo and finished: "Dem's some very serious crimes, cher. Very serious indeed. How you plead?"

This is damn insanity. Every word out of these people's mouths is bigger bullshit than the last. "I plead not guilty to all charges, to everything, I haven't done anything at all. I haven't even committed a crime at all, and you've no reason to arrest me. I'm sitting here thinking you all kidnapped me. It's bona fide," Mateo said.

Lucien patted his arm. "Bounce soft," he whispered. He looked up at the Marshall and reiterated: "We had a rough day is all, I tol' him to slow hisself down a bit, yo' Honor."

"Best listen to your lawyer," the Marshall said.

"He's not my lawyer, 'cause I haven't done a crime and this isn't a court." Mateo said. He was pissed.

"I best explain some o' how dis works down heah, Mr. Anaya. Since the blip, things done changed," the Marshall said.

"I heard your 'Marshall is law' speech. Doesn't make it true," Mateo said. He looked around the courtroom. *When is a court not a court? When it's run by these Cajun kangaroo fucks.*

The Marshall tapped the U-disc on his temple. "See dis t'ing right heah? Mine's yella fo' a reason, cher. I'm workin' to go green. Hear cases, I get green. Render verdicts, more green. Don' matter to me how dis goes. Three months, I'm green, an' I'm out." He nodded.

"What dat mean is it don' make no diff'rence what-so-evah if you fight o' don', I get me green points either way. Now it just happens that I used to be a prosecutin' attorney myself, used to try cases every day back before t'ings turned to shit. What that means is I know how dis works, and I'm here to do it. Stampede, U-Net, the guv'ment says we're authorized to hear cases, we hear cases. They pay for ever'ting heah, they allow us full dis-cre-tion-ary opinions, however we want it. Look 'round, ain' no one here but us. We decide you guilty, you be with us a long time then. I get my points either way. Three months, I get green and I'm gone."

Lucien stood and pleaded: "T'ank you kindly, revered elders and esteemed colleagues. Please allow us our sincere apologies for our rough way o' doin' t'ings. Nous ne sommes pas d'ici comme vous. What my friend heah wants to convey is his profound re-gret for dis-res-pec-tin' your traditions, and he humbly implores your forgiveness. As our be-lov-ed Jesus once said: 'he know not what he do.'" He stood at the table, bowed in reverence.

The Marshall studied them both. "How. Do. You. Plead?"

"Not guilty. There are no charges, and no crimes have been committed." Mateo said defiantly. *Fuck you and your fucking Cajun fucks, you dipshits.*

Lucien shook his head.

"Let's just do dis the straight-fo-ward way, now shall we? As to Charge 1, you bein' a class 3 climate denier, I have you ownin' a Camaro, a gas-guzzlin' one, and using un-approved climate phrases in yo' Stampede feeds. Any counterargument?" the Marshall asked.

Mateo said nothing.

"As to charge 2, you bein' a Republicrat. You deny that?"

Mateo stayed silent.

"As to charge 3, you breakin' out of Probitas Co-rection Center, we have video footage of you doin' so. Wanna see the feed?" the Marshall asked.

Mateo shook his head, no. "I wasn't arrested for a crime, so I walked out. I'm still allowed to do that."

"Noted. As to charge 4, you removin' you own U-disc in an un-authorized fashion, we have as evidence: one, no U-disc, two, scar on yo' temple where a disc should be."

"I tore the damn thing off, so what? It's my head. You force something onto my head, I'm gonna tear the damn thing off," Mateo said. "I'll do it again too."

"Shhhh," Lucien whispered, tapping his arm.

"A confession then. Noted. As to charge 5, the bounty. You claimin' full bounty, Mossback?"

"Full bounty. We did the hard work, we git it all. Two weeks," Mossback said.

"Two weeks. Dat's some serious rations," the Marshall said.

"Oui, mon char. We earned it. We found 'im." Mossback said.

"So you did," the Marshall said. He looked back at Mateo and Lucien and asked: "You gonna present any defense, what-so-evah?"

Mateo growled his response: "No defense, no crime, not guilty of anything. I'm just a Dad trying to see my son is all. That's it."

Lucien just raised his hands, palms flat, at the elders.

The Marshall nodded and said: "Should be easy then. Jus' give us a couple." He turned to the other elders, and they huddled together in a small circle. They whispered and argued, but it was mostly silent. The Marshall did most of the talking, the rest of the elders nodded in agreement.

"Don' look good, 'Teo. Don' look good a 'tall," Lucien said.

"It's a fucking joke," Mateo said.

"Maybe, but no one's laughin' heah." Lucien said.

The elders came back to the table, and the Marshall said: "Will the defendant and lawyer please stand?"

Mateo and Lucien stood.

The Marshall stared hard at Mateo. "I don't sense no regret what-so-evah, Mr. Anaya. A flatlanda down heah, ignorin' Scob law, just spittin' on all o' Scob Nation. We can't let none o' that slide. Our duty to see it don't." He poked his right finger at the table, making his point.

"We, the Elders of Scob Nation, find you, Mateo Anaya, guilty of charge 1, bein' a Class 3 Climate Denier. As to charge 2, we find you guilty of being a Republicrat. As to charge 3, we find you guilty o' escapin' from Probitas Correction Center in an un-auth-o-rized manner, before co-rection. As to charge 4, we find you guilty of removin' your U-disc in an un-auth-o-rized manner. Guilty of all charges," the Marshall said. He banged his skull-gavel four times to signify the guilty verdict.

"As far as sentencin' goes, we give full bounty to Mossback and his crew. That's two weeks full rations. Done. As for your own sentence, we assign you one year climate reprogramming, full construction labor. We also assign surgical U-disc im-plan-ta-tion, with removal only after full confession. Gotta make sure you don't rip off your own damn disc again."

"Non, non, non, please, mercy! Je vous en supplie, don't do dis to 'im, please," Lucien pleaded.

The Marshall slammed down his gavel. "Full confession. One year. An' we'll make damn sure you don't forget it."

CHAPTER 22

CLIMATE CORRECTION CLASSROOM
SCOB NATION CAMPUS

Climate scientist Dr. Tala Rainwater stared at the roomful of students and Professors and wondered how she got there. There was no lectern, no desk, no laptop, no microphone. She stood, alone, in front of the classroom, naked in her ideals.

"You're saying that because you're a rich, white guy," climate student Victoria said.

"In case you hadn't noticed, I'm neither white, nor a guy, I'm a female scientist, or ageyuja digasesdisgi, as we say in Cherokee. There are only two of us in the entire world." She made sure to let the Cherokee dialect linger.

"It's your attitude," another student said. "It's just…wrong. Like you have no morals," student Jerome said.

"My *morals*, I see," Dr. Tala said. She sighed. *It was lesson time. Let's give these kids some context.* "How many of you have ever heard of the Trail of Tears? Anyone?"

The room sat silent.

"Your President Andrew Jackson took our land. Army came in and removed us, moved the Cherokee people from Florida, Georgia, Virginia, Mississippi - all over the southeast - up into Oklahoma. We cried all the way from the Atlantic seaboard into the Oklahoma flatlands, our trail of tears. We lost thousands of my people during that journey, during our resettlement."

"This isn't about that," Jerome interrupted.

"Gadôhvi. It's *all* about that. We live in balance, it's Cherokee spirit. We were taken from our homeland." She sighed to help ballast the strength of her ancestors. "I am not a white man. I am Cherokee. And I am a woman."

The class stared forward.

"Has anyone heard of the treaty of New Echota? No? Tlasqualasdi." *Foolish people. It was our land. White man took it.*

"Ancient history," Victoria said. "That's not why we're here."

"No? Please tell me why we are here then," Dr. Tala said.

"To correct your morals," Jerome said. "To fix them."

"Regarding the climate," Dr. Tala said.

The classroom nodded and murmured. *Yes.*

"Cherokee Nation lived in harmony with the world, with nature, with our environment. We didn't just believe it, we felt it in our spirit. In our souls, in our marrow. It's a part of us, part of who we are," Dr. Tala said. "If anyone needs a change in morals, it's the white man."

"Then how can you say that climate change isn't real?" Victoria asked.

"When have I ever said that?" Dr. Tala asked.

"You write papers that say mankind isn't causing it," Jerome said.

"I conduct research that shows mankind is contributing to it, and we're still working to understand exactly how much. Mankind's burning energy contributes to that. I've been very clear. I've authored thirteen papers saying those words exactly. I've co-authored twenty more," Dr. Tala said.

"Contribute isn't exactly admitting it," Victoria said.

"Contribute is the right word, actually. We're still learning how big of a lever we have. Science on this is evolving constantly. We all use energy, we all contribute to the problem. The responsibility for that is on all our shoulders. It's a continuum, a balance."

"Blasphemer!" Jerome said. "We know it's just 47 companies doing it, it's fact. We read about it in the Doctrine, it says so *right here.*" He held up The Probitas Doctrine and showed it to Dr. Tala. "Or prolly you haven't read it. Says right here: 'fossil fuels *cause* it, Commandment 2. Right *there.* It can't be a Commandment unless it's true." He poked his index finger on the paper.

Dr. Tala scanned the Probitas Doctrine and its Ten Commandments. While she'd seen it before, she hadn't taken it seriously: the idea of a strict set of rules guiding humanity in its dominance over nature flew against Cherokee teachings, against a natural order and balance in the world. To her, this was mankind trying to exert control over which mankind had very little control. It was man playing God, Gadôhv's dominion. It twisted the natural order into a cage, trapping not just truth but the land itself.

She taught:

"So, you believe mankind has dominion over the earth? You believe we are the only things that matter for the climate? That we sit above the earth and all systems and it's here to serve us?" The thought of it tightened her stomach.

"It's written. They're *Commandments*," Jerome said. "Man *causes* it."

"You're creating science that questions it all," Victoria said. "Your studies, your papers, your entire work and all that. You're trying to prove that we can't prove it, that mankind isn't causing all of it," Victoria said.

A Commandment is faith, not science. "The sun shines without our asking, the rain falls without our bidding. The forest shelters us, but we do not command the trees. We are the keepers, not the masters, of the land, just as my ancestors believed. It's why I became a climate scientist: to prove, objectively with science, what my people have always believed," Dr. Tala said.

Victoria dug in: "You're saying mankind isn't causing climate change."

"Mankind *isn't* causing climate change," Dr. Tala said, immediately knowing it would echo.

The students gasped.

"We're influencing it. We don't rule the climate, the climate rules us. Our habits influence it, there's no doubt, but there are other factors at play here. And we, as humans, don't understand all of it. It's why I continue to pursue science."

"That's exactly why you're here then," Victoria said calmly. "You've read it all, you've studied it all, you just refuse to accept it. That's why we have Commandment 4: 'those who question are also the enemy', and 5: 'you're either with Us, or against Us."' she said. "You're the enemy."

Dr. Tala scanned the students for some dot of empathy, but found none; instead, the thirty students stared back at her with hatred and scorn. She had no idea what to do. Normally she would use science and logic to guide her classrooms, to teach her climate students, yet these students wanted no part of it. She was there to confirm what they had all been programmed to believe: there was only one right way to think about the climate, and all of those who didn't were the enemy.

Just then, Professor Richard Talleyman stood and addressed the class. He looked at his two Professor colleagues, then at Dr. Tala Rainwater, then out towards the class.

"This is the face of pure climate denial, students. Pure. Climate. Denial. Study it hard. It doesn't have horns on its head, it doesn't drool or hiss, it stands there and talks clearly, almost rationally, doesn't it?" He looked back at Dr. Tala and said: "She looks almost respectable, doesn't she? Like she'll understand the real truth, if given enough time."

"I am respectable, Talleyman, I've been conducting climate research for twenty-five years, longer than these children have been alive!" she urged. She couldn't believe she was actually hearing this. "How dare you."

Victoria jumped back in: "You claim to be a scientist, but you refuse to accept responsibility for what your research means. People look to you for answers, and you're just giving them more doubts."

"It's not my job to give people answers that soothe their fears. It's my job to uncover the truth, like finding a spring in the desert. Responsibility isn't about telling people what they want to hear; it's about leading them to water."

"Critical thinking, Tala? Or just sowing seeds of doubt to justify your own reluctance to take a stand?" Professor Talleyman asked.

"Taking a stand without knowing the land beneath your feet is dangerous, Talleyman. I stand on the truth, even if it's a rocky path," Dr. Tala said.

Dr. Talleyman stepped forward and approached the witness stand. "Allow me to demonstrate how deep this runs, students," he said. Opening a scientific journal, he read aloud: "Climate change has been attributed to a 37.3% increase in facial hair in post-pubescent male teenagers. The study has been confirmed through peer-review, the link has now been established through scientific consensus."

"There's absolutely no link between climate change and facial hair, Richard – you know that. 'Attribution' – another word for 'blame'. It's just junk science, made up to blame something we already know on climate change, an invented number. And it's easy to call it 'peer-reviewed' if you only show it to people who think the same thing." Dr. Tala seethed.

Student Jerome stood up from his chair and said: "what do you call this then?" He tugged at his sideburns. Another boy stood and tugged at his peach-fuzz mustache. Another stood and pulled at his goatee. Within seconds thirteen boys had stood and were tugging at their teenage facial hair. Jerome looked at them all, mouth open, then said: "She's actually ignoring evidence, right here in front of us. She's *ignoring* it. Like she sees it, but just pretends she doesn't," he said.

"It's not evidence! Every boy your age has facial hair!" Dr. Tala said. It was not in her spirit to yell, but she was being pulled down into the abyss.

Dr. Talleyman motioned with his palms for the boys to sit down. Slowly, they did, Jerome the last. "Denial, students. You just saw it. That is exactly the face of denial, you saw it with your own two eyes. She looked evidence in the face – literally, she looked at all of your faces – and just said no. Blue is not blue, it's actually purple," he smiled, then turned away from her. "But she's not lost, that's why she was brought here. When we're done with her, her disc will shine green," he said. He tapped his green U-disc and smiled.

"You defy natural law, Talleyman. You thumb your nose to the order of things, of nature, of our connection to it," Dr. Tala said.

All thirty students, boys and girls, squinted and whispered about Dr. Tala. All three professors, men and women, squinted and whispered about Dr. Tala. Dr. Tala Rainwater squinted back at her captors and thought about jumping into the Mississippi River.

Later that night, Dr. Tala Rainwater had a dream.

She stood alone at the edge of the Mississippi River, the moonlight casting a silver path across the water's surface. The weight of today pressed down upon her, threatening to pull her into the river's depths. As she gazed into the current, she heard a voice, the whisper of wind through the cornfields.

"You are troubled, Tala," the voice said.

Dr. Tala turned to see Selu, The Corn Mother, spirit of earth and the cycle of life. The visage warmed her.

"Mother Selu," Tala whispered. "I don't know if I can go on. I'm losing my way."

"The path you walk is not easy, child. But the paths worth walking seldom are. Tell me, what weighs so heavily on your heart?"

Tala dipped her toes into the cold river, the water's flow a reflection of her own turbulence. "The world has turned against me, Mother. They mock me, mock my words, mock our people, deny my truth. I've dedicated my whole being to understanding the earth, to seeking the balance that our people have always known. But now…I'm not sure I can continue. The burden is heavy."

Selu stepped closer, her presence comforting and warm. "The river always flows, Tala, always returning to the source. You stand at its edge, contemplating your journey. What is it you seek?"

Tala felt tears welling in her eyes. "I thought…maybe the river could take me back. Back to the earth, from where I came. Perhaps Elohi calls me back."

Selu's expression softened with understanding. "The earth welcomes all who return to it, but your journey is not yet complete. The river flows through you, just as it flows through the land. It does not end, but continues its journey. So must you."

Tala's voice shook. "And if I'm not strong enough? What if I can no longer bear the weight?"

The spirit mother placed a hand on Tala's shoulder, grounding her. "You must remember, child, the great Cherokee nation is one with the earth, with the spirit of sky and fire itself. Your spirit is bound to all things. But you must also remember that the Cherokee is a dedicated and fierce warrior, bound of honor to defend truth and the spirit earth's teachings. We do not seek to fight, but we are fierce when the battle comes. The fight you seek is already within you. You drink from the river of your ancestors, you soak up the land itself.

Continue your journey, child, the fight is still yours. The river awaits your return, but that day is not today. We will be here when you are ready."

CHAPTER 23

ESCAPE FROM SCOB NATION
SOMEWHERE IN WEST MISSISSIPPI

Mateo was held in an eight by ten-foot outdoor cell, with walls made of tall, white bayou reeds. He gripped the thick reeds in his hands and pulled them wider, just to see if he could push his head through. He could, but so what? Even if he broke out, where the hell would he go? He was in the middle of the Mississippi bayou, he had no transportation, no idea where he was or where he would go. Tomorrow he would be assigned to the dormitory, and then his retraining would begin. Tonight, Mateo Anaya was locked up in a makeshift prison cell as a convicted climate criminal.

He sat down on the reeds and pulled his knees into his chest. The helplessness of imprisonment hit him at that very moment, and he began to cry. *This is not how this is gonna end, is it? I'm never gonna see Lauren and Reyes again? I'm just gonna rot away in this Cajun prison?*

A boot tapped on the door and snapped him out of his funk. "Room service," Lucien said.

Mateo looked up, but didn't stand. *What was the point?* He pointed to a rack of cane spears and said: "Just give me one of those, and I can end this right now."

"Naw, Teo, that's not how this is gon' end," Lucien said. His voice sounded reassuring.

Mateo looked around. "No guards?"

Lucien shook his head. "What they need 'em for? Where you gon' go?" he chuckled.

Mateo sunk his face into his knees again. *True dat.*

Lucien crouched down. "Now, you see that forest ovah there? All dem big fat greenery trees?"

Mateo looked, then nodded.

"Turns out dem's some special trees, called Airthorns. Bred 'specially to soak up all them bad greenhouse gases 'n shit. Seems that Scob Nation heah ain't just a penal colony, it also a big fat carbon sponge." He pronounced it like *cah-bahn*.

Mateo shrugged. *Who gives a shit?*

"Also turns out, ma cher, dem trees is like matches, they go up just like that," Lucien said, snapping his fingers. "They maybe soak up all that gas, but also ex-plode like nothin' you ever seen."

Mateo didn't get it. "Why does that matter to me, Lucien? I just don't give one shit about that damn forest." He sat, frustrated and hopeless.

Lucien pressed his forehead to the reed bars and spoke softly: "We gon' start us a fo-rest fire, unna'stand Teo? I'm gonna light up that whole damn thing and we gonna run right outa heah, clean as we can. Already got the boat picked out, already figgered out which o' their boats we gonna sink. Now all I gotta do is figger out if you're up for this. Cuz once it start, it gon' go fast."

Six hours later, when the half-moon rose above the Mississippi bayou, when dark settled in and soaked up everything but the fireflies, when chatter from the holding areas and prisoner dormitories fell to a soft hush, when the shantyboat and other native denizens of Scob Nation finally went to bed, Lucien Dupont torched the Airthorn forest. Turns out his information was correct: he lit one base-brush with a reed torch and flames crawled right up the trunk into the branches. The softest of winds carried the flames from branch to branch, tree to tree, trunk to roots. The crackling heat surged around him, filling the air with the sharp tang of burning sap, thick and suffocating. Within seconds the forest was ablaze, and he turned and ran like hell.

Mateo punched the cage reeds one, two, three times until they snapped. He wrested them back and forth until a hole formed big enough for him to squeeze through, and he did. He caught Lucien in mid-stride, and they sprinted towards the riverbank.

He'd never run so fast in all his life. He sprinted through the outstretched arms of those in the holding pen, past the gasps and gazes from the dorms, and down the dirt steps along the cafeteria. Alarms went off, and he could hear loud yells and screams at the fire scene; in the distance a mechanical voice blurted out through metal loudspeakers: "Attention: the carbon forest has been breached! The carbon forest has been breached! All personnel respond to the Airthorn forest!"

Dozens of Scobs screamed and ran towards the forest, their faces lit with panic. Portable generators were quickly deployed and started, large rolls of drafting hoses were unwound and dunked into the river, their spouts shooting torrents of water onto the flames. As the forest sizzled and smoked, Mateo followed Lucien down towards the riverbed, along the double-stacked rows of shanties and powerboats. He turned to look back one final at the forest – now fully engulfed in flames – and then, suddenly, he fell forward into the dirt, as if he was pushed. Before he could react, his right ankle was yanked, and he was dragged back towards the forest area. Disoriented, he could feel a rope around his ankle and hear the clomps of horses running, and felt the dirt scraping up his back as he was pulled. His foot had been lassoed, and he was being pulled back towards the camp!

Mateo clawed at the dirt but came up with soil and pebbles. Lucien ran alongside the horse slapping at the rider, but that only caused the horse to lurch right, then left, to try and shake him loose. Mateo lurched for and grabbed a long stick, and he used it to poke at the rope around his ankle. Sticking it, stabbing it, he managed to wedge it inside the noose and then, with a hard tug of his wrist, he broke the stick and unleashed the rope. He was free!

Tumbling to a stop, Mateo shook his head and jumped to his feet, only to scream in pain as his right ankle gave way. He hopped on his left leg towards the river, then Lucien put his arm around his shoulder; they ran and hopped together.

Mateo's hand burned, and when he looked over Lucien's shoulder he saw why: his right thumb was completely gone. Somehow in all the commotion his right thumb had been torn off.

They got to the riverbed, then Lucien began poking holes in boat pontoons with a long stick; Mateo grabbed another stick and hopped along, poking holes in whatever boats he could muster. Lucien helped him onto a tall, silver swamp boat then climbed up the bench next to him; he pulled the cord to start the engine, revved the gas, then hit the joystick hard. Mateo and Lucien steered into the Mississippi's deep water quickly, with only the sound of the enormous propeller fan gunning behind them.

Five minutes later, as they zoomed up the river at full speed, Mateo addressed his injuries. His right ankle had been dislocated but had popped back into place, and now looked raw and shiny as a melon. Lucien handed Mateo a bandana and he dabbed at his right thumb, which was, well, gone. It was just a hole. He wrapped the bandana twice around his palm, and Lucien tied it across his thumbhole. It hurt like hell, but was starting to abate as shock set in. Most of all he couldn't get used to the visual: four fingers emerging from his wrist, like tiny fleshhooks that sprouted from his palm. Four fingers, wrapped tightly around a bloody Lil Red.

MEMPHIS CENTRAL TRAIN STATION
MEMPHIS, TENNESSEE

Lucien tossed a Memphis Grizzlies sweatshirt to Mateo and told him to wear it. "Then, you get near Chicago, you're a Bulls fan. Unna'stand, Teo?" he said, tossing Mateo a Chicago Bulls sweatshirt as well.

They had spent the last three hours at Shelby County Medical Clinic, a facility that catered to the homeless and unwashed poor of Memphis. The attending physician quizzed them about the mysterious disappearance of Mateo's thumb, but ultimately succumbed to Lucien's charms: when Lucien said that "my friend heah jus' got hisself caught by a jealous husband and don' want his wife to know 'bout his in-dis-cre-tions" the Doctor simply sutured up the wound. The Doctor had surely heard worse, and closing the thumbhole took a mere fifteen minutes.

Now they sat at Memphis Central Train Station, waiting to board an Amtrak train to Chicago.

"How are you gonna get back, Lucien?" Mateo asked.

"Now, cher, you don' worry y'self 'bout that none. Lucien gon' do what Lucien gon' do," he said. He gave Mateo a huge smile and slapped him on the back.

"So, you're booked as Lucien Dupont, first-class fare all to Chicago. Anyone asks for ID, you just don' got none. The way you look, don't think you'll get any questions what-so-evah."

"You sure?" Mateo asked. "I don't want to make anything worse for you."

"You kiddin' me? You just gave Lucien the best damn story we both evah had, trust me on that. Next time I see Porter I tell him all 'bout our 'Pocalypse Now ride," Lucien said. "I'll be bigger'n Marlon Brando."

Mateo nodded. It was a story, that's for damn sure.

"Now here's da t'ng: I've no idea what's gon' happen when you get to Chicago. Maybe you jus' get on through to DC, maybe they ask you 'bout yo' thumb, or yo' hair, or yo' dignity," he chuckled and squeezed Mateo's shoulder. "You be on your own, cher, but I think you know that already. You can either be me all the way to DC, or you jump off and find you own way. Up to you."

Tears ran down Mateo's cheeks, and he held his head in his hands. The impact of their escape at the hands of Lucien Dupont, his Cajun savior, hit him all at once. He'd known Lucien for mere days, but he felt like a younger brother, being protected from all of life's ills. It was like he'd known him all his life. He just cried and nodded. Finally, he said: "I'll never be able to thank you, Lucien. Really. Don't even know what to say. I've got no way to pay you back."

Lucien leaned in and said, in the softest voice that only they could hear: "I done lost my son already Teo. We doin' this so you don' lose yours. Go save your boy." He stood, kissed the very top of Mateo's bald head, said "a la prochaine, mon ami", then walked away.

CHAPTER 24

Climate HypocRatIST (CHRIST) COALITION
MEMPHIS, TENNESSEE

While Mateo waited at Memphis Central Station, Memphis' Arts District hummed around him with activity. Known for its trendy shops, art houses and deep south historic buildings, the neighborhood signified the full transformation of Memphis.

Seventy-seven years earlier it had been the home of The Lorraine Hotel, renowned for its outdoor patio where Martin Luther King, Jr. was shot. Today, however, inside a five thousand square foot warehouse, sat a collection of tables, chairs, computers, small satellite dishes, and a dozen hackers clacking away at their keyboards. The warehouse was dark, save the computer screens and flickering USB ports.

Jordan Hayes, computer scientist and leader of the Climate Hypocratist Coalition hacker group, began their meeting: "OK people, let's go through the list."

"Natalie Clark, acted in and produced the movie *'Green Horizon'*," hacker Sophie offered.

"That the one where they're like pirates flying around the world saving us from other climate pirates flying around the world?" Jordan asked.

"That's it. Movie ends with her character drowning the oil company boss in a vat of his own oil. Hilarious. 93% on Rotten Tomatoes," Sophie said.

"Make your case," Jordan said.

"Natalie Clark, born Natasha Thompson in Portland, Oregon, in 2003. B.A. from Crestwood University in Hudson, New York, graduated with a degree in Environmental Justice and Community Organizing. With Honors." Sophie said.

"I like her already," Jordan said.

"Founded 'Condiments for Climate' in 2010, has the top three brands in each category. Her Kapitalist Ketchup was used in both the Louvre and Hermitage defacing, Mercenary Mustard in del Prado, and Ransack Relish at the Tate. They're apparently designed to be permanent."

"Permanent how?"

"Uh…they don't come off? Once you throw 'em they stay part of the paintings. Apparently, there's some sort of hardener in them to make it turn solid." Sophie said.

"Nasty. Imagine what that shit tastes like. Plastic containers?" Jordan asked.

Click click clack. "Of course," Sophie said.

"From where?"

"Bangladesh," Sophie answered.

Jordan shook his head, smiling. He stared at her movie star face on the screen. "Not good, Natasha Thompson from Portland, Oregon. Revenues?"

"$24.7 million, 2045 revenues. Jee-*zus*," Sophie said.

Jordan nodded his head. "Travel, and speeches," he asked.

Hacker Dylan clacked at his keyboard and jumped in: "Twenty-three speeches from 2035 to 2044, twelve international conferences, not including movies. Movie production: eight movies, twenty-three international locations." He clacked through more numbers. "Won a 2033 Clammy for Best Climate Documentary Feature: *'Let My Son - Not the Bums - Sell the Sun'*."

"And didn't she do that big online thing?" Jordan asked.

Hacker Dylan nodded. "An oil movie. Live on-stream, all U-Net Event."

Jordan snapped his fingers repeatedly, trying to remember. "What was the name?"

"*'Fucking Dirty, Fucking Oil.'*" Dylan said. He took off his glasses.

Jordan blew out a deep breath. "OK, someone give me a tally. What are the numbers?"

Sophie answered: "CO2 footprint, Condiments for Climate brands, 120 megatons, since its inception. Sourced in

Bangladesh, child labor with a United Nations Exploited Child score of -37, that adds another 83 megatons."

Dylan jumped in: "Movies: eight, fifty-seven times around the world, 1.4 million miles flown, that's 610 tons of CO2."

"And that doesn't even include living," Sophie said. "Doesn't even include anything else." She showed a picture of the actress eating a hamburger and then...*another hamburger.*

"Totals?" Jordan asked.

"Two hundred twenty-three million, one hundred twenty thousand, and one hundred twenty tons," Dylan said.

"Two hundred twenty-three megatons," Jordan said, shaking his head. "How many trees would we need to plant to offset it?"

Sohie answered: "Five-point-four billion. Ish."

"And land?" he asked.

Clack clack clack. Dylan answered: "About fifty-four-point-eight million acres. Essentially, Iowa."

Jordan pulled up a Twittoob feed and displayed it on all eight screens. Climate Activist Natalie Clark was giving a REDx speech to an adoring audience:

> "...we now know that only 47 companies produce over 97% of all global oil emissions. Forty-seven, ladies and gentlemen. Imagine what would happen if we got rid of all those 47 companies...how much cleaner our lives would be, how much happier our children would be, how much more integrated society would live." Images scrolled: waterfalls, multi-racial picnics with children hugging each other, oil derricks being toppled like dictator statues; big, fat, white, oil company executives being hauled off in handcuffs, their castles repossessed. "It's time to redistribute that *dirty* wealth, isn't it?"

Then, more images of crying actors and actresses standing in oil exec driveways, handing out food, cash and deliverance.

He clicked it off. "Fuck, I can't take it anymore. Time for a vote." He clicked his mouse, and all screens went dark; then all member of the CHRIST Coalition voted. In ten seconds, the verdict came in unanimous: "Verdict: Climate Hypocrite. Penalties: FULL."

"Send in your penalties, please," Jordan said. He watched the penalties tally from the eight hackers, scrolling across his screen. Nodding as he read them, he scanned the other faces for signs of disagreement. He let them sink in, then asked: "Are we in agreement? Any dissenting thoughts?"

All heads nodded, with no dissenting voices. It was unanimous. "Alright then, let's read them off. Surveillance first," Jordan said.

Hacker Dylan read the penalty. "Internally, we'll surveil all routers, wifis, U-links, refrigerators, televisions, computers, pads, smart lights, bulbs and plugs. Externally, we'll tap into lights, garage door openers, electronic gates, windows, door-cams, even smart plugs. And of course we'll have full drone-cloak, so we'll record anything inside that veil."

"Ok. Make sure it's higher altitude, the last thing we need is a drone crashing into a window and giving it all up," Jordan said.

Dylan nodded.

"Next, financials," Jordan said.

Sophie jumped back in. "We've got access to all accounts: banking, coins, NFTs, offshore, onshore, trusts, Bam-mo and PayMe. Got 'em all, got 'em teed up. Her investments will include oil – the biggies like Luxxon, Bell and Standard – as well as mines throughout southern Africa and Asia. Turns out she funds the blood diamond trade, seems to love slave labor."

Jordan chuckled. "What about charities?"

"Republicrats 4 Energy, a number of 'other side' groups, along with think-tanks like Manhattan and Kansas Institutes. Got a list of twenty-eight she supports."

"Get receipts," Jordan said.

"Always," Sophie said. "And she's gonna default on that beautiful castle she lives in too," he said, clicking away at his keyboard.

"Damn straight. Travel and logistics, next," Jordan said.

Dylan said: "Passport is locked, driver and air licenses have been put on hold 'pending investigation'. All cards have been hacked, we've upped her limits and have full access."

"Let's have her send cars to congress!" Sophie said. She was bouncing in her seat at the thought. "Like – a Hummer to Senator Abbott and an SUV to congresswoman DiNobli. Deliver them right to Capitol Hill!"

Dylan clicked the orders in and smiled. "Done. Hummer is bright orange, won't be able to miss it. Gets 8 miles per gallon, gas, they'll freak out. Delivery next Tuesday."

"Make sure we get feeds on that, we can feed 'em to socials. And speaking of socials, go," Jordan said.

Hacker Emma, silent until now, smiled broadly and adjusted her dark-rimmed glasses. She pulled her red hair back into a ponytail, banded it, then swung it back and forth. "Hair goes back, Emma's gonna hack," she said.

"I love it when she does that," Dylan said.

Emma ran through the list. "Well, we have Twittoob, WowNow, Stampede and full Umbili-Net accounts, all access, with full privileges. We've locked in all her connections, feeds, friends and family – and all professional accounts. Movie studios, companies, all of them. We've got two hundred and twenty-seven videos patched together that we can start pumping out, we can patch in the network feeds from Capitol Hill, of course drone footage. I'm sure we'll get plenty of audio from surveillance, we can paint the world with 'em. Maybe even turn 'em into ringtones!" she laughed.

"How are the bot speeches?" Jordan asked.

Emma giggled. "Fucking *awesome*, some of my best work. Wanna see?"

The group nodded.

Actress Natalie Clark appeared on screen, speaking intimately at a coffee shop, sipping her latte, engaged in a very private, raw and honest discussion. She was pretty and charming, with a devilish glint in her bright green eyes, and spoke directly to the camera. She leaned in, her voice almost a whisper, and said:

> "We'll root you out, one by one. If you use fossil fuels, we'll find you, we'll get you. We'll shame you and your kids, we'll put you on display. We'll follow you to school, work, the PTA, the gym, your parents' house. We'll even catch you with your lover," she said, giggling. "You won't be able to hide anywhere. By the time we're done, we'll have 'corrected' everyone. We'll clean up this world, or you'll die trying." She put the white coffee mug to her lips and sipped. She winked at the camera. "N'est-ce pas?"

"She speaks French?" Jordan asked.

"Her bot does. Had to give her some clim-a-tude, didn't I?" Emma said. She thwipped her ponytail back and forth.

Jordan leaned back in his chair and put his palms flat on the desktop. He spoke formally: "Let it be known that The CHRIST Coalition has heard the evidence against actress Natalie Clark, born Natalie Thompson in Portland, Oregon, and found her guilty of climate hypocrisy, with full sentencing approved. Let this be the formal notification of the verdict and the approved sentencing, and let our voices serve as final approval."

Jordan asked around the room to each hacker, they responded with "yes" and "aye" and "fuck yeah". When all seven voices were recorded, he finished with his: "Shit-ass guilty. Yes." He clicked the button on his computer and smiled. "Blockchained, baby. Permanent. Fucking. Record."

He stood, held his first out horizontal, thumb out, wobbled it for effect, then turned the thumb down.

"Launch," he said.

CHAPTER 25

UNION STATION
CHICAGO, ILLINOIS

Mateo slept all the way from Memphis, Tennessee, to Chicago, Illinois. He actually had no idea how long it took or how long he'd been asleep: he'd put the ticket stub in the overhead rack, sat down and woke up as the train pulled into the station. As instructed by Lucien, he swapped the Memphis Grizzlies sweatshirt for the Chicago Bulls, pulled the hoodie over his bald head and stepped out onto the concourse.

I am completely alone. No friends, no allies, no nothing. Fifteen hundred miles from home, walking through a landscape I don't even recognize, trying to dodge the U-discs and surveillance cameras. I don't even know what country I live in anymore. America maybe, but nothing I remember.

He traversed the maze of tracks and went into the main atrium of Chicago's Union Station. Mostly he walked with his head down, avoiding all eye contact. He needed two things: food, and a one-way ticket to Washington D.C. As he walked, he noticed that half the monitors were unified with a single message: "Umbili-discs are Now Mandatory for All Travelers." *Shit. How the hell am I going to get a train ticket?*

Mateo felt the weight of eyes on him. It wasn't just the cameras; with mandatory U-discs came a feeling of unmistakable dread, as if everyone was apologizing for their own sins. Public spaces were now confessionals, and the air was thick with a collective guilt – a society walking about, thinking *I may hate myself but I hate you even more.* Paranoia surrounded him, and it was soul-crushing.

In a convenience store, he surveyed the food aisle. Stoink offerings were everywhere: sandwiches, nuggets, even Stoink-on-a-Stick. He finally settled on two peanut butter and jelly sandwiches – *what the hell was up with PB&J, anyway?* – and a couple of unripe bananas. The man behind the counter eyed him, tapping his own green U-disc twice.

Mateo pulled down his hood and displayed his temple scar, and the man squinted and nodded. "I hear ya, brother, we gotta do what we gotta do. Still, they're out there. Just sayin'," he said, tossing the items into a bag.

Mateo turned back, double-checking for a U-call report, but the clerk only nodded. *No friends, just watchful eyes.* He stepped back into the atrium, tearing off sandwich chunks, stuffing them into his mouth like they might be taken from him any second. He caught sight of his own reflection in the glass: a homeless man hungrily devouring a stolen sandwich before he got caught. *That's who I am now.*

To his left, a group of people had gathered around a wall-sized video screen. Conversations buzzed and murmured, and Mateo stepped up to see what they were watching.

Atop the screen scrolled the caption: "ST. LOUIS STANDOFF: CLIMATE PROTESTOR HANGS FROM HISTORIC ARCH."

Mateo initially thought that the St. Louis protestor had hung himself from the arch in protest, a self-lynching climate martyr. But it became clear the man sat in a harness, something a mountain climber or window-washer might use. Mateo thought he looked like a professional dangler, if there even was such a thing. No, this wasn't a suicide; it was just a pissed-off a climate screamer.

Firehouse ladders extended from trucks below, and as authorities tried to reach him the protestor talked to them on his cell phone. He spoke animatedly, said "no, no, no", then finally tossed the cell phone down. As the phone shattered on the pavement, he flipped the authorities off.

Just then, the man's U-disc glowed white, and he clicked his temple and yelled to authorities through his U-link connection. The ladders below extended higher and higher still, but were much too low to reach his dangling feet. His U-disc pulsed through different colors: white, pink, red, yellow. Then, as if it found what it was looking for, the U-disc landed on black and throbbed. *Pulse. Pulse. Pulse.*

The protestor screamed "leave me alone!" He shook his head back and forth, *no no no.*

The ladders below stopped extending. The ladder policemen spoke to each other, looked up, then slowly descended. Their rescue attempt was over.

When the ladders were fully retracted, the policemen climbed off and looked up with all the other policemen, firemen, reporters and bystanders. Cameras and phones captured the sequence in full, high-definition glory.

The protestor yelled down in defiance.

A bullhorn policemen yelled up, with orders.

The protestor yelled back: no.

The bullhorn policemen put down his bullhorn.

A different policeman stepped forward, his chief's uniform adorned with colorful medals of achievement. He yelled up at the protestor.

The protestor looked down and did nothing.

The police chief held up a small electronic device, tapped a button, then looked up one final time.

The protestor yelled, then grabbed the U-disc at his temple. He kicked his legs like a frog in a harness, as if having a violent seizure. His head thrashed left to right, right to left, and as he bucked his left sneaker fell off. And then, just as suddenly, his body went limp. Mateo saw the sneaker fall all the way down, next to the shattered cell phone.

The crowd around Mateo gasped.

"Oh my God, they shot him!"

"What the hell did those bastards do?"

Across the bottom of the screen scrolled the caption: "ST. LOUIS PROTESTOR CAPTURED BY EXPERIMENTAL U-DISC TASER CAPABILITY."

Mateo felt sick to his stomach. He knew exactly what had happened: the protestor had received the very same lightning-bolt-temple-zap he add when he escaped Probitas. It was the exact reason he and Houston had ripped their U-discs off their heads in the first place. He put his right middle finger up to his temple scab and rubbed softly. *This is our new world. This is how they're going to punish us. This is how they're going to control us.*

He needed to get to Reyes. More than ever, he needed to find his son.

The crowd slowly dispersed, and Mateo found the system map and traced his path to Washington D.C. *The Capitol Limited.* Eighteen hours to reach his son. But now what?

He studied the ticket counter, watching as travelers were screened and required to flash their U-discs. He watched couples argue over their different color statuses; a green-virtuous wife berated her yellow-glowing husband, who shook his head in apology. "Those Shining Black Are Required to Travel in Cars 6 through 10," read a sign above the ticket counter. Numbered cars? *Isn't that what they did to the Jews?*

Taking a deep breath, he joined the line.

"Destination?" the teller said, not even looking at Mateo.

"Washington D.C.," Mateo said, pulling the hoodie tighter.

The teller click-clacked on her keyboard and looked at him. "Capital Limited, leaves from Track 14 at 11:34 p.m. Sleeper, First-class, or..." She looked at him again. "Oh, common then."

Mateo fumbled with his wallet, and pulled out cash, trying to steady his nerves. The teller counted it out. "Disc, please."

Mateo took a deep breath, then slowly shook his head. *No.*

She stopped typing, her hands flat on the keyboard. Mateo's voice broke as he spoke: "I've just got to get to D.C. to find my boy." He had nothing left, no excuses, no dignity. Tears ran down his cheeks. *Just let me find him. Please.*

The teller stared, processing. Mateo barely breathed, afraid she might report him. After what felt like an eternity, she spoke into a small microphone. "Tellers to the front, please, tellers to the front."

"Where'd you start, sir?" the teller asked in a soft voice.

"California," Mateo whispered, his voice ragged. "Had a full head o' hair when I began. Had all ten fingers too." He held up his right hand, sans thumb, and pulled back the hoodie to show his bare scalp. *Started with a full head of hair and all my fingers.*

Her gaze landed at the red temple scar. She pointed her chin at it. "You do that?"

Mateo nodded. "Had to. They were going to lock me up for this crazy climate shit. I've come all this way to find my boy." His words tumbled out, thick and uncontrolled.

The teller watched him, then clicked her keyboard with a determined look. Mateo shook his head, his voice now a broken staccato. "Miss, you have no idea. I have nowhere to turn. Please."

She reached for the printer, tearing papers, stamping passes. "This'll get you on. Train 7, upper deck's your best bet. Pull that hood tight and go to sleep, you know what I'm saying? They won't bother you." She handed Mateo the papers, her eyes meeting his.

"They catch you, I'll say you had the disc when I checked you in. But keep that hood up. No disc, they'll arrest you right there. They're stopping everything in Pittsburgh, rechecking. Keep your shoes on, just in case." She pointed to a photo of her son on her desk. "Boards in three minutes, sir. Best hustle."

Mateo made his way to Track 14, then car 7, weaving through the black car aisle. As he looked for a seat, he thought of Stoink Farm, where the robo-cows wandered freely, oblivious to their fate. He envied their engineered ignorance. They knew nothing of the past or the future. *Moot moot moot,* they went. *Just like me,* he thought, finding a seat in the back corner. Sliding his ticket into the overhead rack, he pulled his hood down.

Another lost face in the huddled Scob masses. Just another criminal, bound for correction. Eyes closed, he settled into the sway of the train, willing it to carry him the last miles. Next stop: Pittsburgh.

CHAPTER 26

WINDY CITY TRIBUNE AND POLICE HEADQUARTERS
CLIMATE CRIMES DIVISION
CHICAGO, ILLINOIS

Blonden Viate watched all forty-seven members of the Chicago Police Department mill about, refill their coffee mugs, then take their seats. Interspersed throughout the police officers were a dozen employees of the Windy City Tribune, who also took their seats.

"Is this about that St. Louis shit?" someone from the back yelled. The room laughed.

"The St. Louis Situation, yes. That's exactly why I'm here, to show you what we've built for you." Viate said.

"You gonna zap us like that? Bzzt." another officer quipped, to a chorus of laughs.

Only if I want to, Viate thought. He smiled, then poked his finger out in mock *bzzt*.

Senior Editor Melinda Wohling stood and said: "Come on, Billy, Officer Jensen, please, I know there's a lot going on here. Let's try and get ahead of this, shall we?" She held up a beige U-disc and showed it to the group. While most U-discs were the size of a quarter, hers was big as a hockey puck. She held it up to her right temple, spun it until it clicked into place, then smiled as it glowed green. The room murmured as it shone brightly.

"I guess size *does* matter," another officer joked. Haha.

"OK, funny man, in this case it's absolutely true because, shall we say, some of you are brain-limited. If I try to explain it using words, most of you just won't get it, will you?"

"Oooh, snap!" someone else yelled.

"Listen, really. Yesterday Umbili-Net released their Virident Green program, and I wanted to demonstrate it all to you. Obviously, this one's bigger than the rest of yours, but I wanted you to be able to see it, ok? We're handing out your upgrades, when you get them just go ahead and click them on." Boxes of U-discs were passed about, hands went inside, U-discs were removed and snapped onto temples. Within seconds, the room lit up in a patchwork of green, yellow and black U-disc lights. She stood watching the room, her green hockey puck disc glowing.

Police officers looked back and forth at each other, chuckling, humming, commenting. Officers with black discs tapped on them to make sure they were working, then shrugged when their color didn't change.

Wohling continued. "I have to say, this is one big positive from the glitch. What you're about to see is something that might take us years to implement, to debate, to legislate, to hold caucuses on, all that. But now, we just go right into implementation. What a breath of fresh air. Sad to say it came from a big cyber-event, but sometimes there's a silver lining in those dark clouds. Honestly, it allowed U-net to get us these features within days."

"What does it mean?" a voice from the crowd asked.

"I'm getting to that. She read from the holo-screen in front of her face. "The new Virident Green program has upgraded all the U-discs to be fully climate compliant. These discs will now display your Climate Morality Index Rating instantly, all color-coded them for instant verification. If you're good, you're green. If you have some work to do, you're yellow. And if yours is black, you need correction," she said.

And then I'll blast your brain, Viate thought.

Officers who glowed green smiled and laughed, then teased those who glowed yellow. Members who shone black tapped their discs again, then removed them.

"Explain correction," Chicago Police Chief Brent Benning said. A tall, lanky man with a large Adam's apple, his U-disc glowed yellow.

Editor Wohling smiled broadly. "Green means you're good – your climate thought's in line. Yellow means you've got some work to do, and they've given us a list of classes and other ways to 'get right' and turn that yellow into green. Black means, well, it means you're a climate criminal, and are due for climate reprogramming at an upgrade center."

"What about me? How do I fix this?" Chief Benning asked, tapping his yellow U-disc.

Wohling scrolled through the items. "Honestly, if you turn in your legacy vehicle – says here you have a gold 1999 Monte Carlo? – if you just turn it in, you'll burn green, brother," she chuckled.

The room whooped and hollered in jest. He shook his head then mouthed in silence: "no way".

Viate stepped forward. "If I may, Ms. Wohling. I can help bring this all into focus," he said.

Wohling held her right palm up and offered him the room.

"As Ms. Wohling was explaining, Virident Green is a wonderful new climate sensitivity identification system that will help all of us understand people's climate morality, and more so, allow us to pursue climate criminals at the point of attack," he said, commanding the room.

He waved his palm as he spoke: "Those of you who are green, congratulations, you're got all your climate oars in the water, so to speak. Those of you who are yellow, well you have some improvement work to do, but we, of course, are with you and will help you along your journey. And those of you who are black –" he pointed to the three officers in the room and wagged his finger at them, in jest – "well, you have some work to do as well. And we will welcome you to any one of our Probitas Correction Centers to help with that. Of course."

The group laughed and chuckled. So did he. *But wait, here's the best part.*

"Now I know Ms. Wohling here was going to explain what happens when the discs turn black: not only do they mark you for climate repair, but they also adhere permanently onto one's forehead. I believe U-Net calls it their Temp-Attach feature, and it was just released at our Probitas Center in Boulder two days ago. A quite effective little trick," he said, making sure to minimize its effect and its potential.

"But one of the limitations we've already found with Virident is this: yes, it's a fantastic climate identification system, but it's still just that, an *identification* system. It tells us what a person's status is, but it doesn't go far enough. It still leaves the hard work – the enforcement of climate laws and regulations – up to you. That means all of you, the hard-working people of our police departments across the country, still have to make the arrests. Just like before. And, I would argue, that since people are openly labeled, it might make them more aggressive and secretive. What we're afraid of, potentially, is that a color system like the Virident Program might actually make all of your jobs harder. And we wouldn't want that, would we?" he asked the room.

But don't you worry, my little law enforcement minions, I've solved your problem as only I can.

The room nodded and shrugged. Ms. Wohling's puck-sized disc glowed green, while Chief Banning's eyes squinted with a mix of irritation and wonder.

Viate delivered the coup de grace. "And so, ladies and gentlemen, Officers of the Windy City Police Department, I'm here to announce a brand-new program we've developed just for you. I'm here to announce the launching of our new Climate Action and Enforcement Regime: ProbOnyx."

"Officers shifted in their seats and mumbled to one another; the reporters in the back pressed buttons on their holo-screen and scrolled through recording options. No one had any idea what he was talking about. *Perfect.*

"Ms. Wohling, if you would assist me please? The mannequin head you were going to use to demonstrate. Could you get it please?" he looked at her and waited.

Wohling opened a cabinet and pulled out the head of training dummy and set it onto the desktop. She turned it sideways towards, attached a U-disc to it, then snapped it into place. She nodded and gave him a thumbs up.

"We at Probitas felt that climate identification was, simply, not enough. Why not go all the way, why not move directly into behavioral control? Why not *really* make your jobs easier? So, we got together with the great people at Stampede and developed ProbOnyx, which builds on Virident Black and goes much further."

"The St. Louis arrest," Chief Benning said. "You used this in St. Louis."

Viate nodded, then pointed to the desktop.

All eyes focused on the training dummy head.

Viate pressed a button on his holo-screen. The dummy's U-disc buzzed, then turned black. As he held his finger on the button, the disc buzzed louder and longer, until the head began to wobble. The disc's volume increased, the vibrations intensified, and the dummy head bounced off the desktop onto the floor. The head buzzed and spun around like a fan blade loose from its mount.

"All of the ProbOnyx discs have full Taser Class 2 capability. Very, very sensitive, as you can see. Two seconds and it'll incapacitate a two-hundred-pound man. You saw it yesterday, in St. Louis, the first time we used the Temple-Taze in law enforcement." He was Steve Jobs, launching iPhone version 58. *Maybe I should've worn a black crew neck.*

The buzzing in the room stopped. Officers looked at the spinning head, then at each other, then back up at Viate. The room froze.

Sensing it, Viate walked them back. "What happened yesterday was a last resort, of course, to be used in an extreme situation. With the ultimate discretion, with the proper training, by people in authority. I should let you know that the protestor was rescued safely, and is now resting comfortably under 24/7 mental health watch at St. Louis Presbyterian Hospital. So…it works. It saves lives."

He smiled and let the tension in the room abate.

"But the Chicago Police Department is known for your, shall we say, *more hands-on* approach, and so this is the feature we're really excited about. To show it to you, I'll need some volunteers. Please: those who are shining black." Viate scanned the room for the three Virident black officers, then found them.

The three black-disc officers shifted uncomfortably in their seats, looking at each other. Finally, one said: "No way are you going to zap me like Saint Louie. No goddam way."

"I assure you, there will be no pain whatsoever. My promise to you. I simply want to show you the daily use of this wonderful system." He looked over to Chief Benning, who nodded agreement.

"Please, just relax, and stay where you are. I can demonstrate this all from here." Viate said. Scrolling down through his screen, he took one final look at the three officers, then pressed another button.

The three officers immediately sat up straight, eyes forward, as if at attention. They didn't look happy or sad or angry or anything else, they just sat upright, hands on knees, staring straight ahead.

"What you're witnessing, ladies and gentlemen, is the ProbOnyx feature we call 'Temple Cuffs.' Put simply, this feature puts whomever we choose to under our control. It only works with black temples, of course, only those with severe corrections that need to be made. Rather than have you tussle with criminals, we've put that capability onto their temples. With this new feature, we can have them surrender themselves to your authority without the possibility of physical altercation. Call it self-arrest mode, if you will. We call it Temple Cuffs because they are, essentially, handcuffed."

The three officers tried to struggle, their eyes grew wide, but they could do nothing but sit and stare forward. Viate could see their eyes darting back and forth, the panic setting in, the realization that someone else had complete control over them. *My beautiful puppets, awaiting my command.*

The room fell into a deathly silence, and Viate milked the moment. He was in complete control. He pressed another button and the three officers stood up together, in unison, turned left, then he swirled a virtual spin-wheel and led them to vacant seats at the side of the conference room. He had them face the seats, then turn around, then sit. The officer in the middle's chest was breathing rapidly, clearly in a near-panic state; his eyes were wide and bouncy.

Don't you see? You have complete control of them. And I have complete control of you.

Viate let them sit for three, then four, then five seconds. "Self-arrest. Temple cuffs. With the click of a button."

The room hummed with confusion and excitement. Some stared in wonder and disbelief, others mumbled "some fucked up shit" and other criticism; some even chuckled and laughed at the possibilities for their total control. When Viate knew the entire room understood the power of what he was offering, he pressed the holo-screen button off.

The officers came out of their trances, panting heavily, clearly exasperated. "What the fuck, man?" one of them yelled. A second one, a female officer, stood, looked directly at Viate, then left the room quickly. The third officer just stayed seated, rubbing his forehead. He gently clicked the U-disc off his temple and put it in his pocket.

Chief Benning stepped forward. "This is out now? Like – departments are going to have this?"

"Well we made it for you, even though we had to launch it in St. Louis. A bit abrupt, I have to say. But yes. It's available. Starting today. Here in Chicago." Viate said. He studied Benning, then the room. It hummed with a dull, concerned vibe, like a fog had snuck in and plugged the outlets.

Benning held both his palms up as if to stop the idea. He looked at Editor Wohling, then over to Viate, his eyes a steely-eyed glare: "Melinda, what the hell? The Governor just declared martial law, we're already on high alert, mandatory curfews, all that. Now all travelers are required to wear their discs: so that's all train stations, bus depots and stations, airports, even taxis and Ubers. OK, fine. Then we get this new Virdent Green colors thing, where we have to all understand what the colors mean, how we're supposed to respond, whether or not we even have the training for all this new bullshit. And now…what the hell?"

Viate answered. "Chief Benning, my apologies. These are difficult times, and I know this is a lot to process. The Virident program is an advisory system, but we believe it makes your jobs harder. We built ProbOnyx to help ease these problems, to make it easier for you to do the job the great people of Chicago rely upon you to do." He laid it on thick *And if you don't want this fucking gift I'm giving you, I'll take it to Pittsburgh. I have no time for this.*

Chief Benning tapped his foot with agitation. He look over to Wohling, who spun the oversized U-disc round and round with her index finger.

Viate clapped his hands together gently, then gave a swirly-finger motion to his aides in the corner. Time to leave. "I've miscalculated then, Chief Benning. I thought Chicago was ready for this type of progressive technology. Clearly, you're not. Please carry on." He strode confidently towards the rear exit.

"Wait a minute, Mr. Viate!" Editor Wohling jumped in. "Of course we're interested. We're honored that you chose us for your ProbOnyx launch, that you chose us to create something only we could use." She took the lectern and stared at Chief Benning. "Something that befits our brand and honors the great men and women of the Windy City PD." She glared at Benning, who folded his arms across his chest.

She continued. "I want to reemphasize how groundbreaking this is. If I understand this correctly, we'll be the first major city to finally put the teeth into climate legislation that has been stalled for years. Not only do we have a color-coding system that can classify climate criminals, we have a built-in means to have them self-arrest. Self-arrest! Think of how much time and effort that will save, how many lives will be helped. We can get people the help they need to correct their behavior, and we can save all of you the pain and agony of aggressive arrest procedures. Not only will this help the great people of Chicago, if we do this right, it'll become a model for full federal implementation. And you, ladies and gentlemen, will be the ones that made it happen." She nodded at Chief

Benning, who nodded and walked to the back of the conference room.

"Training!" Benning yelled. "We need days of training for this. I want our arrest success rate to be 100%, understand? Ms. Wohling, you have your marching orders. Now let's go, people."

The crowd murmured and nodded in assent.

Editor Wohling looked vacantly at Viate, who said: "I've brought a team."

What do you think of that, Dr. Forsythe? You think you can keep me out of the loop? You've got Virident, I've got ProbOnyx, and it's a sprint, I'm going to kick your smug ass.

The crowd stood and mingled. Some huddled together and looked at him, mumbling things only they knew. Others walked over the dummy head on the floor and kicked it: one juggled it between his feet like Lionel Messi, then lobbed it to another, who headed it back to him. Still others just stared wide-eyed, like they couldn't wait to get out onto the street and zap people into jail cells. As he studied the officers, Viate's team swooped in to help organize the training.

Pain is just steps on the path to glory. I did this, Daddy, not you.

CHAPTER 27

PENN STATION
PITTSBURGH, PA

Gina stood at the boarding deck for Train 29 and waited for the train to disembark. She and six members of The Flagellantes had parked their e-bus at Penn Station and were there to greet Dr. James as he arrived in Pittsburgh. He had numerous climate facial reconfigurations to perform throughout Nevada, Iowa and Illinois, and had decided that a first-class and sleeper train trip would be just the ticket to reset his demeanor before their final push into D.C. Their Awakening was in three days, and Gina knew they would need the Doctor relaxed and ready to wire up their final touches.

The group had all worn oversized Pittsburgh Pirate or Steelers hats pulled down over their eyebrows, so as not to draw any attention to their circuitry. All wore the customary black cowlneck shirts and jeans, with only two of them showing visible neck bruises where they had self-abused their climate commitment. If anyone stopped them – *and why would they?* – they could just say they were part of a secret vigilante coal-miner's group out of West Virginia.

Dr. James stepped out of the first-class train car, adjusted his brown fedora, then walked up the platform. Gina pulled down the brim of her Pirates hat, then walked towards him. He waved; she smiled back. She thought he looked quite dashing, and it was the first time in their entire relationship that she'd felt, well, sentimental. The brisk cold of the Pennsylvania night air, the anticipation of their life-changing metamorphoses, her understanding that, in three days, she would no longer be able to see the good doctor in any light whatsoever, moved her. The romance of the moment struck her: she was Lara Antipova to his Dr. Zhivago, meeting in Moscow's winter to overthrow dictators and plant freedom. It suddenly felt magical.

She walked eagerly towards Dr. James, then noticed a commotion behind him, to his right. Two cars back, beside the black common cars, were loud noises and people scurrying about. A bald man in a hoodie leapt from the train step onto the platform and began running; he was followed by two police officers chasing him through the crowd. The man bobbed and weaved through people, as did the police officers following him; just when it appeared he was going to turn towards the station's main atrium, he instead turned back towards the platform, towards her. He dodged a couple with a stroller but tripped over the back wheel. He fell onto the cement, rolled into Dr. James and others, and they all fell into a pile. The police officers closed in on the bunch.

Gina ran towards the group and helped Dr. James to his feet. She gathered his hat and handed it to him, then watched the officers lash the runner's wrists together, in front. The agitated man fought against them and yelled: "I didn't do anything! You can't arrest me!"

"We can, and we will, Mr. Anaya," one of the officers said. They pulled him to his feet, did the same with the others, then grabbed his elbows.

Gina stared at the crazed man. *Wait, Mr. Anaya?* she thought. She squinted, looked at the man, stared at him harder, then realized: this is my brother-in-law!

"Mateo?" she said, stepping towards the man.

A police officer turned him away, and said: "Everything's fine, ma'am. We caught him and we're taking him in."

Mateo's head turned towards her. "Gina! Oh my God, Gina! Is that you? Tell them who I am! Tell them I'm not crazy!" His eyes twirled with intensity, his beard was long and scraggly, and she was used to him having a full head of hair. But yes, incredibly enough, this was her brother-in-law Mateo, being arrested at Pittsburgh's Penn Station.

Without thinking, Gina said: "He's with us, officers! Please let him go. We've been looking for him, and here he is," she said. She looked at Dr. James, who gave her a *what-the-fuck* glance.

Gina moved in. "We've been looking all over for him, officers. Thank you for finding him." She replaced an officer's hand with her own and took his elbow. The officer stepped back as she did. He studied Gina's sewn-shut nostrils, then did the same to the rest of her group.

She turned her right temple, shining Virident Green, towards the officers, then motioned for Dr. James and the other Flagellantes members to stand next to her. They did, and the group shone green in front of the two officers and Mateo.

She addressed Mateo brusquely: "I told you what would happen if you got off your meds, didn't I Mattie? See what happens? You run around like a crazy man, have these nice police officers chase you all over the place. And knock down innocent people in the process."

She turned towards the officers. "We lost him in Cleveland, officers, we got out at a rest stop and he took off. Spent three hours looking for him, the group behind us found him and put him on the train. We knew he wasn't doing so well, but we had *no idea*," she said, her eyes pleading. She motioned for Dr. James to take Mateo's other elbow, which he did.

"We have to take him in," the lead officer said. "Protocol."

Dr. James turned to the officer and said, in his most-convincing medical voice: "Officers, I'm Dr. James Westheimer from the Harmony Visage Center in Paso Robles, California. This man is my patient, he's under my care, and I take full responsibility for him. As you can see, his medication has lapsed, and he is in the middle of a serious mental episode that requires my immediate care. As such, he is unable to understand the full gravity of the situation and is, therefore, not fully responsible for the events that have recently occurred." He handed both officers business cards.

The lead officer studied Dr. James, Gina, and the shining green group around them.

Gina continued. "Officer, this is my brother-in-law, Mateo Anaya. He's part of our group heading to D.C., and we lost him. My sister – his wife – is beside herself, she thinks he's off his meds wandering through Ohio. Please, let us take him and get him well again. As you can see, we are all approved." She let the group's green glow wash over him.

"What about his?" the officer asked, pointing to Mateo's scarred temple.

"Self-abuse is the first direct sign of a breakdown," Dr. James said. "I can assure he'll 'glow green' once we right his medication."

The two officers stepped away to confer, and Mateo turned to Gina and said: "Oh my God, Gina, I can't thank you enough."

"Whoever you are, I suggest you shut the fuck up," Dr. James said.

After a couple minutes, the lead officer returned. He said: "He's yours, Dr. James, but we've logged all the details and filed our report. Any other incidents with him or anyone in your group and we'll take you all in, green or not. Do you understand?" He made sure to look at everyone in the group.

"I understand, Officer, and thank you for your professionalism and discretion. It has not gone unnoticed," Dr. James said. He grabbed the rope around Mateo's wrists and pulled him toward the group.

"Leave him tied until you get him back on that train," the officer said.

"Of course, Officer," Dr. James said. He led Mateo and the group away from the landing and into the main atrium.

"What the hell happened to you, Gina?" Mateo asked. He looked at the red laces closing her nostrils, then her eyebrow lights, then the rest of the group with the same. This was the first time he'd witnessed, in person, the completely different woman that Gina had become. Yes, he'd seen her bald, but *lots of women shave their heads.* But now her nostrils were sewn shut with baseball lacing – shut tight! – and her eyebrows were now strips of small LED lights. She was half-robot, half-Gina, and it unnerved him.

"Back atcha, Mat," Gina said. "Seems I just saved your ass, didn't I, Mattie?"

He stared at Gina's nostrils – *how the fuck does that feel up inside her nose?* – then shook his head clear of the fog. "Yes, right, I'm sorry, my God, I have no idea what I would've done if you hadn't come along. What're the odds?" he asked. He sipped the coffee they gave him. *Don't remember a cup o' Joe ever tastin' this good.*

"We can't find Rey, Gina. Ever since the bump we can't find him. Have no idea where he is, so I set out to find him," Mateo said.

Gina nodded. "I know, I've been talking with Lauren every few hours. We're green so we can use the network. Which reminds me, I'm going to temple her," she said. She pressed her U-disc, turned, and walked away. Mateo could hear her talking.

"Tell her I love her. And that I'm OK," Mateo said, stopping himself from crying. He realized how weak he felt at that very moment. Had Gina and her group not come along, he had no idea what would've happened. He sat and sipped.

Dr. James stepped forward and clicked on his penlight. He took Mateo's chin in his hand and turned it, then examined the temple scar. "It's healing OK, you're lucky for that, but the scar'll stay. No way around that." He pointed to Mateo's hand. "What happened there?"

Mateo held up his right hand and watched Dr. James unwrap it. The thumb scab ran vertically up his side palm and looked like the entire thumb itself had been surgically removed. He wondered where in Scob Nation his thumb was at that very moment.

"They did a good job, looks clean, sutures look fine. Hope they got the full joint, can't really tell if they did. How much pain are you in, on a scale of one to ten?" Dr. James asked.

"Thirty-seven," Mateo said.

Dr. James laughed. He took out a needle and syringe, measured it, pulled the fluid into the chamber, then injected Mateo's arm with it. "This'll help," he said.

It did.

Gina returned. "Lauren is freaking out over there, Mattie. She can't find Reyes, she hasn't heard from you in weeks, she has a million questions about what happened and I don't even know what to say to her. I told her you were bald and she freaked out because she had no idea you were bald! And when I told her we found you by accident at the train…"

Mateo held both his palms up flat. "Enough, Gina, I get it. There's nothing you can say I haven't already gone through. Lauren's fine, I've found you, I'm fine enough, and we're heading to D.C." He felt the emotions well up inside him, an odd mix of relief and fear and flat-out helplessness. "I just…need to…get to Reyes," he said. He fought through the sobs.

Gina sat down next to Mateo and leaned onto him. "Hey, brother-in-law," she said, smiling.

He sobbed. "Goddam Gina, I'm so happy to see you. You have no idea," he said. He cried softly into her shoulder. After a minute he stopped, then pulled back. He looked at her nose, her eyebrows, then the same of everyone else in the group.

"What's up with the faces? That thing looks like it hurts," he said, swabbing at his own nose.

"Doesn't, you get used to it actually," she said. "Kinda forgot all about it, to tell you the truth. But these…you wanna see?" she pointed to her eyebrows and smiled.

Mateo shrugged. *I dunno. Do I?*

Gina opened an app on her phone and clicked buttons. As she did, eyebrows lit up across the room. After six clicks, six eyebrows were lit, and she clicked on her own. They all giggled with glee at their eyebrow-light display.

"Stop Oil?" Mateo asked. "All seven of you did this?"

Gina shook her head. "Nope. Five hundred of us did this. And that's not all. We're gonna bring our oil-loving government to its knees. Wait until you see what we do to DC," she said.

"More than this?" he pointed his thumb scar to her sewn nostrils.

"It's not just us, there are groups all over the country who are going to put a stop to oil. Don't you see? It's going to be glorious," she said.

Dr. James interjected: "I'm excited about the Paw Paw gang. They'll bring DC to its knees."

Mateo had no idea what they were talking about, and he didn't care.

Gina looked at the rest of the group, then back at Mateo. "Mattie, listen, we've been talking and you can go with us, but you're gonna have to blend in. Like, we've been approved all the way through to DC, they just scan us and we move right on through. We have it timed perfectly. But if you're like that, we're gonna get stopped and questioned. They're gonna ask lots of questions, and we probably won't make it."

"Um. OK. What does that mean?" he asked. "If I put a disc on, they'll stop us for sure, nothing I can do about that."

"Actually, we can," Gina said. She held up a U-disc and clicked it into Mateo's temple; she spun it back and forth, cycling through the black and yellow, then stopped when it shone green. "See? Now you're approved," she said.

Mateo looked at the green disc in the mirror, then back at her.

"Simple circuit," she said. "Looks good enough, they'll never know. Just keep it on is all, you'll be fine."

"Deal. Easy."

"But these," Gina said, pointing to his eyebrows. "We have to do something about those."

"No way. No way am I doing that, Gina. I don't even know how you did that, and I don't wanna know. No way, no how," Mateo protested.

Gina looked at him, then over to Dr. James.

"We'll just take them off then," Dr. James said. "Anyone stops us and I'll tell them that I'm going to put the lights on at the conference, that we just ran out of time beforehand. But it'll have to look like I prepped him."

And there, in the parking lot outside of Pittsburgh's Penn Station, in the back seat of an all-electric, climate-approved VoltWagon van, Dr. James shaved off Mateo's eyebrows.

I don't even know how I got here, but this is my new world. Whatever waits for me out there, this is the only way I'll get to see my son.

———

Lauren swirled her right middle fingertip across the U-disc's smooth surface as it hummed into her temple. *Just take me there,* she thought.

She sat in a truck, or a car, or a taxi, or an Uber, or a pull-cart, in the middle of a corn field. The sky was cloudy, rain cloudy, but it didn't look like rain. It was cold, but also warm; she didn't know if she should put on a sweatshirt, so she didn't. Stretched before her were hundreds of neck-high cornstalks, all the same height, and as her vehicle sped forward the corn field began to spin. And yet, the more she drove, her position to the cornfield never moved: the stalks stood about her as a swirl, along the dirt road she drove as a swirl, driving about it all in circles. She stopped and looked at a bright green sign: "Welcome to Pennsylvania". Then she moved forward and spun around the cornfield that spun around her, then she stopped again at the sign: "Welcome to Penance".

What?

She looked left and saw a barn, a spectacular freshly painted red number with glowing white beams and cross-stiches. She turned right and saw the same barn, a mirror image.

What the hell?

She looked in the rear-view mirror and again saw the sign: "Welcome to Penitence."

I'm going nowhere. I'm just spinning.

She felt sensations on her back. *Was it the floor carpet, where she lay? Was it the wooden bench she sat on? Was it the bucket seat of Big Red, Mateo's Camaro? Was it the comforting wave of motherhood suddenly coming back to her as she waited for her son?*

Lauren laid in the Pennsylvania corn farm to nowhere, circling, circling, circling, tapping her U-disc.

CHAPTER 28

FREEDOM OIL GUARDIANS GROUP
PAW PAW, WEST VIRGINIA

Paw Paw, West Virginia, is known in baseball circles as the birthplace of the word southpaw. Local lore had it that, in May of 1930, young'un Tommy Miller stood on the mound at St. Regis' Catholic Academy and stared down home plate, which faced west. When little Tommy began his windup, his pitching arm faced south, and when he made it to the big leagues twelve years later, he just became known as Southpaw Tommy. T-shirts throughout Philadelphia were printed with the A's insignia on the left shoulder and Southpaw Tommy on the sleeve.

In river engineering history, Paw Paw is known for their tunnel, which was built in 1850 to bypass treacherous parts of the Potomac River, and which remained a fixture of the Chesapeake and Ohio Canal for over a century. The tunnel also became known for its ghost, the spirit of a canal worker who died during construction and continued to haunt the tunnel. Locals continue to regale tourists with the sounds and frights of the Ghost of Paw Paw Tunnel.

Some say that creating history is in Paw Paw's blood, which might explain the meeting being held on November 12, 2045 in the basement of the First Presbyterian Church.

"Th' whole world's fixin' to be in D.C. in five days," Jackson "Roughneck" Dupree said. He pinned a large, paper map of Washington D.C., up onto the plywood wall, and pulled out a red marker. "We got entrances around the capitol, here, here, and here," he said, circling main traffic chokepoints along Independence and Constitution Avenues. "We can slide in big ole' tankers, right 'long here, y'all."

"Them's the easy ones. The diagonal ones'll be tougher," Coalie Jo said. She pointed her fingers along Louisiana and Delaware Avenues, the diagonals that fed into The Capitol's Reflecting Pond. "But ah reckon we can slide in some other rigs in there."

"Mine'll fit," Cletus Earl said. "Me and the boy's'll take Loosiana."

"I got Delaware," Lula Belle said.

"Conference starts at 8:00 a.m., which means we'll have to do this early. Like at five or six. How're we gonna flatten the tires?" Roughneck asked.

Coalie Joe held up a small, pistol crossbow. "For the eighteen wheelers, have to hit the outside rows first – then wait 'till they flat – then hit them inner rows. Gon' mebbe take twenty points to get 'em all flat. Smaller rigs, can probably get by on four or five," she said.

"How long would it take to move the big rigs once them tires is flat? This an all-day thing or can they just pull 'em back?" Roughneck asked.

"Them'll be there for good. They'll need to hoist 'em out with cranes, and ain' no way they could get cranes in there, especially through the crowds. Once them rigs go flat, they're gon' stay. Ain' nothin' getting' through." Cletus Earl said.

"What about the trucks?" Roughneck asked.

Coalie Jo said: "They can probably tow 'em out, but they'll need the fork tows, can't back into 'em. And even then, they'll have to get up on the sidewalks, with all them people 'round. It'll be a fuckin' mess. If we get three rows o' pickups in there, it'll take 'em half the day to clear 'em out."

"Now let's talk 'bout them pipes," Roughneck said.

Jebadiah Ray stood up and pointed at the map. A retired pipe engineer from Chesapeake Oil & Gas, Jebadiah knew exactly where all the main pipeline valves that fed into Washington D.C. were. He drew big, red circles around Fairfax, Virginia, Hollidaysburg, Pennsylvania, and Lewisburg, Maryland. "These are them," he said. "We sludge 'em and it'll take weeks 'fore they figure it out. By th' time they do we'll have vehicles eva-where." he said.

"Show me what one o' them looks like, Jeb," Roughneck said.

Jebadiah Ray held up a fourteen-inch rod that resembled a small umbrella. At the tip was a ball explosive, activated by wires that ran through the rod. He opened and closed the umbrella a few times, showing what would happen when it opened up inside the pipeline. His crew would drill small holes into the pipeline, insert the rod, then open the umbrella. When ready they would detonate the ball tip, which would cause both oil leakage outward and dirt leakage inward. The umbrella would slow down oil flow, and the dirt ingress would change the mix into an oily slop. The sludge would travel down the pipeline to awaiting stations and depots, would be pumped into cars and trucks, and would last long enough to destroy the engines and leave them stranded on the roads. Since the main pipeline valves would be untouched, it would take CO&G engineers weeks to find the culprits; and by the time they did the pipelines would be useless, the vehicles they powered nothing more than roadside barnacles.

"These things work?" Roughneck asked.

Jebadiah nodded. "Used 'em three times already. Jus' took down a fleet o' taxis up in New York last week. Grounded a dozen of 'em."

"What 'bout them gas plants?" Roughneck asked.

Jebadiah nodded, then smiled broadly. "Differen' beast altogether, but same trick." He held up another insertion rod with a ball on its end, then held a lighter up to the tip. Everybody froze.

"What the fuck you doin', Jeb?" Roughneck asked. He pushed his seat out from the table and faced the door.

"You'll see," Jebadiah said, smiling. Just then, the ball-tip ignited with a flash, but instead of an explosion it started foaming, as if the rod was connected to a hose. He twirled it around and around like a fireworks sparkler, spraying the foam onto the floor like soft-serve ice cream. When the flame extinguished he stepped away, waited a minute, then kicked his boot at the foam structure. It was hard.

"Well, no shit," Roughneck said. He stood up and kicked his boot against the hard foam. "Didn' take no time at 'tall, did it? You invent that, Jeb?"

Jebadiah stood smiling; his cheeks reddened. He nodded. "Imma reg'ler Thomas Edison."

Roughneck turned and addressed the entire group. "Now who says us hillbillies can't get nothin' done?"

"Let's go back through it, sum. We got roads blockt, just jam shit up," Roughneck said.

"Check," the group answered.

"Block gas-o-line pipes with Jeb's special lil 'brella bombs then."

"Check," the group answered.

"Foam up them utility pipes."

"Check," the group answered.

"How long we think they be out fer?" Roughneck asked.

Jebadiah answered. "We get all these working, the taxis and cars should stop by 8:30, forty-five at the latest. Jus' have to abandon 'em in the streets. CO&G'll be able to burn gas for maybe an hour, but by 9:15 it'll clog and it'll black out. No 'lectricity, no cars, no batteries, no nuthin'. By 9:30 it'll jus' be a whole good mess. We'll lock up the whole city."

"Well daggum it, they ain' gon' know what-all hit 'em. A group like the Freedom Oil Group, a bunch o' coon-ass hillbillies, take down all o' D.C. and a entire climate conference in just a matter o' minutes. Jus' don' seem like it could happen in the great U.S. of A now, do it?" Roughneck slapped his knees and laughed.

After a minute, a protester named Drillbit asked: "What kinda story we gon' get out there?"

Roughneck sat back and shook his head. "Not a daggum word about it, is all," he said. "You know how we is. We ain't here to make speeches. They'll see the message loud and clear when them lights go out."

"They want a world without oil? Let's give it to 'em then. Let 'em all see what life is like without it."

CHAPTER 29

SHADOWMERE HALL
ESTATE OF STAMPEDE CEO GORE MECKLENBERG
BETHESDA, MD

Blonden Viate stood in the Grand Atrium of Shadowmere Hall and examined the tall, wooden beams. Covered in rich, deep oak, the walls were adorned with intricate carvings of kudzu vines, southern magnolias, and the faces of plantation owners long gone. Carved into the majestic wall on the right were two faces: the first of Colonel Elijah Alston, cotton, tobacco, and slave owner, original builder of this plantation he called Alston's Keep; and the second of Stampede CEO Gore Mecklenberg, who bought the manor in 2027 and renamed it to Shadowmere Hall. The two visionaries hung side by side, eight feet tall, forever etched into the manor's walls. Just under the carvings was the original brass nameplate that said:

"Alston's Keep
Est. 1852
"A Fortress of Ambition, Built on the Dreams of the Past.
May the Shadows of History Guide Those Who Walk These Halls.
Men Who Lead Live Here."

To his left looped a long, white, curved staircase, to his right its complement, both leading to an upstairs room called, simply, The Sanctum. Standing directly in the middle of the atrium, the two curved staircases gave the impression of a beautiful southern belle opening her gorgeous white legs and welcoming him into her own inner sanctum, her saintly chamber into which only he belonged. *I'll bet Mecklenberg gets hard every time he walks through this front door*, Viate thought.

He gripped the rail's right ending, the newel post, and pretended the round cap was his lass' ankle. Dragging his pinkie along the wood, he tickled her soft, inner calf; when halfway, he leaned down and kissed the flesh of her underknee. She giggled. Continuing up, he slid his palm along her inner thigh, pushing her wider for his welcome. When he reached the top, he released the railing, stood in front of the tall, dark, mysterious Sanctum, pressed his lips to the hand-carved molding, and whispered softly, "Overman is home, my love".

He walked into her virginity, where he would plant the seeds of his takeover.

Walking in, he heard the whispers of his father's ghost swirl in his head. *This isn't your mansion, little B, you had to borrow it from someone bigger, someone successful. Even now in your glory you can't make it happen. Big man? Bah. You'll always be little B.*

Shut up, Daddy!

The red drapes were made from the same batch of charmeuse silk as his robe, down to its sheen and slubby textures. In the center of the expansive room was a round, glass table, lit candles adorning its perimeter, the candleholders made of the same burnished silver as his necklace and medallion. On top of the table was a handwritten note:

"B –

Drink in the history of this building, it has helped guide legions towards their destiny. I trust it will suit your purposes. See you in DC."

- G

P.S. I call the atrium Genevieve."

Viate chuckled, then went to work. He pulled a round brazier from his black leather medical bag and set it on the table. Crumbling the note, he tossed it into the brazier, then lit an edge with a candle. It flickered, then caught flame, then disintegrated into black ash. Smoke appeared for an instant, then disappeared into the hidden air ducts scattered throughout. The Sanctum was built for such moments, down to its removal of any trace whatsoever.

He removed his precious *Thus Spoke Zarathustra,* then a wooden corkscrew, next a red silken ascot, then finally another handwritten note, this one crinkled with worn edges. He set them all down on the table in the same order in which he removed them.

Opening the book, he settled on the first passage.

The wooden corkscrew was burled and heavy in his palm. He ran his fingertips over it, taking time to linger over its length and curls and twists, caressing the carved initials: "From R.V. to V.V." Closing his eyes, he wondered when his grandfather Reginald had carved the words into the screw, when he'd handed it to his father Victor, and on which occasion they'd celebrated. Perhaps it was nothing more than a simple, fatherly gesture, with Reginald carving the words and leaving it where young Victor was sure to look, where he was sure to snoop. Or perhaps it was something more regal, like the acceptance of Victor into Yale, or Harvard, or some other prestigious institution. Cycling through the mental images, Blonden settled on his own invention of the corkscrew's origin: yes, his grandfather Reginald gave it to his father Victor on the day of his own birth, a loving sign of their family's ancestry, a continuation of their lineage. It would be the perfect sacrifice.

He set the corkscrew into the brazier, grabbed a silver candlestick, and lit the screw's tip. As the tip caught fire, he quoted from the book, aloud:

"One must still have chaos in oneself to be able to give birth to a dancing star."

Tears filled his eyes as fire consumed the corkscrew, and he said: "With this I absorb your lineage, I soak up the name, the legacy, the hopes, the dreams of the Viate kingdom. Only I, Blonden, have the power to fulfill our destiny, only I have the chaos to feel it grow. I am the dancing star."

He let the corkscrew burn, let the tears run down his cheeks onto the brazier; they sizzled when they hit flame. When the flame reached its peak, he grabbed the red ascot, smelled it briefly, then tossed it on top. The flames engulfed it.

"I burn the memory of your scent, of your viscera, of your marrow," he said. He remembered his father tying the ascot and how it made him look like a silk-necked rooster, red and cocky, his chin clucking forward, *cluck cluck cluck.*

Tears flowed, the fire burned. When done, he grabbed the last remaining item: the note.

A five by seven piece of cotton rag paper, it was cream colored (officially: soft ivory), 300 grams per square meter, and contained an embossed "VV" atop it, his father's usual. Ink was black, and style was terse, and words acrid. It contained thirteen simple, handwritten words:

"Little B:

"Strength is earned, not inherited. Don't expect my name to carry your weight."

- VV"

Little, as in you will always be smaller than me. Strength is earned, as in I'm the strong one, not you. Weight, as in you're a burden, and heavy to carry. Name, as in it's my name not yours. And VV, as in I call myself Victor, not Dad.

Blonden didn't even remember why or when he received the note, although he'd read it countless times. The reason for its existence never mattered, simply that it existed at all was enough. The undertow of his ancestry stopped here, it stopped right now.

He turned the book to the second passage and held up the note. He didn't crumple it, he actually wanted to see his father's words burn. Instead, he put the tip to the flame, held it up, pulled it close to his face so he could feel its heat, then tossed it onto the brazier. He cried as the ink slowly transformed into ash, and read:

"I am a law only for my kind, I am no law for all."

I make my own laws, I no longer abide by yours. I am the ruler of me, you are no longer. I burn you out of my head, out of my heart, out of my soul. You are no longer my tormentor; you no longer have dominion over me. I am The Overman, you are the ash at my feet. You are gone, I have risen.

CHAPTER 30

CLIMATE ATTRIBUTION RESEARCH AND PROGNOSTICATION INSTITUTE (CARPI) BETHESDA, MARYLAND

Blonden Viate surveyed the climate scientist group with simmering contempt. He'd worked his way through the combined forces of the Windy City Police Department and The Tribune with his usual aplomb, but they were easy. Give the police some brute force and the Tribune a story they could brag about and he could shape them how he wanted.

But the scientists, academics and climate specialists that made up the Climate Attribution Research and Prognostication Institute were, how do you say, more delicate. Yes, they had their PhDs and their lofty titles, but clawing over the top of each other to reach their academic peaks took their toll. By the time they reached the top of their rail-thin pedestals, the air was so thin the only thing they could breathe was ego. And ego, as much as he needed it, could be built or destroyed with praise and funding. He had to make sure to offer plenty of both.

Viate nodded politely as Dr. Marisol Evergreen, Director of CARPI's Climate Attribution Research, effused over Virident's initial success, and made sure to swallow his disdain.

"Thank you, Exalted Master Viate," Dr. Evergreen said. "We're thrilled with Virdent Green. The way you've integrated Scob nomenclature and identification - brilliant! It's a powerful new tool for climate accountability."

"Thank you, Doctor, but that's only the beginning. Virident Green was merely Phase One. While I'm pleased with its success, we're already seeing its limitations. Color-coding is interesting on the cocktail party circuit, but hardly the tools of true change. It's because of that, we developed ProbOnyx, the capability you saw in St. Louis," Viate said.

A murmur of curiosity passed through the crowd. Dr. Evergreen raised an eyebrow. "A bit blunt-force, wouldn't you say? And hardly scientific."

"Perhaps," Viate said, "but isn't moving people towards action exactly what we're all working towards? Isn't that why you do the work you do? To inspire action." He knew scientists bristled at the idea of new systems and thoughts they didn't invent, so he stepped lightly.

"But we do it with science," Dr. Evergreen said.

"Do you? Are you sure?" Viate asked ominously. He knew of the new scientific techniques they'd been working on and the announcements they were going to make at COP. He also knew the liberties they were taking, and the reputational damage they could sustain if these liberties were outed. He had an ace in the hole and they had no idea.

"ProbOnyx will operate alongside Virident Green, building upon the progress we've made and elevating it. It's an advanced model for accountability, with features capable of not just tracking but enforcing climate compliance with far greater accuracy."

Mazel Maven from The Manhattan Machiavellian tapped eagerly on her holo-screen, her voice a whisper of delight. "Did you say enforcing?"

Viate nodded, his eyes narrowing slightly. "Enforcement, exactly so. Virident Green establishes accountability through its color system; its light show is quite effective for that. But ProbOnyx enables *adherence.* Imagine compliance not only highlighted with colors but proactively managed. ProbOnyx goes beyond colored identification and adds active control: climate enforcement officers can actually control people's actions and steer them towards approved solutions. When Scobs shine black, we can physically control their movements to get them the help they so desperately need. I think of ProbOnyx as an autonomous-Uber for the brain, if you will.

Color coding isn't enough; ProbOnyx allows us to physically make them change."

Mazel Maven's eyes sparkled as her fingers clacked away on the keyboard. "This was the point behind St. Louis," she said. Clack clack clack.

"Now I want you to imagine that same capability married with your cutting-edge scientific techniques. Imagine if we not only could instantly identify those who deny science, but also send them to Probitas center for reprogramming. Imagine the power we could put into science."

He let the idea hang in the air.

"Deniers could simply be *fixed*," he offered. "With *your* science, and *my* system."

Dr. Evergreen shook her head, as if trying to eject the idea out of her ears. "Well, you have us all at a loss, Master Viate, as none of us have heard of this before. If ProbOnyx builds on the success of Virident Green, then I'm sure we'll all be very excited to add it to the climate attribution arsenal."

"Indeed, Dr. Evergreen," Viate replied, walking a delicate line between fist and glove. "We'll launch at COP 50, with intensive hands-on training to be conducted within the next few weeks. I believe that CARPI is high on the implementation list." *But we'll launch ProOnyx whether you're excited or not. I've got it in my hands as we speak.*

"Yes, well, that's exactly why we're all here, to discuss our latest work leading into COP 50. These are important times, what with the world coming to our doorstep in two days. Two days! That means we've got barely twenty-four hours, ladies and gentlemen, to ensure the alignment of our Anas specimens in a linear configuration," she chuckled, trying to lighten the mood.

Viate was confused. An aide leaned in and whispered: "ducks in a row." *Gotcha. Climate scientist humor.*

As Dr. Evergreen walked through the introductions of faculty, scientists, post-doctoral fellows and other intelligentsia extraordinaire, Viate didn't give a shit. Let them wallow in their titles and publications, let them peer-review themselves into obscurity, none of them would ever make a difference in the grander scheme. They were merely tools to be used, implements to employ. He was the shepherd, they were his sheepdogs, here to steer the flock at his command.

"Let's start with the newly approved list of events attributed to climate change, then let's move into the ticker. Professor Stone?" Dr. Evergreen said, snapping Viate out of his fog.

Professor Jasper Stone, Lead Scientist for Climate Attribution and Prognostication, said: "It's a nice list, short and tight."

"Study 1: A 23% shift in migratory behavior attributed to climate change, study completed in Malaysia, 2044, full peer-review. Study 2, from Brazil, a 41% uptick in invasive insect species, due to climate change. Peer-reviewed adjacent. Study 3, an interesting historical study using the Inuit tribe in Alaska. Cites a 15% loss in cultural heritage representation because of climate change. Really interesting stuff," he said.

"Sorry if I missed this, but 'peer-reviewed adjacent'?" Mazel Maven asked.

"Sorry, I should have explained that. It's something we just came up with, kinda flying under the radar with it. We're using AI bots to do peer-review, hence the 'adjacent' suffix. We programmed it to meet a 76.45% standard, so, you know, there's some wiggle room. We'll really lean into it hard during the next study cycle," Professor Stone said.

"What's the verbiage I should use to explain that?" Mazel asked. She clacked away at her keyboard then scrolled through holo-screen items on her U-disc.

Dr. Evergreen jumped in. "Well, it's a way to remove the 'fringe element' from peer-review, if you understand my meaning. We continue to have very well-funded scientific incursions from the other side, questioning techniques, really doing nothing more than lengthening the process that is already too long. So, this is a way to 'program out' the noise," she said.

Mazel clacked away on her keyboard, smiling broadly. "Fucking love that," she said. "Using AI to help get minimize

Republicrat misinformation. ProgScience is still the gold standard."

"As you wish," Dr. Evergreen said. "What's that bring the total to, Professor Stone?"

He clicked through his holo-list then smiled: "four hundred and ninety-eight."

"We've got four hundred and ninety-eight events we can now attribute to climate change, with percentages?" she asked.

Professor Stone nodded. "It's a nice list."

"Tell me some of your favorites, Professor," Viate said. He tossed him a softball question, allowed him to have a few moments of his meaningless praise.

Professor Stone clicked his fingers on the desktop. "Honestly, and I'm not pandering here, your Polar Papers are pure genius. Really. Changing rotational axes and even altering time? Inspired. Truly inspired. We would never have come up with that," he said.

Viate bowed his head in appreciation.

"I've always been partial to the 'too fat horses' study," Dr. Evergreen said.

Professor Stone nodded. "Always liked that one too. Climate warming heats up grass fields, causes them to overgrow, causes horses to overeat. So much so they can't run the plows, threatens to bankrupt farmers."

"Yes, it's a good one. I've always liked that one, I've used it in three interviews already. More than a million eyes on it," Viate said.

"Irish farmers," Stone said, shrugging.

Mazel Maven typed away, then clicked off her U-disc. "Genius, all genius. I'm going to livestream every second of this. The front edge of climate science. Brilliant."

"Very good. Now let's move on to new announcements. And this one we're really proud of, we might even be able to compete with the Probitas team here," Dr. Evergreen said, winking at Viate.

Viate smiled. "Oh? Do tell."

"Let me introduce Dr. Serena Raines, on loan to us from Hale University, who was on loan there from Gatebridge University in London. She's recently joined us as Chief of Climate Prognostication," Dr. Evergreen said.

Viate turned to Professor Stone. "I thought you were Prognostication?" *Like I give a damn about any of your titles or why you have them. But I'll stir the meaningless-title-pot anyway.*

"Still working things out," Professor Stone said. He shrugged.

Doctor Serena Raines removed her frameless glasses and set them on the tabletop.

"It's a very exciting time to be here, literally on the cutting edge of things. Let me first say that whilst we launch this new initiative – especially in conjunction with esteemed organisations like Probitas – we can take climate attribution and identification into whole new areas," Dr. Raines said.

"Practicing your conference speech?" Viate asked.

"A bit, perhaps," Dr. Raines said.

Viate held his palms up and shrugged. "Save it for them."

"Right, hop to it then. At COP 50, CARPI will be pleased and honoured to announce a new form of climate science: Climate Implication Science, a cutting-edge method of developing new pathways to investigate climate causality."

"Implied causality," Viate said. "In English, please."

"Science-grounded, informed implications," Dr. Raines said. "The next evolutionary step from attribution."

"I like how you said it better. Give me an example," Viate said.

"Of course, Sir. Let's take a study from Newfoundland, regarding the climate change impact on fishery yields. Standard attribution techniques found that climate change had a 33% negative impact on fishery yields over the study period. But that's where it stopped. With new implication science, we can take it further: with less fish, the local human population will eat less, and will begin to suffer conditions akin to malnutrition, amongst a host of other physical maladies. By opening up the door to implication, we can investigate climate effects much further than we could before. We can dive deeper."

And there was his opening. He'd learned this critical lesson long ago: when ego shows up, honor it. Fan its flames. Caress and adore it. Show it that it's the only thing that matters. Remind them all that only people of brilliance belong inside this room. The only people who think great thoughts are people of greatness.

"Did you invent these techniques, Dr. Raines?" he asked.

"In a sense we did, yes," Dr. Raines said.

"So when the world uses these techniques, it will be CARPI they turn to," he said.

Dr. Raines shrugged. She looked over to Dr. Evergreen, who nodded meekly.

He laid it on thick. "Now now, it's just us friends here. No need to be humble about your groundbreaking work. Let me say it differently to put it into the proper perspective." He teed it up and waited.

The scientists shifted nervously in their seats.

"When the world basks in the warm glow of your insight, when everyone looks up to face the sun, they'll see CARPI. It will be you who lights up our world." He damn near choked on his own word syrup.

The room stayed silent for what seemed an eternity, then they quietly smiled sheepishly at one another.

Perfect. Ego bomb delivered.

"And, of course, it creates access to lots more avenues of funding," Viate said, cutting to the chase. "We can dive deeper into the insurance industry, probably carve out pathways to get into medical as well. Climate change causes undernourished Newfoundlanders," he said.

Dr. Raines nodded. "Well, yes."

"Which means Newfoundland needs lots more money for doctors and hospitals," Viate said. "And medical facilities all around."

"Yes." Dr. Raines said.

"I get it. It's exactly what we need." He smiled. *The Overman approves.*

Dr. Evergreen stepped in. "We've taken the liberty of overlaying some implication techniques on your polar papers. Just, you know, to give you an example of how powerful our two organizations working together could be."

"Three organizations!" Mazel Maven said, clacking away on her keyboard. "Never forget about the Machiavellian!"

"Point corrected," Dr. Evergreen said. "Three organizations, totaling well over a thousand doctors, professors and writers. A new global force," she said.

"Indeed. Walk me through it," Viate said.

"Right, very good, Sir. If I understand it correctly, your 'polar thesis' as it were, attributes the earth moving off its axis due to ice caps melting, all attributed to climate change."

"Something like that," Viate said. *Exactly like that.*

"Implication science can take us further. For example, if we build on the 'shorter days' theme, that would necessitate more artificial lighting, which means more electricity demand, which of course means more demand for all of those products that solve it. More solar, more wind, more batteries. It will also give a jolt to the residential and commercial lighting industries. And of course we'll need factories to build them, and people in those factories," Dr. Raines explained.

"Jobs, jobs, jobs, growth and jobs," Viate said. "Oh, and virtue, of course."

"You seem to understand it very well, Sir," Raines said.

"Think of all the studies you'll be able to fund, Doctors. No one will be able to touch your academic achievements and climate morality. You'll be Top Level for decades," he said, stringing them along.

Dr. Selena Raines smiled. "We *may* have discussed those sentiments, Sir," she said.

"Give me some numbers!" Mazel Maven said.

"Thirteen point seven," Dr. Raines said.

"What's that mean?" Mazel asked.

"If we take the polar thesis out to its implied conclusion, climate change can be implicated in a 13.7% decrease in the lifespan of those within certain geographic boundaries of the ice caps. That could amount to half a billion people," Dr. Raines said.

The time to unite the factions was nigh, so Viate stood to address the communal.

"My dear professor, scientists, colleagues, creators, let me commend you on these achievements. We have been given an opportunity from on high, from rarified air, one we shan't be given again. More than ever the populace aches for the science that you have created, so we mustn't be shy about putting it forward. There is no one – no one! – who understands this better than you, and your wisdom is unquestioned. We must go forth and shape, we must go forth and be strong, we must go forth and carve our paths into the future. Only we are ordained to do it," Viate finished. *And if trick science doesn't work, I'll cook their temples.*

"Hot damn! It couldn't get bigger if Batman married the Joker!" Mazel Maven said.

CHAPTER 31

DISCUSSION BETWEEN BLONDEN VIATE AND MAZEL MAVEN
OFFICES OF THE MANHATTAN MACHIAVELLIAN
NEW YORK, NEW YORK

Mazel Maven (MM): Blonden, thanks for coming down to our offices, just days before the beginning of what could potentially be the biggest climate conference ever: COP 50 in Washington D.C. It's a busy time, for sure.

Blonden Viate (BV): It's my pleasure, we've done so much work I wanted to make sure that we had all the stories straight, that everyone knows exactly how we're shaping the world. It's the least I could do.

Also, just as a point of order, I prefer to be addressed by my Probitas title: Exalted Master Viate. After the NY Roast debacle, it feels like we should allow for the proper decorum.

MM: This is just you and me talking, it's not going to be published. Just a couple of colleagues chatting over coffee.

BV: Still, I don't want it to be misunderstood. The work we do at Probitas and with CARPI and all the other agencies we're engaged with is simply too important to let informality ruin it. ProbOnyx is that big, that transformative. I'm not the boy next door here to take your daughter to prom, I'm leading an organization that's going to guide the world. It helps me to stay on task if we're more formal about it. If it's not too big a problem, that is.

MM: Too cumbersome. How about Sir?

BV: Fine.

MM: You view the work we're doing as shaping the world?

BV: You view the work we're doing as not?

MM: Haha, point taken. You know, I was always fascinated by your background, your upbringing, what it was like to be the son of someone like your father. It couldn't have been easy. He was just so notorious.

BV: Okay.

MM: How did he influence what you do today?

BV: My father influenced me just like every father influences his son. Not sure what to say about that.

MM: Well sure, but a man of his reputation, his notoriety, surely who he was and what he did left a mark on you. And Probitas.

BV: Look, Mazel, you can look all of that up, it's been told ad nauseum. My father was a tyrant, he was ruthless, blah blah blah, everyone knows that. His reputation was notorious. You lead one of the most progressive news organizations in the world, it's all online, I've done a thousand interviews. AI bots can summarize it, you don't need me here for that. If you want to know something specific, ask. Otherwise…

MM: How did the Asheville Collapse flavor the work that Probitas is doing? I always wondered.

BV: Asheville, North Carolina has one of the most advanced telecommunication infrastructures in the country. Viate.Com made sure of that. Hardly a collapse.

MM: Going straight with the spin, I see. That the company line?

BV: It's the truth. One man's spin is another man's perspective. It's how I view it.

MM: Oh, come on, you know what I mean, it's just us here. Viate.Com bought up local providers across the country. Asheville was one of its most visible takeovers, because of the tragedy. It's what people remember about the Viate Vision to take over the world's telecom industry.

BV: We're known for greater things than that. The Viate Vision has resulted in the greatest telecommunication system in the world. That's quite a feat. I know he was proud of that. My father was a lot of things – not all of them good - but he accomplished great things. No one doubts that.

MM: People remember it because people died.

BV: Yes. That winter was brutal. Sometimes people die in winter. Every winter.

MM: Are you saying V-com had nothing to do with that?

BV: Are you saying we did?

MM: I'm not doing a story, I just want to know how the experience flavored your work with Probitas. Certainly there was some effect.

BV: The Viate Vision was to consolidate the entire U.S. communication system under one umbrella. We did that. I learned that it's not enough to have a grand vision, you have to follow that up with action. Direct, sometimes strong, action. Control every step of the process: from the people you select, to the approach you take, to the consistency of message and vision. Don't be afraid of it. You have to get dirty. You have to put boots in the soot.

MM: Boots in the soot, I've never heard that before.

BV: It's a philosophy, really. It's about doing things that others won't do to make things happen.

MM: Sometimes boots trample on seeds.

BV: Sometimes boots trample on weeds.

MM: Is that how you see others who oppose you? As weeds?

BV: They ***are*** *weeds. There isn't another name for them. And it's* ***our*** *climate vision, let's remember. Let's not pretend you're not on board with this. Wouldn't you agree?*

MM: On some level. We do need to put the right stories out there, create the proper blueprints, make sure our energies are aligned. It's why we're doing all the work we are.

BV: Now who's spinning? Journalistic double-speak, if you ask me. Quit softening it, it demeans the work you do, the work ***we*** *do. You don't need to change it into something you can swallow, just be real. It's just us pals chatting, remember?*

MM: I'm not, I'm just uncomfortable with it. Weeds? Really?

BV: That's where you're failing then. That's the difference between us: I see them as weeds and call them exactly that. It's what they are. Deniers grow their roots deep into the aquifers of society and drain them; that's all they do. When you try to pull them out the roots break off and grow ten more plants. They're just in the way. We have to stomp them out entirely. Remove all the roots of doubt. But I've got the balls to say it, and then do it.

MM: That's pretty harsh. Is that how you view the work Jill Forsythe is doing?

BV: Meh. They're small-minded. Forsythe thinks she's safeguarding the Doctrine, but all she's doing is tying our hands, limiting what we can truly accomplish. Green badges and climate color codes? Cute. But cute doesn't change the world.

MM: And you think ProbOnyx does?

BV: It doesn't ask for compliance, it demands it. That's leadership. Forsythe's scared to take the leap. I'm not.

MM: You're going to control people with the click of a holo-screen. George Orwell.

BV: We all want control; your office is a testament to it. This stapler, this paper clip, that laptop, that in-ceiling security system, the hidden microphones you have recording in each room, the buttons you've put underneath the tables so no one sees you doing it. You've built your life – your entire company – on control. Or do you think no one's noticed?

It's what you do. You spin tales, you coopt science, you spin and twist and tell whatever stories you want, under the influence of whomever you choose. The only difference with what ProbOnyx is doing is that we're taking the next, logical steps. We're taking it further.

MM: We tell stories, Blonden, we don't control lives. There's a big difference.

BV: Is there? If you don't see it, you're either blind or lying to yourself. You've already shaped the world in your image. All we've done is refined it.

MM: It's the power of progressive journalism.

BV: It's the power of what you've built. Don't diminish it. It makes you sound weak, like you don't have the stones for the work we have to do. And it's worse: you understand the power of your medium, of your brand, and you're afraid to use it. You like saying shit that makes you sound important, but you stop short.

MM: Not sure that's fair. I'm proud of the work we do. What about the Sunshine Fusion protest? We're front and center with that. We'll get two million hits.

BV: You should be aiming for a hundred. Two million is just pissing into the ocean. We could get so many more. Imagine if you put your back into it.

MM: Still –

BV: Did you know that Niccolo Machiavelli wrote comedies as well as political commentaries? We all know him for The Prince, for his military expertise, leading the Renaissance, but he also had a great sense of humor. He wrote comedies, poetry, even carnival songs. He was quite a man.

MM: I did not know that. That's relevant how?

BV: My point is, he understood how to use every facet of his voice, of his intellect, of his genius, to influence and shape the world. Yes, he was ruthless, but also persuasive. He knew that to influence the masses sometimes deception, manipulation, treachery and yes, sometimes even crimes were needed to achieve his goals. Didn't matter. The ends justified the means. If he lied to get you to move his way, no problem. He used all the tools at his disposal. He had no qualms about it, hence the phrase Machiavellian.

MM: I get it.

BV: Do you?

Your publication is named after him, Mazel. You work at The Manhattan Machiavellian, one of the biggest and most prestigious publications in the entire world, you helped build it into one of the most influential brands ever. Did you do it by being nice, or by being forthright with your guidance?

MM: We built it by being courageous enough to take on the issues.

BV: Bullshit. You built it by telling the people what the fuck they need to hear, in order to help them evolve into their better selves. And most of them have no idea what their better selves even are. You have to tell them. Where would they be without you?

I built ProbOnyx the same way. Do you think I could have done this without all your hard work? We're standing on the shoulders of giants and, I'm telling you, the view is fantastic.

You've controlled minds for decades, now we have the ability to control their actions as well. You helped do that.

MM: You have a point…to a point. I struggle with it though, with what ProbOnyx is doing. Self-arrest? Damn dystopian. I see lines of people marching into their own cells, like cattle into a slaughterhouse. We're not mindless stoinks.

BV: Controlled by people like you. People like you who've already been doing it for decades. Quit pretending like you haven't been doing this already. You have. I'm just formalizing it.

MM: It's mind-control.

BV: It's the next step. You're missing it.

Look, we've been planning this for years. We've written the Bible, the Probitas Doctrine, we've developed the schools and the training facilities for it. And now we have ProbOnyx. We've put all the tools in place, and now the world has opened to give us our chance. The glitch is that chance. It's ***our*** *chance. Everything we've been working on, everything we've thought about, all the preparations we've built, we can put them into practice. Now. Do you think it's an accident?*

MM: I don't' know, Blonden.

BV: I do. The heavens gave us the glitch in order for us to realize our vision. It's been ordained. We've been anointed. We have been rewarded for our vision, for the years of preparation we've put into this. It's our time.

You're mind-control already. And ProbOnyx is body control. If you don't see it then I'll take it elsewhere.

MM: And what happens when ProbOnyx is in the wrong hands? You're not the only shepherd out there. What if the next one decides to lead the sheep off a cliff?

BV: That's why it has to start with us. With me. Because I see the path. Forsythe doesn't. She'll fumble it. You'll second-guess it.

MM: And if you're wrong?

BV: I won't be.

MM: You talk like it's the second coming.

BV: Maybe it's the first coming.

MM: I don't track.

BV: God gave us religion for millennia, to what ends? Has it worked for us? I'd say not. More people have been killed in the name of their God than for any other reason. Religion's failed us. And with that, it's failed God. After doing this for a thousand years, we still don't have salvation.

MM: I don't see the relation.

BV: The first coming of God failed humanity. Does He think we'll give Him a second chance?

MM: I don't have an answer to that. I don't know what God thinks. Do you?

BV: Maybe this is the second first coming. Maybe God, in all His wisdom, has decided that this is the time to hand His will off to man. ProbOnyx isn't just technology; it's destiny. The glitch was divine intervention. Humanity failed to find salvation through God, so now it's our turn to lead them there. We are the architects of this new covenant.

MM: And you're saying that's us? That the work we're doing is what, touched by God?

BV: It's exactly that. He's just given it to us. To those of Us who see, that is. Those of us who don't are willed to wallow in their ineptitude. They'll be the sheep. And we are the Shepherds.

MM: I've never heard these words before. They leave me a bit lightheaded. Breathless really.

BV: That's why I came here today, Mazel, to help you catch your breath. To help you understand the opportunity we've been given, the grace that has literally been handed to us. We are the architects, we can't shy away from it. It's been destined. It's our fate. We have to seize the moment.

My point is simple: if you want to be nice, go work at the Mayberry Gazette. If you want to shape the world, come join us. Jill Forsythe and her ilk will fail. The only paths forward are The Manhattan Machiavellian and ProbOnyx.

MM: I have to think on it. This is heavy shit.

BV: Don't take too long. By the time you're done thinking the world will have changed. And I'll have changed it.

MM: I understand. Sir.

CHAPTER 32

THE MANHATTAN MACHIAVELLIAN

"Strategy over Sentiment"

World Leaders Converge on Washington D.C. for Pivotal COP 50 Summit

By Mazel Maven, Senior Editor and Orchestrator, The Manhattan Machiavellian

In a historic gathering, delegates from 89 countries will convene in Washington D.C. on November 17, 2045, for the 50th annual Conference of the Parties (COP 50). This landmark event promises groundbreaking advancements in the fight against climate change, with the introduction of a revolutionary field known as Climate Implication Science, a pioneering field designed to uncover the cascading impacts of environmental disruption. Central to the event is the unveiling of the ProbOnyx program, a groundbreaking initiative set to transform climate accountability and enforcement. As the world faces unprecedented environmental challenges, COP 50 emerges as a beacon of global cooperation and innovation, signaling a new era in strategic climate action.

Blonden Viate, Exalted Master of the Probitas Group, a global authority on climate morality and policy, offered a candid and fiery preview of the ProbOnyx program:

> "We all know how climate misinformation continues to erode the fabric of society, and how it leads to immoral and unjust distribution of resources. Big Oil executives print money while billions go hungry, all

> because of collective addiction to their slop. Worse, their advocates live among us—hidden in plain sight, spreading lies and subverting the very foundations of our communities."
>
> "But no more. The Probitas Group, alongside our esteemed partners Umbili-Net and Stampede, has developed the ProbOnyx program to eradicate this infestation. Climate deniers will no longer hide in our neighborhoods, corrupt our children, or undermine progress. While the Virident Green system provides a color-coded indicator of one's climate status, ProbOnyx takes accountability a step further. Starting today, Umbili-discs participating in the ProbOnyx program will automatically direct climate criminals to Probitas Correction Centers for re-education."
>
> "If you are a climate denier, your day of reckoning has arrived. If your U-disc shines black, you can hide no longer. Probitas sees you, and Probitas will correct you. Vivate Probitas."

Not to be outdone, the Climate Attribution Research and Prognostication Institute (CARPI), the world's leading center for climate attribution science, also announced an exciting new field of discipline: Climate Implication Science. Frustrated by the limitations of current climate attribution methods, CARPI has created innovative implication techniques to better link climate change to real-world outcomes.

Dr. Marisol Evergreen, Director of Climate Attribution Research at CARPI, described the new discipline as a "climate game-changer.

> "While we are very proud of the 489 events we can now attribute to climate change, attribution science has reached its limitations. Responsible science must continue to evolve, and with this revolutionary technique we can push through these boundaries to

> expand our understanding of how climate change affects every aspect of life."
>
> "For example, we can now properly assign climate blame to Big Oil companies for malnutrition in Newfoundland fish farmers. By linking the cascading effects of their actions to the suffering they cause, Big Oil will no longer be able to evade responsibility. Through Climate Implication Science, we'll save billions of lives and place the burden of care where it belongs: squarely on their shoulders."

They'll no longer be able to escape their responsibilities. Through climate implication science, we'll be able to save billions of lives and put the burden of care where it belongs: directly onto the shoulders of Big Oil."

KEY ARTICLES:

New Science, New Hope: Unpacking the Innovations of Climate Implication Science

Virident Green: Giving Climate Criminals Nowhere to Hide

– MM

CHAPTER 33

50TH ANNUAL CONFERENCE OF PARTIES (COP 50)
NOVEMBER 17, 2045
WASHINGTON D.C.

At 8:53 a.m. on the morning of November 17, 2045, the Washington D.C. Metro, the subway system that ran through the entire city, stopped. Mateo and The Flagellantes, all adorned in black robes, were in Red Line Train 1004, southeast-bound from the Shady Grove Station to Farragut North, when the train dragged to a halt. Lights inside the cars turned red, and a tinny voice came across the loudspeakers: "The train has temporarily stopped. Please remain seated while we restore the cars to full functionality. Thank you for your patience."

If observers looked into the subway car from the outside, they would see it jammed full of different groups: children's soccer teams, businesspeople wearing matching conference-logo shirts, political aides in their customary blazers, black shoulder cases and walking shoes; and of course, they would see The Flagellantes, their black ceremonial robes matching, their black wool caps pulled down over their eyebrows, their breathing ragged through their sewn nostrils. Those observers would see a wide variety of people about to venture into downtown D.C., excited and bouncy to experience the wonders of America's Capitol.

Then, those observers would see Mateo.

He sat alone, missing hair, missing eyebrows, missing his right thumb, clad in a black bathrobe he bought at a Walmart last night. His U-disc glowed green, but tinged more pea-soup than emerald. He could've been a lost cousin who'd been kicked out of the group then abruptly allowed back, or simply a bedraggled and beleaguered brother-in-law, which is exactly what he was. Sitting in the stalled Metro car, Mateo just felt like the bath robed neighbor who'd locked himself out of the house while retrieving his driveway newspaper. He was *that* guy.

But after fifteen minutes waiting in the stranded subway car, *that guy* could wait no longer.

He stood and ran his fingers across the door jamb, expecting it to be soft and responsive like an elevator. Instead, the glass doors were edged in hard rubber, like two windshield wipers had been jammed together. He stuffed his fingers into the rubber, wedged them between the doors, then tried to pry them open; as he did the tinny voice said: "Please remain seated. Do not attempt to open the doors as they could cause injury."

Fuck that. Mateo pulled as hard as he could, and the right side opened. He gave it a yank, the frame bent, and it stayed open. *Voilà*, he thought, remembering his friend Lucien.

He turned to Gina and the group. "Now's the time, Gina. Now's the time for all of us. We've come this far, it's time we go the last mile. Come on." He stuck his head out through the door and stepped out onto the platform.

The interior of the Farragut North station was lit red like the subway cars, with strobe lights flashing throughout: down the tracks, across the platforms, up the stairs. Gina and The Flagellantes followed Mateo out onto the platform, and they quickly huddled together. Once passengers saw doors opening, more doors opened, and passengers streamed out onto the platform. Within minutes the station was packed full of riders, their faces glowing red, wandering about, rushing towards the stairwells.

"Let's just get up to the street," Mateo said. He grabbed Gina's hand, found the "Connecticut Avenue & K Street NW" exit sign, then started walking up the stairs towards daylight.

Stepping out of the K Street exit was like entering a circle of Dante's Inferno. People and cars filled Connecticut Avenue, and while traffic was stopped, it was different than the daily jam: most of the cars were abandoned. Cars sat with doors open, passengers in various stages of exit; and those cars that moved at all did so slowly, ignoring traffic signs, hopping onto sidewalks to navigate through the jumble of people and steel. It was like all of the city's foot and auto traffic had followed Mateo up the subway stairs and vomited out onto the street: it hummed with activity, but was without purpose. It was a nest of buzzing confusion.

"Is this for the conference, Gina?" Mateo asked, though he already knew the answer.

"I don't know *what* this is for, Mattie," she said. She held hands with Flagellantes group members and turned south, towards Lafayette Square. As jammed as Connecticut Avenue was with cars, Lafayette Square was a morass of humanity. Thousands jammed the Square and overflowed towards the White House and down the Pennsylvania Avenue diagonal. Stoplights flashed red but didn't actually direct any traffic, and impatient drivers abandoned their vehicles and walked away. Pennsylvania Avenue, the city's main traffic artery, was completely clogged. Traffic police waved their hands above their heads like referees, but people simply flooded past them without notice. Most officers just gave up, but one stalwart maintained his vigil: he stood firmly in the middle of the Pennsylvania Avenue and 13th Street intersection, pointing to and fro, blowing his whistle, pretending that he was actually making a difference. Finally he relented, put the whistle into his front pocket, then merged into the crowd.

The group snaked through the crowds along the Pennsylvania Avenue diagonal, southeast towards the Capitol. At 12th Street, in front of The National Archive, protestors surrounded an oversized display of the Constitution: one climbed a ladder, held up a bucket, then poured red paint all over it. Another screamed through a bullhorn: "Time to bring climate criminals to justice! No more oil!"

The Flagellantes pressed on.

Two blocks farther, outside the National Gallery of Art, more protesters gathered and screamed. The gallery's plaza, famous for its fountain and its three I.M. Pei-designed glass pyramids, was stuffed with people and condiments: naked protesters bathed in the fountain, while others sprayed ketchup and mustard all across the pyramids. Just across the plaza stood a thirty-foot-tall blue rooster sculpture, being scaled by more protesters carrying a "Don't Eat Me" banner.

And still, The Flagellantes pressed on.

Another block farther, they reached the first truck barricade, at the intersection of Pennsylvania and Louisiana Avenues. Three broken down pickups had been parked and abandoned, staggered so they blocked the entire intersection. Their tires were flat, punctured with arrows throughout. A forked tow truck pushed into the first truck but struggled; it gave up and went to the second instead. Up the diagonal to their left – at the major intersection of Louisiana Avenue – sat an abandoned oil tanker, its back tires up onto the sidewalk, its front tires pushed into incoming traffic. All eighteen tires were also flat and pierced with arrows. Mateo had no idea what happened, but it was clearly intentional: he imagined snipers sitting atop a belltower somewhere, aiming their bows at imaginary buffaloes, thwacking arrows into the herd. An industrial crane-lift sat in traffic two blocks away, but there was no way it was getting through. The oil tanker would stay, the intersection would remain blocked.

When Gina saw the Ulysses S. Grant statue at the base of the Reflecting Pond, she began to run. "This is it, this is it, oh my God this is it!" she screamed.

The other group members ran after her; Mateo took his time and stepped through traffic. The Flagellantes gathered at the statue, hugged and cried, then gathered into a makeshift formation. They formed a single file line, faced the Capitol, took their cue from Gina, then pulled their robes open in unison. Mateo saw the eight Flagellante members, robes open, naked and bruised, giggling and smiling, and stood confused: he had absolutely no fucking idea what they were doing. But at this point, he didn't really care.

Mateo was just three blocks away from his son.

The Capitol Plaza was abuzz with activity, chockablock full of people. The power outage had delayed the COP 50 opening ceremonies, and conference organizers scrambled everywhere replanning stages, moving seats and cameras, and managing the long queues of people. Eight robed protesters blended into the thousands of attendees awaiting the arrival of politicians, celebrities, and other climate persons of interest. Hundreds of robot-cops spun on their wheels, randomly saluting trees and pylons and Viszlas and anything else that moved; a small group of engineers moved from robot to robot, pulling out switches, rebooting them, then ultimately painting a red X or green O on each. Bullhorns emerged and activated, while "testing 1-2-3" filled the air. Three teenagers stood to the left of the Reflecting Pond, looked around, then jumped into the water. They breaststroked their way through the pond and made it halfway across before Capitol Police fished them out.

Standing atop a pole in the middle of The Capitol Plaza was a lit sign, blinking red: "The Opening Ceremony of COP 50 Will be Delayed until 4:00 P.M."

Gina ran back to Mateo, giddy with excitement. She hugged him and cried. "This is it, Mattie! This is what we've worked for - it's everything. Can't you feel it? We're finally going to show them."

Mateo hugged her, then began to cry as well. "I have no idea what you're into, Gina, but I hope it's everything you wanted. The whole flashing thing?" he asked.

"Lauren asks, you never saw *any* of that," she chuckled. "There will be five hundred of us," she said, hugging him tight.

"Ok Gina. I hope it…somehow works for you. But you know I have to go. I have to get to Reyes. Can't thank you enough, you know that." He lifted the brim of her wool cap and kissed her eyebrow lights. "Good luck."

Gina pushed her shoulders back and stood tall. "Go get him Mat. The whole world is going to see us. You will too. Godspeed."

Mateo turned and sprinted. He turned right on Constitution Avenue, past the oil tanker blockade, then up the Maryland Avenue diagonal towards Stanton Park. Past the park he hit C Street, NE, and ran past 7th, 8th, and 9th Streets. When he hit the Slow Nickel Laundromat, he stopped. Gathering his breath, he walked up the street towards Reyes' apartment.

He imagined himself escaping from the Probitas Climate Center in Boulder, Colorado, crashing through guards towards his own climate freedom. He imagined himself recapturing stolen treasure in the Texas countryside, riding horseback, firing backwards into banditos, awaiting a hero's welcome when he returned the money to the townsfolk. He imagined himself rescuing climate Scobs down in the Louisiana bayou, piling them onto his swamp boat and racing up the Mississippi towards freedom.

He imagined himself driving his 1984 red Camaro, Big Red, up California's winding coastal highways, windows open, hair blowing in the cool spring breeze.

He imagined himself running fingers through his hair, back when he had hair, back when he had all his fingers. And eyebrows.

He imagined how good it was going to feel to see Reyes' face again.

He knocked on the door of Apartment C, at 903 D Street, NE, in Washington D.C.

He heard steps behind the door, saw the peephole go momentarily black, then saw the door swing open quickly.

"Oh my God, Dad!" Reyes Anaya said. "How'd you find me?"

Mateo stood at the doorway and could not make a sound. He tried. His mouth was open – he could actually taste the cold air – but no sound escaped. He just stood there in silence, mouth-agape. *Maybe someone stole my tongue*, he thought.

My God, I forgot how beautiful you are.

Reyes quickly pulled him into the apartment and shut the door. He hugged Mateo and spoke.

I know you're talking, but I can't hear you. Sounds like buzzing. Bzzzzzz.

Reyes spoke – his mouth bounced up and down – and Mateo could feel fingers on his chin, wetness down his neck.

Maybe I'm bleeding. Maybe I'm crying. Am I? I don't really know.

Then, suddenly, he was on a couch. He could see Reyes srunning into the kitchen, then a glass of water, then a feeling at his lips. Cold water at his teeth. Wetness on his tongue. His thumb-scar pulsing.

"Dad! Dad! Are you hurt? Answer me!" Reyes was yelling now.

"Reyes. It's you. You're...*here.*" Mateo finally said. He heard his own voice, though it didn't really feel like he said it.

Reyes hugged him on the couch, burrowed his head into his temple where the makeshift U-disc had been attached. It fell into Mateo's lap. *Reyes can heal me.*

Mateo ran his fingers over his bald head. *Reyes is here.*

Reyes talked.

Mateo touched the U-disc wound on his temple. It hurt like hell, but was comforted by Reyes' touch. *Reyes is here.*

Reyes said more words.

Mateo felt the pain of his missing thumb pulse, and he looked down at the scar. It was pink and swollen, yet healing. He shoved his hand into his pocket. *Reyes is here.*

Reyes patted his cheek, then the top of his head, then buried his chin into Mateo's shoulder.

Mateo held up the small red car. He couldn't grip it, so he just cupped it in his palm. *Reyes, here.*

Reyes squinted at the car, looked back, then shrugged. "Dad?"

"I thought you might need Lil Red," Mateo said.

They hugged.

Lauren lay on the bare tile of her kitchen floor and hummed in U-disc glory.

She pressed her thumb along the base of the Thomas Jefferson Memorial. The white marble was cold and unflinching, like the Washington D.C. winter. Reyes laughed. *Hummm.*

She was a butterfly atop the Vietnam Veteran's Memorial wall, flitting atop its joints, dancing her tarsus along its black granite shimmer. Mateo jumped up to high-five her, but she fluttered away. *Hummm.*

She was round and pregnant, her breasts full, with Reyes crawling out of her umbilical into the real world. He jumped out, smiled at her, then jumped down onto the tile of the Lincoln Memorial. He smiled at President Lincoln's carved face, ran down the steps and jumped into the Reflecting Pool. He swam a backstroke. *Hummm.*

Reyes is here. Reyes is here. Reyes is here. Hummm.

At 16:40 p.m. on November 17, 2045, Gina and all five hundred members of The Flagellantes formed a circle around the Capitol's Reflecting Pool and faced west, towards the setting sun.

At 16:48 they dropped their ceremonial robes to the ground and revealed their bruised fleshpalettes to the media cameras. They showed the square grids inked all over their naked bodies, each square signifying a ton of carbon dioxide they had emitted in their lifetime, each bruise a cleansing step in their repentance.

At 16:50 the group tilted their faces up, opened their eyes, and stared directly into the setting sun. Within twelve seconds their retinas seared into useless crisps, blinding them all. Their solar panel corneas soaked up the sun's last rays, powered up their nose battery implants, then lit up their eyebrow ridges. When the sun set behind the Lincoln Memorial, conference attendees surrounded the group and gasped at their commitment; and when full darkness hit, five hundred forehead lights shone brightly and illuminated the United Nations flags with the words "STOP OIL."

At 16:52, all five hundred members of The Flagellantes emerged as their Pure Selves in front of the world, butterflies breaking free from their cocoons, united in their climate despair. They stood bare in purity, bruised in penance, blind in commitment, their eyebrows lit in Nazarene glory.

It was magnificent.

EPILOGUE

BLONDEN VIATE AND DR. COLLEEN FORSYTHE
UMBILI-CALL: TEMPLE TO TEMPLE
LOCATIONS UNKNOWN

Blonden Viate templed Dr. Colleen Forsythe at exactly 11:43 p.m. local time. Yes, it was three hours earlier at her west coast office, so she was sure to still be awake and engaged. The exact time wasn't really important. What mattered was that he called forty-three minutes past his own cut-off, well beyond the boundaries she'd grown comfortable exploiting. His international reach swelled by the day, and time no longer held power over him. Let her worry about time.

"Late for you, Viate," Dr. Forsythe answered, combing her fingers through her hair.

Viate waved it off. "The world is moving too fast to worry about time."

"An unusual position for you to have, given your-"

"Irrelevant," he interrupted. *Time is now my bitch, not the other way around.*

"I'm looking at orders for ProbOnyx from Sao Paolo, Bogota', Berlin" – he scrolled through his holo-screen – "hell, we have orders from Lower Antilles. We're global already."

"I didn't know you launched outside of the U.S.," Forsythe said.

"We didn't," Viate said. *Look how much people want what we offer.* "And yet, when the people ask, we provide. It's our duty to help them. I've got three years of production right in front of me."

Forsythe seemed to hold her composure, though her fingers stalled mid-air on the holo-screen. She blinked once, too slow for her usual efficiency.

He leaned back, savoring the stillness in her hands. *Even now, in defeat, she was trying to recalibrate, calculating odds that didn't exist. She doesn't even realize how completely I've dismantled her. To her, losing isn't even possible. Until it is.*

"It's certainly validation for the vision we had," she said.

"It's validation for the system *we* built," he said.

"We're going to limit the Virident Green backbone to the U.S., for now. We want to make sure we continue to offer the stellar service we're known for. Not to throw water on your parade, of course, just that we'll have to temper the plans. We won't be able to support your expansion," she said. Forsythe played her card.

Viate laid down his four aces. "I understand your limitations, so we've taken care of all that. With the advanced orders we've been able to secure funding for new manufacturing. ProbOnyx will be able to go global, alone." He let the words hang in the air, then continued: "Although we do see room for regional capabilities like Virident to continue. In some capacity we've yet to determine. I'll of course let you know when we make that ultimate decision." *Don't worry, I'll make sure to let you know when you're out of business.*

Forsythe's lips tightened briefly before she nodded. "If there's nothing else, I'll grant your leave then."

You grant nothing. I won, you lost, Viate smiled in syrupy victory.

Forsythe's finger moved to click off the holo-screen.

"Oh, one more thing, and I almost forgot," Viate said.

Forsythe paused and raised her eyebrows.

"Janet. I spoke with her," he said

Forsythe's eyes bulged quickly before she steadied them. "You spoke with my daughter? Why on earth would you do that?" she asked.

"She expressed an interest in what we were doing, and it just so happened we had an opening for our international expansion," Viate said.

"Your…international…expansion," Forsythe said. She looked genuinely confused, all the more so as she scrolled through her holo-screen to find details.

"Australia. She's going to head up our Australia operations. Should be there by Wednesday," Viate said.

"I see," Forsythe said. "I'm sure it's quite an opportunity."

And ten thousand miles away from you, Viate thought. "Vivate Probitas. Overman out."

He ended the call and leaned back, feeling the U-disc hum through his temples. Reaching for his Louis XIII cognac, he took a slow sip, savoring the burn as it rolled across his tongue and slid down his throat. The warmth pooled in his chest, a baptism of fire and success. Victory purred through his temples.

I did what you couldn't, Daddy. I built an empire. And this time, it's mine.

Made in the USA
Coppell, TX
18 February 2026

71714566R00134